THESE NAMES
MAKE CLUES

THESE NAMES MAKE CLUES

E. C. R. LORAC

With an Introduction
by Martin Edwards

Poisoned Pen
PRESS

Published by Poisoned Pen Press, an imprint of Sourcebooks,
in association with the British Library
P.O. Box 4410, Naperville, Illinois 60567-4410
(630) 961-3900
sourcebooks.com

These Names Make Clues was originally published in 1937 by Collins, London, UK.

Library of Congress Cataloging-in-Publication Data

Names: Lorac, E. C. R., author. | Edwards, Martin, writer of introduction.
Title: These names make clues / E.C.R. Lorac ; with
an introduction by Martin Edwards.
Description: Naperville, Illinois : Poisoned Pen Press, [2022] | Series:
British Library crime classics | Originally published, 1937.
Identifiers: LCCN 2022029623 (print) | LCCN 2022029624
(ebook) | (trade paperback) | (epub)
Subjects: LCGFT: Detective and mystery fiction. | Novels.
Classification: LCC PR6035.I9 T48 2022 (print) | LCC PR6035.
I9 (ebook) | DDC 823/.912--dc23/eng/20220624
LC record available at https://lccn.loc.gov/2022029623
LC ebook record available at https://lccn.loc.gov/2022029624

Printed and bound in the United States of America.
SB 10 9 8 7 6 5 4 3 2 1

INTRODUCTION

These Names Make Clues is an intriguing detective novel written at a time when its author was establishing herself as one of the leading exponents of the genre. The book was first published in 1937, under the prestigious Collins Crime Club imprint. Remarkably, however, this is one of E. C. R. Lorac's novels that has been almost forgotten. At the time of writing this introduction, I cannot trace a single copy for sale on the internet—anywhere in the world. Nor have I been able to discover any critical commentary about the novel in reference books. Quite a mystery.

This neglect is all the more surprising given that, of all the Lorac books I have read, *These Names Make Clues* is the novel most closely in tune with the mood of traditional detective fiction of the kind we associate with the Golden Age of Murder between the two world wars.

That mood is struck right from the start. It's April 1936, and we encounter Chief Inspector Macdonald at home. He's about to read a popular travel book by Peter Fleming (whose younger brother Ian was at that time unknown; this was long before he created James Bond), but first he goes through his correspondence.

Amongst his letters is an invitation from Graham Coombe, a publisher, and his sister Susan. They invite Macdonald to "join in a Treasure Hunt. Clues of a Literary, Historical and Practical nature will be provided. It is hoped that detectives, both literary, psychological and practical, will compete in their elucidation." In an accompanying letter, Coombe challenges Macdonald to forget his professional dignity and "measure your wits against those of the thriller writers, and others, who are competing."

This is the sort of set-up that is more commonly associated with writers like Agatha Christie; one thinks, for instance, of *Cards on the Table* (in which Hercule Poirot is invited to a bridge party in the company of murderers who have escaped detection), first published in November 1936. As the seasoned reader of detective fiction knows, such a scenario inevitably leads to fatal consequences.

Macdonald debates with his friend, the journalist Peter Vernon, whether to accept the invitation, and after tossing a coin, he decides to do so. Once he arrives at the Coombes' party, the complications come thick and fast. The host has invited people to adopt pseudonyms, and one of the first challenges for the Scotland Yard man is to work out the real identities of his fellow guests. The clues in the treasure hunt are equally convoluted. Suddenly the lights go out. Candles are lit, but matters take an even darker turn after it becomes clear that a man calling himself Samuel Pepys is missing. Macdonald and Coombe go in search, only to discover his corpse in a small telephone-room at the back of the house.

The dead man is actually Andrew Gardien, "author of a dozen detective stories. The 'Master Mechanic' the reviewers called him, owing to his ingenuity in inventing methods of killing based on simple mechanical contraptions... Springs and levers and pulleys had been used with wonderful effect by the quick brain which had once animated that still body." But how exactly did he meet his end—and was he the victim of murder, or did he die of natural causes? Before long, another death is discovered and this time there seems to be no doubt that the victim was murdered. Yet in a Golden Age detective novel, things are seldom as they seem.

These Names Make Clues is an example of the traditional "closed circle" mystery, with a limited group of suspects, as with *Bats in the Belfry*, which Lorac published earlier the same year, and which has been reprinted as a British Library Crime Classic. For those tempted to indulge in a little literary detection, it seems highly significant that 1937 was also the year in which E. C. R. Lorac was elected to membership of the Detection Club.

The Detection Club was the world's first social network for detective novelists. Founded in 1930 by Anthony Berkeley, the club adopted a constitution and formal rules a couple of years later, by which time it had already made a significant impression on the literary world, broadcasting two radio serial mysteries, and publishing two highly successful collaborative detective novels, *The Floating Admiral* and *Ask a Policeman*, which remain in print to this day. The first President was G. K. Chesterton; after his death in 1936, he was succeeded by E. C. Bentley, author of *Trent's Last Case*, the novel which was the catalyst for the Golden Age style of cerebral whodunit. Leading figures in the club included Dorothy L. Sayers, Father Ronald Knox, John Rhode, Agatha Christie, Milward Kennedy, and Baroness Orczy. The aim of the club was primarily social, but members were also keen to elevate the literary standards of the genre. Election to membership was—and remains to this day—highly prized.

Lorac was elected the year after the club elected its first American member, John Dickson Carr. In the same year, she was joined by Christopher Bush, Newton Gayle (a pen-name for Maurice Guinness and Muna Lee), and Nicholas Blake (the name under which Cecil Day-Lewis, who later became Poet Laureate, wrote detective fiction). No more members were elected until 1946, by which time the world had changed. Lorac continued to be a proud and enthusiastic member of the Detection Club to the end of her life, travelling down to London after the war from her home in Lunesdale to attend meetings. For a number of years, she served as secretary of the club.

It seems highly likely that *These Names Make Clues* drew inspiration from her experiences and encounters on becoming a member of the Detection Club. Andrew Gardien bears a resemblance, both in physical appearance and the type of mysteries he wrote, to John Rhode (Cecil John Street in real life), who was a pillar of the club and evidently very good company. Suffice to say that Gardien's personality and behaviour were different from Rhode's, and I imagine that both he and Lorac were highly amused by the liberties she took with the character. It would not be a surprise if it were discovered that Rhode, who was generous with his expertise, gave Lorac the idea for the murder method in this story. It is possible to detect touches of other club members, such as Baroness Orczy and the husband and wife team of G. D. H. and Margaret Cole, in the characters. There may also be a hint of Billy Collins, Lorac's publisher, in the portrayal of Coombe.

Pseudonyms and games with names play a significant part in this story, and in fact E. C. R. Lorac was itself a pseudonym. It concealed the identity of Edith Caroline Rivett (1894–1958), who also wrote a lengthy mystery series under the name Carol Carnac. She was known to her friends as Carol, and when she started writing crime fiction she simply turned that name back to front so as to become Lorac.

Detection Club members prized "fair play" in their detective fiction, and Lorac's reluctance to present certain vital information necessary to enable the reader to solve the puzzle until rather late in the book may have raised a few eyebrows among her colleagues. Nevertheless, this is an entertaining story which has been out of print for far too long. The British Library reprints of Lorac's novels have led to a huge resurgence in her popularity, and it is a pleasure to rescue this book from the obscurity in which it has languished for more than eighty years.

—Martin Edwards
www.martinedwardsbooks.com

A NOTE FROM THE PUBLISHER

I

CHIEF INSPECTOR MACDONALD, STRETCHING HIS LONG limbs in an adequate chair by his own fireside, was prepared to enjoy the sort of evening which he preferred to any other. His own company, a book (he had just got Peter Fleming's *News from Tartary*), a pipe, and a wood fire—these promised a perfectly satisfactory evening.

Before he began the book, however, he opened the letters which had arrived while he was out. The first three he tore up after one glance—a prospectus of a newly-floated company, an offer of a "complimentary sitting" from "Violette," a Court photographer (the description made Macdonald grin; his own criterion of the word "Court" was very different from that of the photographer), and a begging letter from that hardy and unashamed pickpocket, Jeff Baines. Jeff always expressed a belief in the kind-heartedness of the police officer who had first caught him out in his skilful handcraft, and Macdonald indulged in a second grin over the optimism of the cheerful rogue. The fourth letter did not follow the previous three into the fire. It caused the chief inspector to sit with a look of rather comic perplexity on his lean, long-jawed face. The large square envelope contained a card on which the copper-plate inscription ran as follows:

Mr. Graham Coombe and Miss Susan Coombe invite Chief Inspector Macdonald to join in a Treasure Hunt. Clues of a Literary, Historical and Practical nature will be provided. It is hoped that detectives, both literary, psychological, and practical, will compete in their elucidation.

Cocktails 8.15 p.m.   All pseudonyms respected.
April 1st, 1936.   Caroline House, W.1.

A note was included with the card, which ran:

DEAR CHIEF INSPECTOR,—*I hope this sort of thing is not beneath the dignity of Scotland Yard. When we were discussing the impractical nature of the clues set forth by thriller writers at Simpson's the other evening I had no idea who you were. On being enlightened I chuckled a bit, and then it occurred to me that our party would be immensely improved if you could be induced to come and measure your wits against those of the thriller writers, and others, who are competing. We hope for a jolly evening, and my sister and I would be much honoured if you will join the chase, pseudonymously, if you prefer it.*

Sincerely yours,
GRAHAM COOMBE.

It was about a week ago that Macdonald had met the writer of the letter. Dining at Simpson's with a barrister named Parsons, Macdonald had been introduced to a bearded man whose aspect was rather don-like—the fine domed head and thoughtful eyes denoted learning, though Coombe's face lighted up occasionally with an impish gaiety rather at variance with his general impressiveness. The conversation had turned to detective stories, and Macdonald had uttered a few trenchant criticisms of the methods employed by the author of a new thriller which was enjoying a brief furore as a best seller. It was not until after Coombe had left them that Parsons informed Macdonald that the donnish-looking fellow was Graham Coombe, the publisher, whose firm had produced *Murder by Mesmerism*, the novel which Macdonald had criticised.

After receiving this information, Macdonald had felt rather chastened. He had had no intention of being a spoil-sport, and writers of detective stories had ample justification for their pursuit—a living to earn on the one hand, and the public to entertain on the other. He had wished that he had been less censorious. With Coombe's invitation in his hand, he felt that he was hoist with his own petard. He was offered hospitality by a publisher who turned the other cheek to the smiter, and who at the same time challenged the critic to use his wits in practical combat against those whom he had derided. Frowning, Macdonald cast the card aside and filled his pipe. If he went to the party he would probably end by looking a fool, as well as feeling one, for it was highly probable that the "thriller merchants" would deal with clues "literary and historical" far more swiftly than he could himself. If, on the other hand, he refused to go, he could imagine Graham Coombe chuckling over the pusillanimity of a critic who funked a battle of wits with those whom he had criticised. He was still debating the point in his mind when he heard the bell ring at the door of his flat, and a moment later a long-limbed young man strolled in, observing:

"Don't say damn. I'm not stopping long. Oh ho! You've got a card from Graham Coombe. What about it?"

The speaker was Peter Vernon, a journalist from whom Macdonald had acquired useful tags of information on certain occasions, and the chief inspector pointed to a chair with his pipe.

"Sit down, laddie. Are you one of the treasure hunters?"

"No such luck. Coombe sent me a card, but I've got to go up north that week for the T.U.C. meeting. I've never been to one of Coombe's parties, but I've heard that they're the last word in the way of a good evening, and he's spreading himself over this one. It's going to be a damn good show. Coombe's idea is to see if the thriller gang can live up to their pretensions and do down the straight authors over picking up clues and reading ciphers and all the rest."

"Let 'em get on with it," replied Macdonald. "I'm not an author. It's not my idea of amusement."

"Like that, Queen Vic? Not amused? Cold feet, Jock? More shame for you."

"Those are my matches, and you can take them out of your pocket," replied Macdonald. "Why on earth should I spend a good evening racking my brains over stuff that's not in my line, to provide amusement for a crowd of nimble pen-pushers? I don't see myself."

"Do you a power of good, Jock. You're getting too high-minded. Pen-pushers! I like that! Ever heard of Ashton Vale, the economist? He may be going, and Digby Bourne, who wrote that book on the Australian hinterland. Then V. L. Woodstock's going—the historian. I like to see you sitting in a large arm-chair being superior. I'd give my wig to go."

"Ashton Vale? Good Lord! I've always wanted to meet him; but—a Treasure Hunt!"

"Why not? I like parties with a point to them. Coombe'll give you a run for your money. He'll set the clues, but you'll have the run of his library to get the facts if you don't happen to know them, and the sight of Ashton Vale working out a numerical cipher's enough to cheer a man up."

Macdonald groaned.

"Numerical ciphers! Losh! I've forgotten all the algebra I ever learned, and a log table's as much good to me as Plotinus."

Puffing away at his pipe, Vernon laughed to himself. "Graham Coombe's got the laugh on his side this time, Jock. Although you criticise his choicest authors in the manner of one having authority, you take good care to keep out of their way when you're given a chance of demonstrating your superior 'methodology.' Ca' canny!"

Macdonald laughed in his turn. "Oh, I can see all that without having it pointed out to me. I'm cast for the clown, whether I go or not. The one thing I like about the whole show is the idea of meeting Ashton Vale and seeing him doing a bit of funny stuff in the treasure-hunting line. What's this about 'pseudonymity,' or whatever the word is?"

"That's a touch of astuteness on the part of Coombe. I don't know exactly who's going to show up at this do, but most of them won't know the others by sight. You won't have the faintest notion if the chap who pips you at the post is a thriller writer or a pukka scholar. When you arrive you'll be handed a card to wear on your coat, inscribed with the name of some dead and gone literary colossus. You'll find yourself labelled as Erasmus Esquire, or Sir Thomas Mallory, while Ronile Rees will be Currer Bell or George Eliot, and Nadia Delareign will be Mrs. Aphra Behn or Sappho, and every one will look at every one else with a glare of suspicion. Of course, Coombe will get most of the fun, because he knows who everybody is."

"Yes. From his point of view there's plenty of entertainment value in the party," groaned Macdonald.

"Why not from yours? If you and Ashton Vale and Digby Bourne can't make Ronile Rees and Co. look funny, you damn well ought to. Coombe's not a fool. He'll set you all posers which you'll have an equal chance of guessing. However, it's your pigeon, not mine. I'm fed to the back teeth that I can't go myself. What I really came for was to recover a book I left here last month. A yellow jacket, one of the Left Societies' publications."

"Take it away. It's behind Gibbon on the top shelf. I don't like the look of it. But you didn't come in because you wanted that book. You came in to see if I'm going to Coombe's party. Why?"

"Because I want to hear about it, and if you go you'll be able to tell me all the choice bits. For a chap who's fond of posing as a flat, you see a surprising amount that other folk don't see; and, what's more, you remember it. I'm not certain if there's more to this party than meets the eye. What a lark

if Ashton Vale turned out to be the author of Ronile Rees'
books. You never know with these blighters. They just chuck
off a thriller or two in their spare time."

Vernon got up from his chair; being very long in the legs,
he had a habit of twisting them round one another like a
contortionist, and strolled over to the bookcase to remove
his "yellow back," while Macdonald picked up Graham
Coombe's card and studied it. At last he said, "I'll toss for
it. Heads I'll go, tails I'll stop at home. May the good Lord
send it's tails."

He flicked the coin into the air, and it spun up and
down again.

"Heads," whooped Vernon. "You're for it."

Macdonald nodded. "I'm for it. I shall go—and look a
fool. If I'd refused to go I should have felt one, so Coombe
gets his own back either way."

Caroline House lay in that quarter of London bounded
by Marylebone Road to the north and Oxford Street to
the south, a locality in which a few small Regency houses
still survive, unexpectedly blocking the ends of the quiet,
straight little streets which are now mainly occupied by
nursing homes and a few good residential hotels. Caroline
Street began at Wigmore Street and looked as though it
ought to run right through to Regent's Park, but at its
northern end the low widespread bulk of Caroline House,
shaded by a large plane tree and a fine catalpa, stretched
a dignified façade across the end of the street. Macdonald
had often seen the pleasant stuccoed front, with its elegant
pilasters and fine double door, and had wondered to whom

it belonged. A nice place to live in, he thought, as he rang the bell on the evening of All Fool's Day—spacious and quiet, a typical Nash production.

Relieved of his hat and coat in the outer lobby, he was led into a wide lounge hall, shut off from the entrance lobby by heavy swinging doors, and Graham Coombe came forward to greet him.

"Nice of you to come," said the publisher, and when he smiled the wrinkles round his dark eyes puckered up and took on the mischievous aspect which was so unexpected when his face was in repose. Inclined to baldness, his lofty brow gave Coombe the professorial look which had struck Macdonald on first seeing him, and the neat, dark imperial added a look of the foreigner. Coombe looked the very type to occupy a chair of Spanish or Italian literature at one of the older universities—very "*soigné*," somewhat given to using his hands in an apt gesture to reinforce his words, and of a melancholy aspect when his face was in repose.

"This is your nom-de-guerre," he added, proffering a card to which a pin was attached. "You're Izaak Walton for the duration of the evening. You can claim your own name and rank later, just as you wish, or retire unknown."

"I shall probably be only too glad to conceal my ineptitude, and go home as Izaak," replied Macdonald. "Thanks for the charitable thought. I admit that your card caused me misgivings, but it seemed only sporting to give you the chance to retaliate. If I'd known who you were, I shouldn't have been so captious the other evening."

"I'm glad you didn't know, then," replied Coombe; and Macdonald noticed that his pointed ears twitched a little when he smiled. "My sister's receiving the victims upstairs. You'll be announced as Izaak Walton, of course."

At the head of the wide stairway Macdonald was taken in hand by a merry-faced young man who led him to the door of the drawing-room and announced him as the author of *The Compleat Angler* in a fine stentorian voice.

The lady who received him with a bow and a charming smile was very much like her brother, but without his unexpected puckishness. Macdonald had armed himself for the fray as best he might by acquiring all possible information about those whom he might meet. Miss Susan Augusta Coombe was revealed as a personality by a few lines in *Who's Who*. That she was a socialist, humanist, and pacifist was indicated by her published works. She had worked for the cause of Women's Suffrage as a young girl, had nursed in France during the war, and had occupied herself in political and social work since. Her age Macdonald would have guessed as under forty, had he not been better informed. White skinned, with her black hair brushed smoothly back like a man's, she was clad in a beautifully cut gown of rich black moiré with very full, long skirt. A row of pearls fitted close to the base of her throat, and pearl-button earrings decorated her small ears. The fine dark eyes which smiled at Macdonald as she greeted him were very bright and very observant, and Macdonald found himself thinking that she had the typical look of the convinced pacifist—an aspect both spirited and a little aggressive.

"Miss Fanny Burney was just advancing a theory that Fascism and Communism are fundamentally the same," observed Miss Coombe, and Macdonald took a glass of sherry from a tray which was advanced to him. In a very few moments he began to enjoy himself. The preliminary canter of conversation with which the evening was to begin gave him a chance to observe his fellow-guests. It also put him on his own guard. It would be all too easy to give away his identity by a misguarded word showing the attitude of the official to those twin diabolical "isms" which belabour the world of to-day, and that was just what he did not mean to do. Keeping his end up in the conversation, he studied those around him and tried to place them. There were nine people in the room, including Miss Coombe and himself. Of the three women-guests present, one was quite a girl, very fair, dressed in a gown of shot green and gold silk, cut low to the waist at the back. Her hair was dressed in a plaited bun low on the nape of her neck, and a little golden fringe curled on her forehead. So youthful and guileless did she seem to be that Macdonald decided to guess by contraries and to credit her with the production of bloodthirsty thrillers of the gangster type, especially as she was labelled Jane Austen.

Fanny Burney, who was advancing theories concerning the essentials of Communism and Fascism, was a much older woman, with slightly grizzled red hair, a square face, rather lined and weary, but still comely. A thoughtful type, meditated Macdonald, with a liking for facts and also a slight tendency to instruct. The Historian of the party, he decided. Finally there was Mrs. Gaskell, a beautifully clad woman with crisp fair hair and very blue eyes. Her voice told Macdonald that she was a Scot, and he was pretty certain that Mrs. Gaskell drew the same conclusion concerning himself, despite his efforts to talk "London English."

Of the men, Thomas Traherne was the most striking, a tall

dark young fellow, with the type of good looks which might well indicate a poet, and a fluency of speech which outdid all the other conversationalists. His vocabulary indicated scholarliness and a cosmopolitan upbringing. Samuel Pepys was a man of fifty inclined to stoutness, a bit of a "*viveur*," Macdonald judged, and none too well at ease. His fingers showed that he smoked incessantly, and his eyes were restless, but betrayed a disposition to dwell on Jane Austen with marked appreciation. Macdonald promptly disliked him, though admitting to himself that if a girl has a lovely back and displays it to the waist, it was only to be expected that a certain type of man would eye it appreciatively. Remembering Peter Vernon's assertion that Ashton Vale and Digby Bourne were to be at the party, Macdonald considered the two remaining men. Bourne he picked out because of his physique and deeply-tanned face. The *nom-de-guerre* of Ben Jonson undoubtedly covered the famous cartographist. This left Laurence Sterne to be identified as Vale—also a man of good physique but grey-haired and almost excessively thin. His shrewd, grey-green eyes met Macdonald's with a twinkle which seemed to indicate that the Izaak Walton label amused him on account of its aptness.

A few minutes after Macdonald had entered, two other guests were announced in quick succession. Madame de Sevigné was a handsome, effusive woman in a marvellous gown of gold lamé, with puffed sleeves and a train. Anna Seward was a grey-haired lady with a severe profile and a shingle, who wore a little ermine cape over a beautifully-cut black gown. Her alert eye and quizzical expression made Macdonald suspect the "thriller" writer—with just such an expression of severe impersonal curiosity should the creator of skilful murderers face the world.

After the entrance of Anna Seward, Graham Coombe entered the room, and the folding doors of the drawing-room were firmly closed by the announcer, who called:

"*Messieurs et Mesdames!* The Ceremonarius will now address the Treasure Seekers."

The publisher, his eyes twinkling, took up his stand in the middle of the room.

"Ladies and gentlemen, you have done us the honour of meeting here this evening for a battle of wits. Each of you will be handed a clue to unravel, which will, when deciphered, lead you on to the next step in the game. In the event of any of you wishing to supplement your personal stores of information, my library is at your service. Clues may lead you to the library, the dining-room, or the entrance lounge, all on the ground floor, where is also the telephone room with guides, timetables, and so forth. The phone is, of course, at your disposal. In the small room at the turn of the stairs above this floor an additional store of books will be found, all published by the firm over which I have the honour to preside. In all these rooms you will also find refreshments to assist your labours. Eventually, when the Treasure has been unearthed, a final test will take place. All of you, save two, have had books published by Coombe at one time or another. To the best of my belief you have none of you met one another before."

Here he glanced rapidly round the room, and Macdonald fairly chuckled at the guarded expressions on the faces of the guests.

"During the evening you will have the chance of conversing

with and observing one another. At the conclusion of the Treasure Hunt, each guest will be allowed to ask six questions of each fellow guest, and make an attempt to place his or her name and status, direct questions as to name and authorship being barred. You are, by agreement, set upon an evening of detection. I hope that you may derive entertainment from the pursuit."

There was an outbreak of laughter and cheerful comment. Laurence Sterne was heard to raise his voice.

"I take it that it's part of the game that we all endeavour to conceal our personalities, while being under an obligation to answer questions truthfully when it comes to the final round?"

"Exactly," beamed Coombe. "This is a competition. To give away points to your rivals is against the spirit of the game. My sister, the major-domo here, and myself, are at your disposal to answer all legitimate questions. Paper and pencils are provided on the table under the window. I will now present you with your initial clues."

As Graham Coombe began to hand out slips of paper, Jane Austen turned to Fanny Burney:

"Treasure Hunting, or a General Knowledge paper set to the whole school," laughed Jane. "We can all feel that we're back at school again, guessing our way through exams. My Science Mistress once told me that my ability in pure guess-work amounted to inspiration. She meant to be crushing, but I took it as a compliment."

Fanny Burney studied the speaker with a thoughtful air.

"An inspired guesser ought to be disqualified on this occasion," she said severely, and her pedantic voice amused

Macdonald. "It's like trying to be telepathic at bridge," she went on, "quite improper."

"Are you telepathic, Miss Burney?" asked Jane Austen in her most impudent manner. "So am I. Shall we call quits and cancel out?"

"If you want to practise telepathy, Jane," began Samuel Pepys, but Miss Austen cut in:

"I don't—and I won't, so don't be optimistic on my account."

She took a slip of paper from Graham Coombe and turned to Macdonald.

"I hope there's a booby prize," she said to him. "I'm the world's densest at paper games, and as for clues, I shouldn't know one if I met it. If I tell you the books of the Old Testament, will you oblige with geography bits?"

Macdonald, who was at her elbow, laughed.

"My knowledge of geography is limited and specialised," he retorted, recognising the gambit and knowing that she was fishing for Digby Bourne. "Losh! If this is algebra, I'm done!"

It wasn't algebra. The first "clue" was a simple cipher, which ran as follows:—

"*Each separate numeral represents a letter. E is the most frequent letter.*

"*The words 'on' and 'no' are reversible.*

"*2=the letter N.*

"*The letter K occurs thrice, once as an initial, twice as an ultimate.*

2.3. 4.2.3.5.6.7.8.9.7. 2.7.7.8.7.8. 1.7.7.4. 3.2. 7.2.8. 3.1. 8.7.1.4.*"

Each guest was handed a similar slip, and Macdonald assumed (rightly) that each cipher differed from its fellows. He could not help laughing to himself at the manner in which the company set to work, though even as he deciphered, he kept an eye open to observe the others. This might be an easy game, but the prize would go to the speediest, and Macdonald backed Laurence Sterne as the likeliest winner. As it fell out, three people made an almost simultaneous move to their next clues, of whom the quickest was Jane Austen, who completed her cipher a split second before Laurence Sterne and Izaak Walton.

The latter, bidden to seek a desk, realised at once that no such piece of furniture was in the drawing-room. He hurried out to the library downstairs and found a copy of *The Compleat Angler* lying on the end of the desk. This contained a small cross-word, headed "Walton" and Macdonald sat down to the desk to solve it. A moment later he was joined by Anna Seward who gave an exclamation of despair as she took her next clue out of a copy of Boswell's *Life of Johnson*.

"Oh, this is hopeless! The thing's all based on Holy Writ. I never could do Scripture. What do I do now?"

"Bag the Concordance before the others get here," said Macdonald helpfully. He felt happy because he was well up in the sons of Jacob, and recognised that Jael, the wife of Heber the Kenite, was the lady eulogised as "Blessed above women," and he was pretty certain that most of the competitors would go astray by misreading the quotation and putting in another name of four letters. He was half-way through his cross-word, held up by "served by Ahab a little but by Jehu much," when Thomas Traherne strolled in.

"This is utterly beyond my capacity," he groaned. "A drink's the only hope and a little inductive reasoning. Some one spread a rumour that a pukka C.I.D. man's here. I place him as the stout merchant, Samuel Pepys. His feet are about right for beetle crushers. I say, what's the land of Uz? or is it a leg pull? Do Bibles have indices?"

"Sons of Israel… How odd of God to choose the Jews," murmured Anna Seward. "Really I am painfully slow, and the articulated skeleton's just finished the second round— Laurence Sterne, you know. I met him on the stairs and he told me that anything I said would be used in evidence against me. Does that indicate anything? He's a bit sinister—so long and thin, and much too clever. Did Gad live in the land of Uz? I think so. Mrs. Gaskell's much more of a rapide than you'd think from the look of her. I place her as 'crime,' but Madame de Sevigné's still sitting in the drawing-room looking blank."

"The Austen kid's going to win this. She's a mover," said Thomas Traherne. "Lord! You're not through?" This to Macdonald, who had picked out the letters indicated in his cross-word as instructed in a footnote, and was making for the door. *Lycidas* was his next clue and he had noticed a vellum bound copy of Milton upstairs in the drawing-room. Hastening back there, he passed Laurence Sterne, inspecting the lettering on a cross-stitch sampler, while Ben Jonson sat at the bottom of the staircase working steadily at the cross-word. A glint of golden green and a low laugh indicated Jane Austen at the back of the lounge, and Fanny Burney stood beside her.

"Do you feel like Archimedes when you've seen your way

through a clue?" inquired Jane's fresh young voice, and Fanny Burney replied:

"Still feeling that you're in the fourth form, my dear, hearing about—Eureka, I've got it?"

"So I have, got it in one and no questions asked!" laughed Jane, as she hastened toward the library.

Digby Bourne was gazing thoughtfully into the recesses of a grandfather clock at the turn of the stairs, inquiring idiotically, "Have you ever met a nude plum?" as he detached a slip from the pendulum.

In the drawing-room, Madame de Sevigné was still looking in a puzzled way at her very simple cipher, and Graham Coombe was assuring Samuel Pepys that the land of Uz was well authenticated in a famous English classic. Seeing Macdonald hastening towards the bookcase on which lay the vellum bound Milton, Coombe chuckled.

"I've laid ten to one on you and Jane Austen being the winners, Izaak Walton," he said. "Don't disappoint me."

"Wait and see," replied Macdonald, who found himself gazing at a line of music whose melody was not beyond his power to hum. "Hymns A and M," he murmured. "Number 165. St. Anne. That's a gift. Now where did I see that da Vinci cartoon?"

II

IT WAS ABOUT AN HOUR LATER THAT MACDONALD entered the small room which held the volumes published by the firm of Coombe. He had worked his way through a variety of clues, having been held up once through ignorance of the fact that Angostura was an alternative name for Boliver, and that the latter town was situated on the river Orinoco. As the major-domo pointed out, the bottle of Angostura which provided the clue provided bitterness in more senses than one.

Macdonald, being well in the running in the Treasure Hunt, had decided to acquire a little data concerning the authors published by the house of Coombe. It was his ignorance of these which might land him at the bottom of the list when it came to question time, and since he had entered into the spirit of the game and was intent on winning if he could, he wished to get all the information which might assist him in the final test.

A copy of *Coombe's Quarterly* lay on the table, and he

inspected it for photographs, and in the hope of biographical details which might prove useful at question time. Immersed in his research, he fairly jumped when a quiet voice behind him observed, "Old Graham's rather a peach. He does give us a chance to use our grey matter, even though his *mot-croisées* are a bit amateurish."

Turning, Macdonald saw Jane Austen sitting just behind the door, concealed from any one who entered the room until they turned their back on the fireplace opposite. She was laughing at him with evident enjoyment.

"Two people present have never had a book published by the firm of Coombe," she quoted, "and you're one of them. All Coombe's authors get a copy of that *Quarterly*. They don't need to study it here. Q.E.D. You've been very snappy over clues and things, Izaak Walton. You lost time over Angostura, but you hared through the little questionnaire about police procedure in a manner that was highly incriminating. The proper study of mankind is man. Ben Jonson had to go to Whitaker & Co., to look up about coroners and procurators fiscal, but he knew that Bolivar was on the Orinoco, because he'd been there."

Macdonald bowed. "Your verdict, madam, is strictly according to the evidence," he replied, "but why make me a present of the information?"

"It's a fair cop so far as you and Ben Jonson are concerned, isn't it?" she pleaded. "I'm not being altruistic or anything goopy like that, but I want a quid pro quo. I've spotted you as one of the 'non-authors' and I'm nearly certain about the other. You're a Scot, you gave it away first when you said 'Losh,' and when you've finished a clue your *r*'s roll like kettledrums. I'm willing to bet on your occupation, rank, and name, but I want to know if Mrs. Gaskell talks Glasgow or Edinburgh. Can you tell me?"

"I've got my own ideas on the subject," replied Macdonald, "but what about my quid pro quo? You haven't told me anything I didn't know."

"Said he scathingly. I'll give you a clue to Mrs. Gaskell, if you'll answer my question about her accent."

"I don't know if it's in the best traditions of Treasure Hunting, but I'd say she hails from the Highlands and went to school in Edinburgh," replied Macdonald, and Jane Austen laughed.

"I'm right then. Is imagination the most noticeable feature of a Scotswoman?"

"No, not in the sense of literary imagination, if that's what you mean."

"Scots are always heads of departments, aren't they?— having critical constructive and methodical minds. Ask old Graham if his best reader isn't a Scotswoman. That's your quid. Tell me, before you came to this party, did one of your friends come and spill the beans about who might be present? I think that was arranged beforehand, but photographs and personal descriptions were strictly *verboten*. Cunning, wasn't it? The carrot which brought me was Scotland Yard."

Macdonald began to laugh in his turn.

"That's called a double cross in gangster circles," he chuckled. "You're handing me the office that you're a detective writer after inside information, and you're much too canny to give yourself away like that. I shall ask you if you took a first in history at Oxford. You pipped me over Marie Thérèse and Pragmatic Sanctions in clue 7. I remember now."

Jane Austen threw back her head and laughed so that her small white teeth gleamed between her parted lips and made her look younger than ever.

"We're both fifty per cent up in the final test," she chuckled. "Personally, I enjoy the deductive method as applied to my fellow beings much better than working out paper clues."

"So I have observed," said Macdonald. "Your asides have been most helpful."

She looked at him with raised brows. "I'm sorry about that. I ought to emulate Anna Seward, who talks a lot without telling you anything. I just can't place her." Getting up, she added, "We'd better get on with it or we shall be also-rans. I hate looking things up. I always guess or cadge information on a fifty-fifty basis. You owe me another small return. What was the origin of the quotation, 'darkness which may be felt'?"

"There's a very good dictionary of quotations—" began Macdonald, but he got no further. As though in answer to Jane Austen's query, the lights went out, and the small room became black save for a rectangle of fading red which was the electric fire, also dimming to blackness.

"Mercy!" she laughed. "I didn't do that. Honest to God, I'm not being funny. I hate being in the dark, so if you did it—"

"I didn't," said Macdonald. "The main fuse must have gone… You'd better stay where you are for the moment. Don't move about, or you'll knock things over."

A confused clamour came from below. The stairway was in darkness, and startled voices were calling and exclaiming. A crash of glass followed by a voice saying "Hell! I'm sorry. I say, what the devil's happened?" occurred on the landing close below where Macdonald was standing, and then Graham Coombe's voice made itself heard.

"I'm awfully sorry, everybody. This isn't part of the entertainment. There must have been a fuse. Will everybody stay put until we can get some illumination. Sorry, old chap. Better stand still a minute."

Macdonald had got a lighter in his pocket but no matches. The tiny flame at least made a focus of illumination. At the door of the drawing-room Ben Jonson held a lighted match in his fingers for a moment and it shone on the startled face of Mrs. Gaskell just behind him. After it went out, eyes growing accustomed to the darkness could see the firelight shining through the open doors of the drawing-room.

A voice from the stairway said, "Are you there, Val? I've made hay with a whole tray of cocktails and stamped on the sausages. Are you all right, angel?"

"I don't know where your girl friend is, or who she is," retorted the spirited voice of Jane Austen, "but don't go being familiar, Thomas Traherne."

"I say, wouldn't it be rather a lark to have question time now, before the lights come on again?" inquired Laurence Sterne's voice. "It'd make rather a good inquisition in the firelight."

"Don't they grow candles in this house?" inquired a superior female voice on the stairs just above Macdonald. He did not recognise the lady's voice, but drew aside to let her pass, observing the glint of her reddish grey hair just before his rather futile lighter expired. It was Fanny Burney, looking not too amiable.

"Don't mind me. I like being trodden on," said another

voice. "My first question is, do you weigh twenty stone or twenty-five? Oh, hooray! Some one's found a candle. What do you bet that Mr. Coombe's first edition of *David Copperfield*'s been lifted in the melée? Not a bad plot, darling. You could throw the loot out of the window to an accomplice on the pavement."

Laughter gradually spread among the startled company as Graham Coombe and a parlourmaid appeared, the one bearing two very dilapidated looking candles, the other an electric torch.

"Ladies and gentlemen, follow the torch bearers into the drawing-room until repairs are effected," cried the voice of the major-domo. "First aid will be rendered in case of need and stimulants in plenty... Oh, excellent! Music is being provided to calm the company."

Some one in the drawing-room had begun to play the piano and Macdonald heard the liquid notes with pleasure. Bach's first prelude, delicately played, seemed to smooth out the awkwardness of the situation. He stood where he was, and Jane Austen passed him, whispering:

"I say, doesn't it get the old professional instincts all on the qui vive? Darkness always makes me suspicious. You never know, you know!"

Seeing Coombe going downstairs again, after having left the candles on the drawing-room mantelshelf—a quaintly inadequate illumination in a room over thirty feet long—Macdonald following him said, "Can I do anything to help? I'm fairly handy with fuses."

"Thanks very much, but I think it's a case for the Electric Light Company," replied Coombe. "It's the main fuse, we can't get at it. Everything in the house has gone, including the cooker. If you'd come and hold this damned torch while I telephone, I'd be glad. We're not used to this sort of thing. We ought to have candles somewhere, but no one can find them. What a picnic! The phone's in here."

"No harm done," replied Macdonald, "and the authorities are generally very quick on occasions like this. I'll hold the torch while you phone."

"What the devil do I look for?" said Coombe, hunting in the telephone book. "Marylebone? St. Marylebone?... Town Hall... Damn it, that's no good, Meters, Emergency calls...that's it. Doesn't it strike you a bit fishy?" he added as he dialled. "Been here for years. Never known anything like this happen before. Hullo! Speaking from Caroline House..."

The authorities having promised to send a man immediately, Coombe cheered up a little. "I hope there hasn't been any funny stuff going on here," he said. "Can't quite understand it. Heard of a burglary done the other day, a pile of stuff cleared off while the whole household was in darkness... Jolly sporting of some one to start playing the piano up there... Funny thing—people can't talk normally in the dark. Nice touch the chap's got too. What's that? Haydn, isn't it?"

They went back into the drawing-room and found the company gathered round the fire, save for the pianist who was playing in a shadowed corner. Ben Jonson was sitting on the floor close to the fire, his brow corrugated over a paper in his hand. "Bloody hand," he murmured meditatively, "where have I met that one?"

"Try Macbeth, old drink-to-me-only," said Thomas Traherne mendaciously, and Macdonald noticed that the young man was sitting on the arm of Jane Austen's chair. Laurence Sterne was standing by the corner of the mantelshelf, his thin face looking dreamy in the candlelight as he listened to the music, obviously oblivious of his fellows. Anna Seward was murmuring to Madame de Sevigné, "My dear, what a tragedy, such a lovely frock too!"

Macdonald noticed that Madame de Sevigné's golden gown was sadly marred by a stain which spread right down the front of it, as though a glass of wine had been upset on it. He also saw that the lady's hands were trembling a little, and heard her murmuring in reply:

"Oh, that doesn't matter, but I do feel a bit weak in the knees. I was in the lounge when the lights failed, looking at those books in the case by the grandfather clock, and some one banged into me and knocked me right over. I'm a perfect fool in the dark, I always get a sense of vertigo when I can't see anything, and I was frightened. It's all right now, but I could have screamed at the time. Something uncanny about darkness… How well that woman plays! I do envy people who always keep their heads in an emergency."

"I was a bit shattered myself," murmured the low deep voice of Anna Seward. "I'd just popped into the pay-a-penny, you know, and I couldn't get out. At first I thought it was a rather inconsiderate clue, and decided to look for that book of Guy Thorne's *When It Was Dark*. All these young people would scarcely have heard of it."

A diversion was caused here by the entrance of the two maids, the first carrying a very antiquated oil lamp and the second bearing a branched candelabra complete with lighted candles. Miss Susan Coombe followed them talking cheerfully.

"I do apologise to everybody. I feel that this contretemps is a reflection on my housekeeping. We always keep candles—lots of them—only it's so many years since they were needed that we couldn't find them. They'd got hidden behind the soaps and sodas in the store-room cupboard. Oh! my dear Thomas Traherne! Whatever have you done? Is that a cut?"

"Bloody hand! Got you! Own up!" boomed Ben Jonson.

In the comparatively bright light which now filled the room, everybody blinked a little. Thomas Traherne, Macdonald noticed, had got a handkerchief twisted round his hand, with marks of gore on it.

"I'm awfully sorry, Miss Coombe. I cannoned into a tray of drinks in the lounge and I'm afraid I did an awful smash. I cut my hand a bit, but it's nothing. I'm terribly sorry about breaking your glasses."

"Oh, bother the glasses! They don't matter. Geoffrey, take Thomas Traherne upstairs and find iodine and lint. You know where things are in the medicine cupboard. I do hope there aren't any other casualties."

Laurence Sterne was looking round the room with his quick bird-like stare.

"We seem to be a man short," he observed. "Where's Samuel Pepys?"

"In the dining-room, making the best of his opportunities," suggested Ben Jonson. "Do we now resume the status quo and get on with the clues? I've remembered my 'Bloody Hand' poser and I'm ready for the next."

"It's anagrams that get me down." It was the pianist who spoke—Fanny Burney—"I haven't a synthetic mind."

"I'm afraid the Hunt will have to be in abeyance until the

electrician comes," said Coombe. "We're getting candles put everywhere, but they're not very adequate in a house this size."

"Personally I'm only too glad to give my wretched wits an interval of repose," said Anna Seward. "Though I'm going to ask Ben Jonson if he had much trouble with the Customs when he landed at Southampton last month."

There was an outburst of laughter and general conversation and Macdonald heard Graham Coombe's voice beside him.

"I say, have you seen anything of Samuel Pepys? We'd better find him."

Macdonald stepped from the room with his host, and they stood together on the dimly lighted landing where a couple of candles glimmered among the shadows.

"I don't seem to have seen him since the word 'go,'" he replied. "Perhaps he found Treasure Hunting not to his taste and folded his tent like the Arabs."

"I think I'd better make certain," said Coombe. "I was a bit put about earlier on. I'm afraid Samuel Pepys got a bit fresh with Jane Austen and found he'd made a mistake. Confound the fellow!"

"If Jane Austen ticked him off, it's quite reasonable to suppose that Samuel Pepys packed up and went home," replied Macdonald. "If so, his hat and cloak will have been taken from the cloak-room. Let's think, how many men guests have you here? Ben Jonson, Thomas Traherne, Samuel Pepys, Laurence Sterne, the major-domo and myself. Six."

"No. Five. The major-domo is my secretary, Geoffrey Manton, and he lives here, I got him to do the announcing touch. I'll take this candle and go along to the cloak-room. I hope to the deuce that electrician gets a move on."

Macdonald went with Coombe to the men's cloak-room

which opened from the entrance lobby, and looked round in the light from the candle. Five hats and caps on the pegs and Macdonald made a guess at the owners of the different hats. The Gibus he attributed to Thomas Traherne, the black Trilby to Laurence Sterne. The rather shapeless dark velour looked like Ben Jonson's, and the dark Homburg was his own. Coombe lifted down a bowler and glanced inside it.

"This belongs to Samuel Pepys," he said, "and here's his coat. He's still in the house. It's damned odd, isn't it?... Oh! thank the Lord! Here are the lights again. Quick work, what!"

"Very quick," agreed Macdonald. "If Samuel Pepys is still in the house, we'd better find him. Speaking without prejudice, he looks as though he could lower a few. Shall we try the dining-room? He wasn't in the drawing-room, or on the stairs, or in the small library."

They went back into the lounge hall, and Coombe opened a door which led into a panelled room with a fine rosewood table and Sheraton sideboard. The curtains were drawn across the windows, the room immaculately neat and obviously empty. Coombe chuckled nervously as he bent and looked under the table—the only place where a man could possibly be concealed. "This is a sort of Mad Hatter's Party," he said. "I set my guests on a Treasure Hunt and end by hunting for one of them myself. Damn the fellow! Where is he? He can't have taken it into his head to go upstairs and have a snooze. Try Susan's sitting-room."

Miss Coombe's study—a workman-like looking room with built in bookcases, filled cabinets, and a big kneehole desk, did nothing to assist them. No one was there, and Coombe looked nonplussed.

"This is silly," he observed. "The chap wasn't in the library when the lights went out, because I was there myself, and I was alone. Laurence Sterne had just been in looking up a clue, and he went out a minute before the lights failed. I turned the key in the door when I came out and shut it, because I didn't want people blundering about there in the dark."

"You've probably locked him in then," replied Macdonald. "We'll just look in the telephone-room again to make sure before we go on."

"But damn it, we were in there just now, and the room was empty," expostulated Graham Coombe.

"We didn't really look. That electric torch of yours throws a very small beam," replied Macdonald. "Might as well make sure."

They went again to the small room at the back of the house and Coombe threw open the door, saying irritably:

"Of course he's not here."

There was a desk by the window, on which stood the telephone. A large arm-chair stood in the middle of the small floor space, and against the wall facing the window was a fine mahogany bureau, whose heavy front was pulled out, though the flap was not let down. Pulling aside the chair a little, Macdonald said, "I'm afraid he is here. Very much here." Coombe wheeled round and stood looking down at the floor with horror on his face. In the space between the arm-chair and the flat-fronted bureau Samuel Pepys lay on the floor his arms flung wide, his eyes staring at the ceiling. Macdonald knew at a glance that he was dead.

"My God! How ghastly. Chap must have had a heart attack when the lights failed," groaned Coombe. "Get some brandy, there's a good chap. I'll ring up a doctor. I hope to God it's not as bad as it looks."

"I'm afraid it is. Just as bad," replied Macdonald. "Stand by that door, sir. We don't want any one blundering in here."

Kneeling down beside the big man on the floor, Macdonald felt for a pulse which he was certain had stopped beating. He went further, and loosened the fine tucked shirt and felt for the heart, then tested the temperature of the hands with his own. They were already cold, though the large body retained enough heat to tell that death had only occurred a short time ago.

"He's quite dead," said Macdonald quietly. "It looks as though you might be right. He probably died within the last quarter of an hour—as the lights went out, perhaps. I think it'd be best if I telephoned for one of our own surgeons. It'll be simpler in the long run."

Graham Coombe looked appalled. He mopped his lofty brow with his handkerchief as he replied:

"Do just as you think best. My God! What a frightful thing to happen. Shall I go and tell the others to clear out?"

"No. Not yet. There's bound to be an inquiry, and it will be better if every one stays on for the time being."

Macdonald went to the telephone and dialled a number, adding to Coombe, "Don't touch anything, sir. It may be quite simple and straightforward, but it's better to leave everything as it is until the surgeon's seen him. There's glass on the floor there, he probably had a drink in his hand and dropped it... This is Chief Inspector Macdonald speaking. That Wright? I want you at Caroline House immediately. Three minutes from Harley Street. Know it? Good. Quickly, there's a good chap."

Just as Macdonald replaced the receiver, some one opened

the door, which was brought up short by Graham Coombe's shoulder, and Laurence Sterne's laughing voice said:

"Sorry, am I butting in? My last clue is quite beyond me and the telephone seems indicated as the quickest way of cadging information."

"So sorry, old chap, just a minute," stammered Coombe, but Macdonald, quick to make up his mind, put in:

"Let him come in, sir. He may be a help."

Coombe stood away from the door, and the tall thin figure of Laurence Sterne slipped in through the door, and he closed it behind him.

"Good Lord!" he ejaculated, his angular brows twitching oddly. "That looks bad. Fit? Heart? The poor chap looks a goner."

Macdonald nodded. "I'm afraid so. A doctor will be here inside ten minutes. You're Ashton Vale, aren't you? Will you help to keep things going up stairs? Say that Samuel Pepys had a tumble in the dark, but a doctor's been sent for, and Mr. Coombe hopes that every one will carry on."

Ashton Vale—who carried the label of Laurence Sterne— looked back at Macdonald with a question in his keen eyes which he did not put into words. He gave another glance at the figure on the floor, and then put his hand on Graham Coombe's shoulder.

"Tough luck for you, old chap, rather than for him. We've all got to pass out sometime, and he got his call without knowing it, from the look of things." Turning to Macdonald he added, "I get you. I'll do my best. You're the C.I.D. wallah, I take it? Thought so."

He slipped out again, and Macdonald knew that the

Economist's quick wits had taken in everything—the reason for his request that the party should "carry on," and the possibility that "heart" was not the only explanation to account for that still figure on the floor.

Turning to Coombe, Macdonald said:

"I will stay here, sir. Would you be at hand outside when Dr. Wright comes? And if the electrician is still on the premises, get him to stay. It will save a lot of trouble if we anticipate questions by getting the facts in order."

"Yes, yes. Of course—but it's pretty obvious, isn't it?" said Coombe nervously. "I know that Gardien had some heart trouble, he mentioned it to me a short while ago."

"Quite," murmured Macdonald, glancing at the door, and Coombe took the hint and hurried out.

So Samuel Pepys was Andrew Gardien, author of a dozen detective stories. The "Master Mechanic" the reviewers called him, owing to his ingenuity in inventing methods of killing based on simple mechanical contraptions. "Heath Robinson murders," another reviewer had styled them, involving bits of cord and wire and counterpoises, all nicely calculated to tidy themselves up when their work was done. Springs and levers and pulleys had been used with wonderful effect by the quick brain which had once animated that still body.

Turning the key in the door, Macdonald bent over Gardien's body. He covered the face with the man's own silk handkerchief, and studied the hands with a frowning face.

III

Dr. Wright, attached to the experts department of the C.I.D., lived in Poland Court, W.1., and he arrived at Caroline House within twelve minutes of Macdonald's call. Having briefly examined the body of Andrew Gardien, he said, "Heart failure apparently. Been dead about half an hour. No wound as far as I can tell. No signs of poison. Were you with him when death occurred?"

Macdonald explained the circumstances, and Wright looked down thoughtfully at the dead man.

"It looks as though you found him about ten minutes or so after he died," commented the doctor.

"If it had been poison, it would have had to be something of the nature of prussic acid, or one of the cyanide group. Nothing else would have acted quickly enough. It wasn't one of those. No smell, no corrosion. You say he seemed perfectly fit an hour and a half ago, and you found him dead about ten minutes after the fuse occurred. He looks as though he might have been a heart subject. Any reason for supposing there was anything else to it?"

"No. Nothing you'd call a reason. Have a look at the palms of his hands and see if you notice anything."

Wright bent and examined the dead man's hands and then took a lens out of his pocket and peered through it.

"Looks as though he'd scorched them a trifle. There's a bit of a mark, nothing much though. What's in your mind?"

"Those marks showed much more plainly when I first looked at him," said Macdonald. "It just occurred to me— probably a wild idea—but there was an almighty big fuse for no apparent reason, and if the chap was a heart subject, an electric shock might have finished him off quite easily."

"True enough, but why should he have monkeyed with the fittings? You don't get an electric shock unless some of the fixtures are faulty."

The doctor looked inquiringly round the room. An electric fire stood in front of the fireplace and he made a move towards it.

"Don't touch it for the moment," said Macdonald. "It's still warm but only just perceptibly. It's been turned off for some time. A stove that size keeps warm for the best part of an hour after the current has been switched off—warm to the touch that is, so that you can tell it's been alight."

"I suppose it does. Are you assuming the stove leaked?"

Wright had an inquiring mind. Having glanced at the stove, he followed up the flex which connected it with the point in the wainscot whence the current was derived. This point was not set in the wall close to the fireplace, but was in the adjacent wall, close to the mahogany bureau. The plug at the end of the flex was not now fitted into the point, but lay on the floor a little way from it, although the electric switch was still turned down to supply the current.

"Oh ho! Do we see daylight?" inquired the doctor. "I remember that I once tripped over the flex of my own electric fire and jerked the plug out of the point when the fire—all three bars—was full on. The result was a blue flash a yard long and a complete fuse of everything in the house. The electrician told me that such a fuse would almost certainly occur when the wiring was bearing a heavy load if the plug was jerked out with the power full on. That what's in your mind?"

"Something of the kind," said Macdonald, and Wright went on:

"Let's see. You imagine the flex got in the fellow's way, and he tripped over it, came down on the stove and burnt his hands a bit, and staggered up and collapsed from shock a moment later? Short circuit in his own system as well as in the electric doings. Quite a possible explanation, though I don't quite see how the flex got in his way. Still, at these Treasure Hunt dos, people grovel in corners and hunt behind pictures and all the rest. However, I suppose you'll have a P.M. and work out probabilities after that."

He went to the table and bent and sniffed at the pieces of glass Macdonald had collected from the floor.

"Nothing wrong there, so far as I can tell. Get them analysed to make a job of it. Liqueur glass, apparently. Cherry brandy. Shall I get him moved right away?"

"I think so. I'll go through his pockets to see if he'd got any of the Treasure Hunt clues on him. Coombe seemed to be surprised to find him here. There were no clues leading to that bureau and there doesn't seem to have been any reason why he should have opened it."

"Oh, you're trying to be too reasonable. If you ask people

to a racket of this kind, it's only to be supposed that they'll look anywhere and everywhere."

Macdonald agreed. After a few moments further consultation, he rang up his own department to ask for a photographer to be sent at once, so that the body could then be moved to the mortuary, and left Dr. Wright in charge in the telephone-room until these matters were settled.

Graham Coombe was walking up and down the lounge when Macdonald reappeared, and he hurried towards the chief inspector with an anxious look on his face.

"Dr. Wright thinks death was due to heart failure following shock," said Macdonald. "I think it would be a wise move to question all your guests and try to determine Gardien's movements from the time the hunt started."

The publisher looked still more worried.

"Is that necessary?" he expostulated. "Things are pretty wretched as it is. Every one will be upset, and if you get on the warpath it'll put the lid on it. Devil take it, the man hasn't been murdered, or anything like that."

The last sentence sounded much more like a question than a statement, but Macdonald avoided answering it.

"It's a bit puzzling, sir. You say that none of the clues given to Gardien would have caused him to go into the room where we found him."

"That's true, but I told every one the telephone was there, at their disposal, that is. In a game of this kind, it's quite legitimate to ring up your friends and ask for information."

"Yes. I see that, but I can't see why Gardien should have opened the bureau in order to telephone if there was no clue to lead him to do so. I don't want to worry you unnecessarily for I realise quite well how distressed you feel, but I do consider it's important to get the facts established as fully as possible while events are still fresh in people's minds. However it's for you to decide. I'm not speaking as an official, only as a guest who happens to have first hand knowledge of the requirements of coroners. If you'd rather, you can ask Wright to report to the local authorities and let them carry on. I shall then be merely a witness among other witnesses, but it's up to me to tell you what I consider the wisest thing to do, and the most likely to save people further trouble."

Coombe's forehead puckered up unhappily.

"I've no doubt you're right," he said. "Have it your own way. Make any arrangement you like."

"First, whom must you notify among Gardien's people? His wife?"

"He hasn't got one, not to my knowledge. My dear chap, I don't know the first thing about him," groaned Coombe. "I don't even know where he lives. In the country, I believe. I always send letters to his agent. I've talked to Gardien at my office once or twice, that's all. Wife?—how should I know?"

"It would be best to get on to his agent, then, and learn Gardien's address," said Macdonald. Coombe was beginning to get really agitated and evidently needed assistance.

"Won't be at his office now. Mardon-Elliott, that's the man. A new agent. Lives in Surrey somewhere, God knows, I don't."

Coombe ran his hand through his thinning hair with the gesture of one distraught, and then exclaimed, with an expression of sudden enlightenment:

"What mugs we are! Of course Gardien will have a card on him. We must look in his pockets."

"I've tried that already. There's a card-case, but no address, only his name. Don't bother about that any more for the moment. I'll see to it later. It might be as well to put Gardien's overcoat in the telephone-room, there will probably be an address in one of the pockets. A man doesn't carry much about in evening clothes. Meantime will you arrange for me to have the small library upstairs, and let me see people one by one?"

"Yes. I'll see to it. Good Lord, this is more than I bargained for! I undertook that there should be no publicity when I organised this stunt. Jam for the papers, that's what this will amount to."

Macdonald went back to the men's cloak-room and collected the hat and coat which Coombe had indicated as Andrew Gardien's. A quick search produced gloves and handkerchief, rammed carelessly into the large pockets, a pipe and tobacco pouch, a small bottle of tablets, with Boots' label—evidently made up to a prescription—several bus tickets and a few bills for cash purchases. In an inside pocket was a small bundle of letters, but those which were still in envelopes were all addressed to Gardien, care of his agent, Mardon-Elliott, Thavies House, Strand. Not a sign of a private address.

"Odd," thought Macdonald. "However, that can wait. It's this house that matters now."

He left the coat in the telephone-room, where Dr. Wright was still looking down at the electric fire with a thoughtful air, and went up to the small library on the first floor. Here he found Jane Austen standing by the fire talking to Graham Coombe, and the publisher said:

"I expect you'd rather I left you to it. I've explained to

everybody more or less, and they're quite willing to answer questions. This is Miss Valerie Woodstock."

The fair-haired girl smiled at Macdonald.

"We guessed one another early on, didn't we? I still feel as though this is all part of the game and believe old Graham's doing a leg pull."

"I wish that were so, but it isn't," replied Macdonald. "The evening began as a farce and has ended in a tragedy. I want to work out the movements of the man who was labelled Samuel Pepys. You know his real identity I take it?"

"No. I haven't the least idea. Mr. Coombe's been very careful not to tell anybody anything. Who is he?"

"He was Andrew Gardien." Macdonald used the past tense and left it at that. "Did you see anything of him during the evening?"

"Yes. I saw him at the back of the lounge as the clock struck nine."

"What was he doing? Sitting? Standing? or just passing on his way?"

"Do you want all the i's dotted?"

"Yes, please, and the t's crossed."

The girl's shrewd eyes met Macdonald's full. Her appearance might indicate the society miss, interested only in clothes and a good time, but her expression showed a very different personality. Valerie Woodstock had recently leapt into fame for an erudite piece of historical research, and Macdonald knew that a first-class brain was hidden behind that frivolous exterior.

"We'd better wash out the Samuel Pepys' label and call him Gardien now," she observed calmly. "I think he was slower off the mark than some of us. I had done up to clue four before he made a move from the drawing-room. I'd got to 'Integrity is decorative and silicular' and I was hunting round for a vase of honesty. There's some on a table in the corner of the lounge under the stairs—honesty and Cape gooseberries in a big blue jug. I rescued my clue from the pot and sat down on a tuffet to read it. Gardien came round the corner of the stairs, and began being fatuous. Not feeling that way disposed, I removed myself from his vicinity and went back into the drawing-room where Miss Coombe was encouraging Madame de Sevigné. It was just after nine o'clock then. I heard the clock strike. I didn't see Mr. Gardien again. He seemed quite well then."

"Did you see where he went when you left him?"

"No. I wasn't interested."

"Was there anybody else in the lounge at the time?"

"Denzil Strafford—labelled Thomas Traherne—was there for a moment or two."

Once again their eyes met; Macdonald's grey, expressionless, but very steady, the girl's blue and bright, and very alert.

"And Mr. Strafford observed that Mr. Gardien was— fatuous—to use your expression?"

"Is all this necessary?" Valerie Woodstock's voice was indignant and a little impatient and Macdonald replied:

"It's not personal inquisitiveness on my part, Miss Woodstock. I happened to be here, and I can't very well ignore the whole situation. My own opinion is that a preliminary clearing of the decks may eventually save trouble all round. You are under no obligation to answer questions, it's purely voluntary—and of course unofficial."

"I never supposed that personal curiosity was your motive," she said dryly, "but I think I am justified in showing a little impersonal curiosity too. If the man is dead, what killed him?"

"Heart failure—so far as the doctor can tell."

Her arched eyebrows shot up. "A formula, isn't it? Most deaths can be put down to heart failure finally."

"There were no indications to lead to any other reasoning," replied Macdonald. "I asked you—or was about to ask you—if Mr. Strafford spoke to Mr. Gardien in your presence?"

"Of course he did," she replied. "You've shown me already that you're quick at seeing things. You heard Denzil call out to me just after the lights went out, didn't you? He was at Trinity when I was up at St. Elizabeth's. Mr. Coombe didn't know we were friends. However. There it is. Denzil ticked off Gardien good and strong—but I don't imagine that Gardien had a heart attack on that account."

"Thanks. I see the general outline. Only one other question. Was there any one else in the lounge at the time?"

"Not to my knowledge. In fact I'm sure there wasn't. I was furious—with both of them. I'm quite capable of looking after myself. Is that all?"

"That's all, thank you."

Macdonald went steadily through his self-appointed job. He found that the party consisted of four "thriller" writers, four "straight" authors, in addition to Janet Campbell, one of Coombe's readers who had the label of Mrs. Gaskell, and himself.

The four thriller writers were as follows:—

Ronile Rees (Fanny Burney)
Nadia Delareign (Madame de Sevigné)
Denzil Strafford (Thomas Traherne)
Andrew Gardien (Samuel Pepys)

The four straight writers were:—

Valerie Woodstock (Jane Austen) History
Mrs. Louise Etherton (Anna Seward) Romance
Digby Bourne (Ben Jonson) Travel
Ashton Vale (Laurence Sterne) Economics

Of all the guests, only two pairs were previously acquainted, Valerie Woodstock and Denzil Strafford; and Ashton Vale and Mrs. Etherton. (Macdonald was sadly out in his first estimate of that lady as a detective writer. Despite her pronounced profile and severe manner she was the most popular "heart-beat" romantic on the market.) None of them had previously met Andrew Gardien, and none of them had guessed his identity. There was plenty of evidence to prove that Gardien had not moved out of the drawing-room until shortly before nine o'clock, when he had followed Valerie Woodstock down into the lounge. Concerning the matter of that meeting, young Denzil Strafford was perfectly explicit. The latter had gone into the telephone-room to ring through to a friend for information concerning the nature of a pseudo-carp (which proved to be an apple) and on emerging into the lounge had heard Valerie Woodstock's voice addressing Andrew Gardien. Strafford had got to the back of the stairs in time to see Gardien trying to kiss Valerie, and had promised to bash his face in at some future time. Gardien was a big fellow, and the manner in which he had got hold of Valerie made the younger man's blood boil. "The blighter had been swilling cocktails ever since he came, and he reeked of whisky then," said Strafford. "If it hadn't been that we were guests in Coombe's house, I'd have run him out on to the pavement and socked his jaw then and there. When the lights went out I thought at once that it was some low trick of Gardien's and I made a dash for the stairs. That was when I collided with that tray of drinks. I thought Gardien was after Val again."

"After Miss Woodstock had gone upstairs, did you see what happened to Gardien? Did he move on, or stay in the alcove under the stairs?"

"He stayed there. I went upstairs again—Coombe was just coming down—and I thought of telling him that Gardien was drunk—but I didn't like to—I wish I had now."

"Yes. I wish you had," said Macdonald.

When Nadia Delareign appeared to be questioned, the first thing that Macdonald noticed was that she was no longer wearing her golden frock which had had a glass of wine upset over it. She wore an evening cloak over a dark blue silk frock.

Macdonald expressed sympathy over the damaged gown, and she replied:

"Very nice of you to be so sympathetic. Susan Coombe was a brick. She sent it off straight to the 'day and night cleaners'—those people in Baker Street who advertise that they're always open. She thought the stain would come out if it were cleaned immediately; but a little thing like that doesn't matter. What a dreadful tragedy to have happened here when we were all so gay and thoughtless. Such a very fine-looking man Mr.

Gardien was, too. His brow reminded me of Beethoven's. I was just saying to Miss Coombe that some of the finest intellects among modern writers find satisfaction in the technique of the detective story. The problem…"

"Undoubtedly," said Macdonald dryly. "And I am very glad to have such experts to present the necessary evidence. Would you be kind enough to tell me when you last saw Mr. Gardien? We are trying to find who was the last person to see him."

"I was talking to him in the drawing-room for quite a long time. I found him *most* interesting and most sympathetic. We almost forgot the Treasure Hunt in discussing our experiences in the East. Indeed that was how I deduced that Samuel Pepys hid the personality of Mr. Gardien. His last book but one had India for its setting, and there was no mistaking the first-hand knowledge involved. As a matter of fact, I stayed a night at Colombo on my way home at the Galle Face, you know, and Mr. Gardien was staying there, too. A curious coincidence. I didn't tell him, of course, but when I said, 'Oh, you must be Andrew Gardien; I realise it from your knowledge of India,' he just smiled and admitted it most charmingly. I think we must have been chatting for nearly an hour."

"Not quite, I think. Mr. Gardien was in the lounge at nine o'clock," said Macdonald. "I think that you were downstairs when the lights failed?"

"Yes. A most terrifying experience," said Miss Delareign with a shudder. "We all have our weak points, and though I am generally a most fearless woman in the face of danger, I am very sensitive over darkness. Somehow I felt that something terrible was happening, and I was puzzled about that grey-haired man. Apparently Miss Rees and I were the only people who saw him, but I thought at the time it was very odd. I am sure that he was not among the guests when the first clues were distributed, and he did seem to move in a furtive way. When the lights failed some one knocked into me most violently, and I lost my balance and fell down. I thought at once of that peculiar-looking man. Have you found out who he is?"

"I have heard nothing about him," said Macdonald. "Where did you see him?"

"At the far end of the lounge, just as I was going towards that bookcase under the stairs. I'm afraid that I don't know anything about the popes, and it never occurred to me that Leo was just a joke and I was supposed to look for a lion, and I thought the *History of the Papacy* might help. As I went downstairs I said to Miss Rees—she was labelled 'Fanny Burney,' you know—'Who *is* that man? I'm sure he wasn't upstairs.' He was just going into the telephone-room. It would have been about a quarter of an hour before the lights went out."

"Did you see him again?"

"No. I was hunting for my clue, and I found a book of ghost stories, a most amusing book, and one of the stories gave me an idea. With a little manipulation it suggested an idea for a new plot—no plagiarism, of course, just a train of thought following on a particular incident. I'm afraid I forgot the time. I was so absorbed in my inspiration, and when I get an idea…"

"Quite," interpolated Macdonald. By dint of keeping the scatter-brained lady severely to the point, he arrived at the following facts:

Miss Delareign had stayed in the large drawing-room until Andrew Gardien went downstairs. She had then moved into the small room which was connected with the drawing-room by folding doors and had talked to Janet Campbell (labelled as Mrs. Gaskell). She had gone downstairs a few minutes later, passing Miss Rees (labelled as Fanny Burney), and had commented to her on the grey-haired man. Miss Delareign had gone to the alcove of the lounge under the stairs some time after Gardien and Strafford had left it, and she was still there when the lights failed. Since it was half-past nine when the fuse occurred, Miss Delareign had presumably been in the alcove for twenty minutes by herself. When she was coming away a glass of wine or liqueur had been spilt over her frock. She accounted for this by saying that some one had left a glass of wine on the table, and that this had been knocked over when some one rushed violently into her in the darkness. Asked by Macdonald if it were a man or a woman who had thus collided with her, she replied that it was certainly a man; the force with which she had been flung over left no room for doubt.

Breathing a sigh of relief when the verbose lady had been shown to the door, Macdonald asked next for Miss Rees. Miss Delareign was a confused and unreliable witness, but he had hopes of Miss Rees. Judging from her conversation at the opening of the evening, she was a logical and clear-headed woman who should be a reliable witness. Miss Rees was as explicit as any detective could wish, and set forth her own movements lucidly. She had been in the drawing-room or the lounge until eight forty-five, having then dealt with a cipher, a cross-word puzzle and an acrostic involving the names of towns situated on certain rivers. (General knowledge seems to be the lady's speciality, Macdonald noted. She knew much more about rivers than he did, and quite as much about the sons of Israel and the jewels of the Apocalypse.) She was quite sure of the time, having a watch on her wrist, and was timing herself for the different clues. At eight-fifty she had gone into the library to look in a dictionary of quotations. At nine o'clock she had entered the little book-room on the stairs to work out a numerical problem involving the dates of the Kings of England. (Macdonald felt that he was saved from an inferiority complex by her admission that she had borrowed a John Richard Green's *Short History* from the library to refresh her memory.) At nine-ten precisely she had gone downstairs and rescued her next clue from the fruit bowl in the dining-room. On the way she had met Miss Delareign, who had drawn her attention to the grey-haired man walking into the telephone-room.

"I put him down as the detective," she said in her calm, matter-of-fact voice. "I had been told that a C.I.D. man might be present, and I thought that we were supposed to deduce him. I put you down as Andrew Gardien—which shows how misleading appearances can be. The man could certainly write," she added, with an air of one offering a sop to Cerberus.

"I suppose he could," replied Macdonald with a smile. "Can you describe this grey-haired man more precisely?"

"About five-foot eight in height, very broad shouldered and flat-footed," she said. "His back was towards me and I did not see his face. He wore a dinner-jacket and his hair was rather short; I should describe him as bullet-headed. I can't tell you any more than that. I came upstairs again then, and went into the drawing-room again. Miss Coombe was there and Laurence Sterne, whom I understand is Ashton

Vale. Just about this time I realised that I had a bad headache coming on. I only mention this personal detail to explain why I went upstairs. I seldom go out in the evenings, and I had found this party a little exhausting. I had some aspirin in my bag, and I went up to the landing above, where there is a small settee, and I rested there for a while. I was still there when the lights failed. Quite honestly, I should have been glad to sit in the dark for some time, but I thought that I ought to come down. As I reached this floor some one struck a match by the drawing-room door. He was labelled Ben Jonson, I think. Another man was standing in the doorway here with a cigarette lighter in his hand, only I could not see who he was. Judging by their voices, Mr. Coombe was close to the library door at the time and Mr. Vale was on the staircase."

The pleasant deliberate voice ceased, and Macdonald saw with some sympathy the movement of the speaker's hand across her forehead. Miss Rees looked tired, and her eyes gave evidence of the headache of which she had complained.

"Thank you very much for the trouble you have taken," said Macdonald. "You have been most helpful."

"I can't see what difference it all makes," she said wearily. "I understand that Mr. Gardien died of a heart attack. It is only to be hoped that he saw a doctor recently. If that is so, Mr. Coombe may be spared the distress of attending an inquest. If that is all the information you need from me, I should be very glad if I might go home. It's a long time since I have been to an evening party, and it will certainly be a very long time before I go to another."

Macdonald murmured a word of sympathy and assured

her that she could go home at once. He felt grateful to Miss Rees for her admirably explicit evidence, for he put no trust at all in the effusiveness of Miss Delareign.

The story of the grey-haired man was the chief point which required elucidating at present, though Macdonald had had a hunch ever since he saw Andrew Gardien's dead body that quite a lot of elucidation would be needed before a satisfactory explanation could be arrived at.

Unofficial as his present inquiry was, he intended to pursue it before the small events of the evening could become confused in the minds of the guests.

IV

IT WAS HALF-PAST ELEVEN BEFORE ALL THE GUESTS HAD departed from Caroline House, leaving the Treasure unlocated. The key of the telephone-room was safe in Macdonald's pocket when he was joined by Graham Coombe in the small library for a final conference. The publisher looked nervous and melancholy, but Miss Coombe—to all appearances—as placid as she had been when she received her guests. Macdonald got up to assist her with a tray which she was carrying, and she observed:

"I belong to the old-fashioned school. A good strong cup of tea is more to my liking in times of emergency than gin or whisky. Will you have a cup, too? Well, Graham, I said beforehand that I disliked the idea of your party. Too clever by half. The only sensible thing you did was to ask the chief inspector."

"Really, Susan," began Coombe irritably, but the lady went on firmly:

"I'm only too thankful that somebody's here who can get

things straightened out. You are no good at all over complications of this kind."

She turned to Macdonald. "Sugar? I think I've got one point settled. If there were a stranger in the house this evening, I can tell you just how and when he got in. No grey-haired man was admitted at the front door, but there is a possibility that some one may have got in at the servant's entrance. The housemaid, Gladys Smith, admitted that she slipped out just before nine o'clock to see if she could meet the postman; they are devoted to one another, it appears. Gladys walked to the corner of William Street, and left the back door opened while she was out. Obviously any one could have got in."

"Does Gladys make a habit of slipping out to meet the last post?" inquired Macdonald, sipping his tea, and Miss Coombe nodded.

"She does. I asked that particularly. The cook knew she went and just let her, saying, 'Girls will be girls.' I don't mind Gladys making a date with the postman, but I do object to her leaving the back door open. Of course, you're thinking that some one could have watched the house and got to know that Gladys left the door on the crack, so to speak."

Macdonald nodded, and Miss Coombe went on:

"Well, it's all very odd and mysterious. I expect we shall find it boils down to common or garden burglary when we've had time to look into things, but I don't see that there's necessarily any connection between the intruder and poor Mr. Gardien's death, do you?"

"No, not necessarily, though there may be some connection between his death and the fusing of the lights."

"The fuse was burnt out, not removed," put in Graham

Coombe. "That is to say it was caused by an accident or some fault in the wiring. I'm of the opinion that Gardien's death was due to shock. The lights failed, and he was so startled that he jumped up too quickly, or made some sudden effort, and just passed out, as heart cases sometimes do."

"Let's hope you're right," observed Miss Coombe. "But all the same I should be interested to know if the inspector succeeded in locating everybody when the black-out occurred."

"Yes. I've got everybody accounted for," replied Macdonald. "Oddly enough, no one seems to have seen Mr. Gardien since a few minutes after nine, when Mr. Strafford left him in the lounge. At the time of the fuse people were placed like this."

He held out a sheet of paper to his hostess, and she read it aloud as she studied it:

Miss Woodstock and Macdonald.—Small library on first floor.

Miss Delareign.—Alcove under the stairs, ground floor. Alone.

Miss Rees.—Second floor landing. Came downstairs on to first floor a moment or so after the fuse, and met Macdonald.

Mr. Strafford.—On the stairs between ground floor and first floor.

Mrs. Etherton.—Upstairs in ladies' dressing-room (alone).

Digby Bourne.—In drawing-room annexe.

Miss Janet Campbell.—In main drawing-room.

Ashton Vale.—In dining-room (alone).

Geoffrey Manton.—In study on first floor (alone).

Mr. Coombe.—In library (alone).

Miss Coombe.—In housekeeper's room in the basement.

Mr. Gardien.—In telephone-room (alone).

"Thirteen in all," observed Miss Coombe. "I'm not a superstitious woman, but I do prefer even numbers."

"Don't talk rubbish!" snapped the publisher. "I should be glad if the chief inspector would answer one question for us." He turned and glared at Macdonald. "Have you any reason for supposing that Gardien's death was due to anything other than natural causes?"

"Nothing so substantial as a reason," replied Macdonald. "Two abnormal events happened, apparently simultaneously. The current failed, leaving the house in total darkness, and a man was found dead. Perhaps darkness makes me suspicious. We all react to it in some way. I felt that something was wrong. When you told me that Mr. Gardien had no clue which led him to the telephone-room, and certainly none which would have led him to open a closed bureau, I wanted to account for his presence in the room and for the opening of the bureau. Finally, an intruder was seen in the house shortly before the lights failed, and Miss Delareign was knocked down by somebody rushing across the hall just after the fuse. Taking things all together, I think an investigation is indicated."

"I quite agree with you," said Miss Coombe. "I believe myself that the intruder engineered the fuse by interfering with the current in some way, and that Mr. Gardien saw something happen which caused a shock resulting in his death. He may even have got a real shock—an electric one—if he happened to have been touching any of the fittings when the fuse occurred. Wouldn't that be possible?"

"It seems quite reasonable to me," replied Macdonald. "I have been very grateful to you and your brother for co-operating with me in a purely unofficial inquiry. I think you will find it justified in the event of a further investigation. I know just how difficult it is for people to be accurate over details some time after an event. They confuse what actually happened with what somebody else told them."

"Don't I know it!" said Susan Coombe, in her deep, sensible voice. "How many people can give an accurate account of even the simplest transaction? One in ten? Take Miss Delareign—I wouldn't believe a word that woman told me without some corroboration. She just gabbles, and she's as blind as a bat and too conceited to wear spectacles. If the presence of the grey-haired man rested on her evidence alone, I should be inclined to disregard it; but Miss Rees—she's a very different proposition. She struck me as a most able woman, quiet, level-headed, observant, and intelligent. If *she* says she saw the man, then he was there."

"Pure feminine bias," growled Coombe. "Miss Delareign is a most logical writer."

"She may be logical on paper, but in conversation she's thoroughly stupid," said Miss Coombe firmly.

Macdonald got up at this juncture.

"I want to have another look at the telephone-room," he said, and Graham Coombe replied:

"I thought that was coming. I've been wondering all this time why you didn't concentrate on that. It's obvious that you think there's some problem to be solved over Gardien's death."

"I may be quite wrong," said Macdonald; "but all I have done is cautionary. I rang up both my own department and the division authorities, and they concurred in my putting through a preliminary inquiry, even though it may be proved redundant. As for the room—that stayed put. It won't change its mind in the interval. People's minds and memories don't stay put. They take colour from their contacts."

Miss Coombe finished her second cup of tea with satisfaction. "I'm obviously the first to regret that such a deplorable accident has happened to one of our guests," she observed in her calm way, "but I can't help being intelligently interested in the investigation. If I were you, Graham, I should go and check up your first editions. I've had the silver counted already, and I know my own bits and pieces are intact. I locked my bedroom door," she observed to Macdonald. "After all, I didn't know any of these people, and I do like to be on the safe side!"

Macdonald controlled his mirth with difficulty. Obviously Miss Coombe ran her brother's house most efficiently, but Macdonald guessed that the publisher had some difficult moments with his plain-spoken sister.

Unlocking the door of the telephone-room, Macdonald stood and looked at it. Save for the fact that Gardien's body had been removed after photographs had been taken, everything was in the same position as when Macdonald and Coombe made their grim discovery. The drawer of the bureau was half pulled out, the electric flex trailed loosely on the floor. The table under the window, which held the telephone and telephone books, stood pushed into its place against the wall, though it had been moved when the window had been shut. When Macdonald had first inspected the room after finding Gardien's body, the window had been open at the top.

Standing with his back to the door, Macdonald had thought out possibilities involving the presence of the intruder. The latter had been seen to go into the telephone-room. Conceivably he had been occupied in going through the bureau when the door opened. The relative positions of door, arm-chair, and bureau would have made it possible for the searcher to drop into concealment behind the big chair. Gardien, on entering the room, might have sat at the table under the window or (more probably) in the large arm-chair, his drink within reach on the stool beside him, while he pondered on the "unsporting" nature of such promising looking damsels as that learned historian, Miss Valerie Woodstock. Following that line of reasoning, Gardien must have sat in that arm-chair for best part of half an hour—smoking a cigar, perhaps; an ash-tray and its contents had been scattered on the floor, and the butt end of a cigar lay under the bureau. The intruder, concealed behind the chair, must have got very stiff, weary, and anxious. Some involuntary movement on the latter's part startled Gardien, who jumped up. Some sort of fracas might have followed which involved one of the men with the line of flex and the plug was then jerked violently from its socket, causing the fuse in the manner which Dr. Wright had suggested (and in which the electrician had concurred). Whereupon Gardien had collapsed from heart failure, and the intruder had rushed out through the hall, and had collided with Miss Delareign by the stairs.

Not an entirely satisfactory reconstruction, Macdonald meditated, even assuming that everybody had recorded the exact truth. Why should the intruder have rushed to the back of the hall, instead of making direct for the front door—a much safer exit? Leaving his place by the door, Macdonald went and stood by the bureau and considered it. It was a good piece, built of fine dark mahogany, a hundred years old, perhaps. Closed, it formed a solid-looking rectangular shape, flat fronted and flat topped, with cupboards below, and a flap above which closed flush with the cupboard doors. To open it, or use it as a writing desk, it was necessary to grasp the metal ring handles of the flap and draw them towards you; the flap could then be let down by pressing metal buttons on either side, inset in the interior sides of the bureau. At the moment the flap was pulled out, but not let down, and the little drawers within, each with their ivory button, were all closed.

Turning the beam of his electric torch on to the interior of the flap, Macdonald examined the workmanship of the handles. The metal ring handles were each held in a lion's head boss on the front of the flap by nuts screwed on to short rods which ran through the thickness of the wood. Torch in hand, Macdonald stood and stared down at the nuts, his mind working furiously. A few tiny shreds of fine copper wire shone in the beam of the torch; they were held in the nuts in the same manner in which the wires of a flex are screwed against the poles of an ordinary electric fitment. Resisting the temptation to touch the nuts and see if they could be easily unscrewed (he had no pliers at hand), Macdonald bent his head this way and that to make certain that he was not woolgathering, and then went and sat down on the chair by the telephone table and stared at the wall opposite to him, with the partly-opened bureau and the electric-power point in the wainscot.

"Well, if that's the explanation, it's about as neat as anything could be," he meditated. "A minimum of apparatus and mechanics of the simplest."

Neat and workman-like with his own fingers, possessing enough knowledge of electric fitments to do repairs to his car and domestic fittings, Macdonald saw how that desk could be turned into a death trap. Some one brought in a plug to fit the power point. Connected with this plug was a stout flex or miniature cable capable of carrying the full available voltage. This flex was divided into its component sections, some yard or so before its end, and the bared wires were then screwed under the nuts of either handle inside the flap of the bureau. Thus arranged, even with the power on at the source, the thing was harmless—until some one was induced to pull open the flap. Grasping both handles firmly, they would then complete the circuit, and the current would run through their body as through the wiring. The only apparatus to be brought into the house would be the plug and length of flex, easily concealable in a man's pocket or woman's bag. A couple of minutes to loosen and rescrew the nuts with the wires inserted behind them, and all would be complete. The flap could then have been almost shut, and the extra flex, running down by the side of the bureau farthest away from the door, would have been out of sight.

Sitting staring at the bureau, with its wrought bronze handles, Macdonald envisaged the full possibilities of the diabolically simple scheme. It would not have been necessary for the organiser of it to have been in the room when the victim was electrocuted. Some message which would have ensured that Gardien would open the bureau would have been enough to complete the business, and Macdonald could not help realising how simple it would have been for the organisers of the Treasure Hunt to lead a seeker to the bureau. Any one opening it would instinctively grasp both handles to pull forward the heavy flap.

Dismissing that line of thought for the moment, the chief inspector went back to the matter of the fuse. It seemed probable that this occurred when the contact was abruptly broken as Gardien's grip on the handles gave way when his body fell on the floor, but the fuse and consequent "black-out" might well have come as a total surprise to the ingenious murderer. It would not have been foreseen, and it was probably the darkness which had been the cause of the piece of negligence which now proved the certainty of foul play—the leaving of the broken particles of wire behind the nuts on the bureau. Once the electric current had done its work it was necessary for the murderer to remove his flex, and the darkness had made him (or her) nervous. Instead of unscrewing the nuts and removing the wiring carefully, the murderer had tugged the flex away in a panic, removed the plug from the point, and fled. Wisdom would have decreed replacing the plug from the electric fire in its proper point—but in the darkness who would have waited to fumble for a point in the wainscot, when any movement might mean discovery? That sudden fuse must have meant a shock for the murderer. What was forgotten? What remained that should have been removed? Nerves might well have paralysed memory and ingenuity in the "darkness which may be felt." The memory of the phrase flashed back into Macdonald's mind. Valerie Woodstock had asked him the origin of the phrase just before the lights failed. "Let there be a darkness over the land of Egypt, a darkness which may be felt." Macdonald's retentive memory went back to the book of Exodus. Spoiling the Egyptians… Had there been a grim humour behind the game which had been played that evening? Treasure seeking, or death in the dark?

Dismissing this train of thought also as out of place for the immediate present, Macdonald took his torch again and bent to examine the power point in the wainscot. The fuse had left its trace here, for the white porcelain was blackened round the circular slots. The plug from the stove which lay on the floor was bright and untarnished, showing no such signs. Remembering the marks which he had seen on Gardien's hands when he first examined him, Macdonald thought it possible that his grip had tightened on the two handles as the current ran through him. There would have been a mechanical contraction of the flexor muscles at first which would have caused the fingers to shut more tightly. Then as the legs collapsed, the weight of the falling body would have dragged the hands away. That the current might have heated the metal handles in its transit, Macdonald was reasonably sure. The narrow-beaded edge of the elaborate ring handles was of a different metal from the handle itself, and the difference in resistance to the current of the two metals would have resulted in heating that with the higher resistance as the current went through it. The beaded edge of the handles might well have heated up while the circuit was complete, and thus left their marks on the gripping hands. Macdonald thanked his stars for the impulse which had led him to call up a medical man on whose promptitude he could rely. Dr. Wright had come at once—but even so, the tell-tale marks had nearly faded out by the time he examined the body. What proof had he, Macdonald, got that murder and not natural causes had resulted in Gardien's death? Barring those marks on the dead man's hands, and the minute frayings of copper wire—nothing. If an electric shock had caused death, it was probable that a post-mortem examination would tell nothing. A weak heart had ceased to function—that was all.

Going to the telephone, Macdonald put through a call to his own department. He intended to have this room watched during the night. Even with his hand on the receiver, another thought made him pause. He remembered his own voice saying to Peter Vernon, "I shall feel a fool either way, if I go or if I stay away."

Was he to have been fooled—a murder committed under his very nose and a verdict of natural causes to ensue? Not if he could help it. The message he put through was different from that which he had first intended.

Turning back to the door at last, he locked it behind him and went into the lounge. Graham Coombe was standing by the fire, and Macdonald saw the publisher jump as the door opened.

"My God! I'm glad to see you again," said Coombe. "I'm getting the dithers over this evening's performance. If you had gone and had a heart attack in the telephone-room, too, it would have about put the lid on the entertainment. You seem to me to have been in there for hours! Any further light on the events of the evening?"

"I have been studying the electric fittings," replied Macdonald. "It seems very probable, in my opinion, that Mr. Gardien's death was caused by an electric shock, and the possibility of foul play must be taken into consideration. I'm afraid that the nature of my report will make a full investigation inevitable."

Coombe groaned aloud. "What you mean is that the man was murdered. Consequently, every one who was in this house this evening is under suspicion. The only comfort is, that there was an unauthorised stranger in our midst. It seems common sense to connect that up with your 'possibility of foul play.' But why in the name of all that's reasonable should the chap have chosen my house to stage a murder in? Beats me altogether!"

Miss Coombe at that moment came sailing downstairs, her wide moiré skirts swishing pleasantly as she moved.

"I have never yet had a party without finding somebody's property left about afterwards," she observed. "People are amazingly careless over their possessions. Item: one evening bag with no name in it, but I believe it's Miss Delareign's. Item: one cigarette-case, with the initials V. W. on it, or is it a repair outfit? Item: one pair of long gloves. I always put them into the lost property box there, and wait until people claim them."

She indicated a box-stool by the wall near the fireplace, on which stood an ash-tray. "And heaven knows I provide enough ash-trays for an army, but people *will* balance their cigarettes on tables and ledges. Look at that—sheer vandalism."

She pointed to a charred mark on the edge of the "lost property box." "Disgusting habit!"

Moving the ash-tray, she opened the box, which formed the seat of the stool. "Such odd things people leave in the house. What on earth is this? A skipping rope?"

She pulled out something from the box and Macdonald laid a hand on her arm.

"No. It's not a skipping rope. It's electric flex—and a pretty powerful one at that."

"Oh, Lord," groaned Coombe. "This is the sort of thing which we can expect now. I wish to God some one had electrocuted me if they wanted a little practice at that sort of thing. I shouldn't have minded an investigation then."

Miss Coombe stared at the curving line of flex in Macdonald's hand, her eyes very bright and clear.

"I suppose that settles it?" she said. "Now you'll be on the warpath for a full electrocution outfit? 'Just hold this for me for a moment, dear' sort of thing. And to think I led you to it in the best 'planting' style. Well, Graham. 'Curiouser and curiouser.' It looks as though we're for it."

"Miss Coombe, nobody realises better than I do how unpleasant the situation must be for you and your brother," said Macdonald quietly. "If you will accept a word of advice, I think you would be wise to go to your rooms and rest. I am afraid that the only thing for me to do is to get a man sent down by my department to search the lower part of the house immediately. It would be much better to get it done now while the servants are upstairs and before anything has been moved for cleaning."

"So far as I am concerned, you can search anything and everything," replied Miss Coombe. "You want me out of the way and I want to go to bed, so we'll say good-night. I don't pretend that there are not a multitude of questions I should like to ask, but for the time being they can wait. So far as I can see, the less Graham and I do in the way of talking, the better."

With the calmest of bows, she turned towards the stairs again, having put her collection of lost property in the box stool, and she walked upstairs without turning her head.

Coombe gave a deep sigh. "Susan's a wonderful woman," he observed. "She's seen so many strange things in her life that she seems incapable of being startled any more. She was one of the first hunger strikers in the suffragette days, and used her prison experiences to write a memorandum for the Home Office on desirable reforms in women's prisons. From being a militant in politics, and a nurse in war-time, she has become a logical pacifist in her maturity. She will probably write another memorandum after this, on the possible efficacy of women inspectors in the C.I.D. Frankly, I haven't her strength of mind. I want to know what has happened in my house, and what you are going to do about it."

"The answers to both questions, so far as they go, are obvious," replied Macdonald. "A death has occurred here, and the electric circuit was interrupted. I believe that the two events were connected. The length of flex which your sister found strengthens that belief. Since I was here on the spot, the authorities instructed me to undertake what investigation seemed indicated. I want to search all the rooms used by your guests this evening, and to study the staircase and exits. That is the immediate programme. You have promised to let me have a complete list of the clues made for the Treasure Hunters, and to-morrow I shall hope for a conversation with you concerning every one who was here this evening."

Graham Coombe's face puckered in a frown of distress.

"I ought to have followed Susan's lead and not begun to ask questions," he said. "I asked for a snubbing, because it's obvious that you can't answer questions. But one thing does seem to stand out unpleasantly: If the wiring system of this house were used to bring about Gardien's death, it looks as though some one familiar with the house were responsible for it. To the best of my knowledge and belief, I am the only person in the house who had ever seen Gardien before. Far from desiring his death, it was to my advantage to have him alive. He was a very profitable addition to my list."

His troubled face showed a glimmer of its mischievous smile. "Really, my dear chap, the situation's ridiculous. I ask one of my most valuable authors to my house in order to murder him, and I invite a C.I.D. man to see me do it. It's the sort of situation which Miss Rees could write up to perfection." He faced Macdonald and looked at him steadily. "Susan always tells me that I talk too much; but I find it rather a relief to get things into words. It's quite obvious that I must be suspect number one, and I bear no resentment about it, but I shall find the situation less uncomfortable if we both face it—you and I. Having told you that I expect to be suspected, I shall be able to talk to you with less embarrassment than if we both walked round the nasty thought in circles." Coombe actually chuckled here. "I always cheer up when I look worries in the face," he added. "It's the business of appearing hearty when I feel frantic that gets me down."

Macdonald smiled, too. He liked Coombe. There was something very attractive about his mobile face and habit of impetuous speech, and there was clear thinking behind the seemingly hasty utterance.

"Now I'll leave you to it," added the publisher. "If you want me you'll find me in my bedroom—second floor back. Consider the house is your own and do exactly as you like in it. I shall only cramp your style by hanging around and helping you to find things." He grinned quite cheerfully now. "I generally finish by agreeing with Susan," he added; "but a man must put up some show of independence. I'm glad it was she who found that flex and not me. She would certainly have blamed me for interfering if I'd found it. You'll let me know when you're through? There's a bed in the spare room if you'd like it."

"I'll come up and tell you when I've had a good look round," replied Macdonald. "I shall post a man in the telephone-room until the morning, just as a precautionary measure."

"Post an army if you like. Poor old Gardien! He'd have enjoyed this much more than me," sighed Coombe as he turned towards the stairs.

V

AFTER THE COOMBES HAD BOTH GONE UPSTAIRS, silence settled on Caroline House. Macdonald stood by the fire, thinking over the events of the evening while he waited for Detective Reeves to put in an appearance. It was an essential of detection to regard every contact in a case as dispassionately as the symbol of an equation; the likes and dislikes of a detective had to be kept apart from the reasoning mental processes whereby he assessed probabilities. With one side of his mind, Macdonald liked Graham Coombe and his sister. They were a friendly and amusing pair, whose qualities, imaginative and whimsical in the former, practical and sensible in the latter, made a good foil to one another.

With the other side of his mind, Macdonald had to consider how either—or both—would fit as culprits in this evening's work. The points against them were as follows:

They had the best opportunities of arranging the very simple mechanics involved.

By means of clues in the Treasure Hunt it would have

been easy to ensure that Gardien opened the bureau. Both Graham Coombe and his sister were alone when the fuse occurred, and might have found time to remove the flex. The fuse and resulting black-out seemed to Macdonald to have been an event which the murderer could not have foreseen, but it might have made a change in tactics inevitable. Had the lights remained on, the company would not have reassembled immediately in the drawing-room, and Gardien's absence might not have been noticed for another hour or more. Even though anybody had gone into the telephone-room to use the instrument or to consult a timetable or directory, it was by no means certain that they would have seen the body behind the chair. The fuse did two things. It made it essential for the murderer to get into touch with the rest of the party as quickly as possible, and it also covered people's movements.

Macdonald argued that the murderer, knowing that the fuse indicated the time of Gardien's death, would have had a fear complex lest the connection between fuse and death should become apparent, and would seek to establish an immediate alibi. In point of fact, the fuse *had* worked to the murderer's disadvantage, because it had immediately put Macdonald on the qui vive. "Something wrong somewhere," had immediately suggested itself to him when he saw that not only the lights but the electric fire had failed also, because an ordinary fuse is much more localised in its effects. The lights from the roadway outside had shone above the curtains enough to show him that the failure of current involved the house only. There was no failure at the power station while the lights were still burning outside.

Going back again to the problem of the murderer

confronted with the unexpected darkness, Macdonald decided that the first essential would have been to remove the flex and plug, and get them concealed. Doubtless some careful plan had been worked out to dispose of these suggestive objects, but the darkness had prevented that plan being put into operation. The plug must have been cut off with pliers and concealed in one place, the flex hastily thrust into that box in the hall.

Visualising the box as he had seen it earlier in the evening, Macdonald remembered it as standing farther towards the left, close to a tray of glasses.

He was interrupted in his cogitations by the sound of a motor horn outside—a short, sharp blast contrary to the bye-laws now in force. That would be Detective Reeves, awaiting instructions outside. Macdonald went to the front door and admitted him. With his impersonal, professional acumen now relegating all personal likes and dislikes to the background, Macdonald again changed his plan of campaign. He had intended to let Reeves keep an eye on the telephone-room all night, to see if anybody came to remove the fragments of copper wire from behind the nuts in the bureau, but since the flex had been produced from the box, such a course had no point. In one sense the action of Miss Coombe could be interpreted as stating, "Since you've cottoned on to the fact that the electric current was responsible for Gardien's death, you might as well have a bit more to go on. Ecce! The actual flex, discovered by me, of course. Your move, I think."

Admitting Reeves, Macdonald led him to the telephone-room.

"We'd better have what fingerprints there are, although I

don't suppose they'll be any help to us. Next, whoever worked in here must have had pliers and a plug to fit that point. It's more a matter of determining that they're not in here than expecting to find them. Then I want any slips of paper like this one." He produced one of the Treasure Hunt clues which he had tucked into his pocket and added:

"You may find one anywhere, inside books or vases or drawers. Just make certain if there are any of them about, but do the fingerprints first, including the wainscot and floor around the power point."

Going back to the lounge to begin his own search there, Macdonald's quick ear caught a sound of something rattling in the direction of the alcove under the stairs. Even as he remarked it the sound ceased, but a movement at the turn of the stairs caught his eye. The "major-domo"—Geoffrey Manton—was standing at the top of the first flight, some papers in his hands. He came down quickly as he met Macdonald's eye.

"You were asking Mr. Coombe for the clues handed out to the treasure hunters this evening," he said. "I had rough copies of them, as we made them up between us. I've been copying out some of the illegible ones. I think they're all here."

He held out the sheaf of papers, and Macdonald thanked him as he took them. An idea came into the chief inspector's head as he glanced at the well-built figure of the young man beside him, concerned with the possibility of a grey wig, a coat with padded shoulders, and shoes of a Charley Chaplin tendency. A possibility that the supposed "intruder" was an inmate of the house?

In the immeasurable fraction of time in which an idea can

flash, half formed, across the thinking brain, Macdonald met the other's eyes and sensed a tension about him, a guardedness in that apparently frank look. Earlier in the evening Manton had been playing the cheerful clown, a smile on his lips and merriment in his eyes. Seen now, without the smile or the social mask of welcoming courtesy, he looked much older than he had previously done.

As he took the papers, Macdonald heard the same sound from the back of the lounge, that foolish little rattle which somehow suggested a child's game, and Manton exclaimed:

"There it is again. I heard it just now."

He took a step forward, but Macdonald held out a warning arm. "Do you mind going upstairs again? It only confuses matters to have several people on the job."

Manton shrugged his shoulders and turned back towards the stairs, while Macdonald hastened to the back of the lounge. There was a door here, concealed by a large folding screen, which gave on to the service stairs at the back of the house, and it was from the half-open door that the rattling noise issued. The lights were burning on the stairs, and Macdonald could see that there was nobody on either landing or stairway. As he stood listening, the rattle began again, almost at his feet, and he gave a start as something rolled in a curve across the polished floor. Ludicrously, an object like a large polished cotton reel rolled to Macdonald's feet, and a black kitten leaped from behind him and pounced on its toy. Macdonald made a grab, but the kitten was quicker than he. With a pat it had propelled the reel across the landing and down the service stairs which led to the basement, and rap, rap, rap, the absurd object bounced down the stairs, with the kitten in hot pursuit, leaping and bounding like a mad thing. Macdonald raced after it, making futile grabs, but, with the perversity of kittens, it managed to roll its toy under a chest against the wall in the basement passage, and, since there were only a few inches of clearance between the floor and the bottom of the chest, Macdonald had to stretch himself flat in order to get his arm under the chest and grope for the reel. Since he was anxious not to grasp the elusive object in his hand, he had quite a lively duel with the kitten, which fastened joyfully on to the fingers of an unexpected collaborator in a vastly pleasant game. By the time Macdonald had collected the particular "treasure" on which both he and the kitten were intent he was laughing to himself from the very absurdity of the business. Carefully grasped by one of its brass contact rods, he held an electric power plug—adjustable, he noticed, to any fitting—from which the flex had been cut with pliers.

His official "search" was being turned into pantomime. Miss Coombe had produced the flex from the stool-box, with the air of a conjurer producing a rabbit from a hat, and her kitten had obliged with the missing plug. It only remained for Graham Coombe to find the pliers in the bathroom, and the apparatus would be complete.

Looking down at the still hopeful kitten, which was circling round his feet with tail rampant, Macdonald said:

"If you could only tell me where you found the thing, you might be really helpful. For all I know, you have patted it all over the carpet before you got it on to the polished floor. Or did some one offer it to you on the end of a string, trusting to your capacity for drawing attention to it?"

Leaving the kitten to pursue its own tail in default of other attractions, Macdonald carried the plug upstairs to Reeves. The latter was a competent all-round detective, notably skilled in two arts. One was the technique of fingerprint work, the other the technique of Jiu Jitsu—both of which arts made him a valuable lieutenant on occasions. Putting the power plug down on the table by the window, Macdonald said, "I might send this to the lab, for the department to do their best with; but, knowing what's likely to be on it, I don't want to give them occasion for mirth. Try it, anyway."

The result of the trial was, as Macdonald had foreseen, excellent prints of kitten paws. The kitten had evidently enjoyed a plentiful and greasy supper before it stalked its valuable piece of evidence, and the polished surface of the plug showed a series of little greasy pad marks all over its surface.

"That's that," said Macdonald. "I'll send it to the lab, all the same, for the pleasure of getting their report. Nothing on the power point, I suppose?"

"Nothing," said Reeves, "and the slab of the bureau's been rubbed over pretty thoroughly. Nothing there. Plenty of markings on the table and phone, but so confused as to be pretty useless. There are two of your chits in the waste-paper basket, but I haven't treated them yet."

He pointed to two crumpled slips of paper which lay on the table beside a pair of forceps, which had been used to unfold them. Both slips held the cross-word, one with the initials J. A. in the corner, one with S. P.—Jane Austen and Samuel Pepys. The first was filled in—correctly, as Macdonald knew, having solved the same problem himself. The latter was a complete muddle, with hardly a word filled in correctly.

"You'll get prints from these all right," said Macdonald, "but I doubt if they'll help us much. We seem to be getting all the data and it's leading us round in circles, like that confounded kitten."

Leaving Reeves to his job, Macdonald went back to the lounge and made for the "lost property box." He had an idea which offered to complete his search for the "apparatus" in logical fashion. Fishing out the evening-bag which Miss Coombe had put away, he loosened its cord and tipped out the contents on to a table. It contained a lace handkerchief, unmarked, a powder puff and lipstick, a small box of Balkan Sobranie cigarettes, a menthol stick—and a very small but well-made pair of pliers.

"As might be expected," said Macdonald to himself. "That's the lot. Flex in the lounge, plug by the alcove, pliers in a bag in the drawing-room." He continued his researches into the lost property collected that evening. The cigarette-case which held powder and lipstick in one compartment and cigarettes in the other was obviously Valerie Woodstock's. Her first clue—the numbered cipher—was tucked in among the cigarettes. The long gloves were marked by their owner's name in marking ink, just inside the top—Miss Delareign's. The pliers went to the patient Reeves, to be packed up and sent to the experts of the fingerprint department. Macdonald guessed that they would have been wiped, but hoped that some traces might remain on the smooth metal which could be developed by the chemists.

Standing again in the now silent hall, with the grandfather clock ticking slowly as the only sound in an apparently sleeping house, Macdonald considered afresh the lie of the rooms and those who had been in them at "zero hour"—the time of the fuse. Beyond the double doors which shut off the outer lobby from the lounge was the men's cloak-room—empty, according to all accounts. Standing with his back to the double doors, Macdonald had the doors of the dining-room and telephone on his left, those of the library and Miss Coombe's sitting-room on his right. At "zero" Graham Coombe had been in the library—alone and therefore uncorroborated. Ashton Vale had just entered the dining-room in search of a "sterile farinaceous Berry," which he had correctly interpreted as a banana. Vale also was alone. In the alcove, concealed from the lounge by the stairway, was Miss Delareign. A good strategic spot, that, thought Macdonald. Somewhere in the neighbourhood of the fireplace in the lounge, Denzil Strafford had been ruminating helplessly on the clue of "Antique beaver"—with a pot of "old man's beard" (wild clematis) at his elbow—but Vale had not seen Strafford in the lounge when he crossed from library to dining-room, neither had Miss Delareign in the alcove been aware of Strafford's presence near at hand. Assuming that everybody—with the exception of the murderer—had been intent on elucidating the clues of the Treasure Hunt, it was quite natural that they should not have noticed each other's proximity. Macdonald knew that while he had been concentrating on some of the longer clues in the Treasure Hunt, he had been quite oblivious to his surroundings.

He could not expect to get any more positive evidence about the relative positions of the party than he had already got from the guests, neither could anything infallible be argued from such details as the broken and upset glasses. A tray of glasses had been knocked over near the electric fire in the lounge and one broken. Another glass had been found lying in the alcove, but the parlourmaid had picked it up when the lights came on again and taken it to the pantry with the tray which had been overturned near the electric fire in the lounge. It seemed reasonable to argue that the first of these had been knocked over by Miss Delareign, and stained her frock, the second by Denzil Strafford, when he blundered towards the stairs in the dark—but a third glass had been knocked over and smashed in the telephone-room itself.

Pondering deeply, Macdonald walked upstairs to the first floor landing. On this floor, the long drawing-room, with its smaller arched-off recess, stretched across the whole front of the house. The study (which the Treasure Hunters had not been invited to enter) was at the back, and the little library where Macdonald had been at "zero hour" opened off the half-landing above. It was to the study door that Macdonald went, and knocked lightly on the door. It was opened immediately by Geoffrey Manton, who looked prepared to see a ghost.

"Oh!—er, you. I was reading, not feeling like sleep yet awhile. Do you want to look round in here? I'll clear out and go upstairs."

"No, don't do that. I thought you might still be about," said Macdonald. "Do you mind coming downstairs and helping me with an experiment?"

"Delighted." The young man spoke dryly. "What do I do? Rattle a cotton reel in the alcove?"

"No. The kitten does that quite efficiently, thanks." Macdonald chuckled a little as he spoke. He turned towards the landing. "I just want you to walk about in the lounge a bit, while I look on."

They walked downstairs together, softly, thoughtful of the presumably sleeping household above. A sound as of a chair being moved came from the telephone-room, and Manton started like one on edge.

"It's all right. One of my men is in there," said Macdonald. "There's nothing to get bothered about. I'm going to stand in the lounge, no matter where. I want you to go into the library and then come out again a moment later and cross into the dining-room and stay there. Read this slip of paper as you walk and try to understand it. Tell me what you make of it later. Don't look at it until you begin to move out of the library."

Manton took the paper, on which Macdonald had scribbled a line from Shakespeare with the words incorrectly divided, so that it read like nonsense. "No wist he wint ero, fourd I scon tent," which he calculated might hold Manton's attention while he crossed the lounge. Prepared to enter into the experiment in the proper spirit, Macdonald took another slip of paper himself and set to work to express 17/6¾ in decimals. He took up his stand on the farther side of the fireplace as Manton entered the library and played fair, concentrating on his calculation. Three minutes later he looked up. The lounge was empty, the library door set wide, but he had neither seen nor heard anything. Going quietly into the dining-room, he saw Manton standing by the table staring at the slip of paper in his hand.

"I can't make any sense of it," he said, and Macdonald answered, "No matter. Where was I standing in the lounge when you crossed?"

"God knows, I don't. I didn't see you because I was trying to read this. What is it?"

"Richard III., first line," chuckled Macdonald. "Your wits aren't functioning. Did you take trouble to walk more quietly than usual?"

"No, I don't think so."

"I didn't hear you. The carpets are thick and your pumps are quiet. If any one concentrates on a treasure hunt clue they are oblivious to other people. There were three people in the lounge or crossing it when the lights went out, and none of them saw or heard their fellows. Quite understandable."

"Quite," said Manton dryly. "Their word wasn't good enough to satisfy you?"

"It is not I who has to be satisfied," said Macdonald quietly. "Do you mind reversing the walk this time, and going from here to the telephone-room door? You can look about you this time, and observe where I am standing. I shall be concentrating on my clue, and you're to try to do your walk without me seeing you."

Manton's forehead showed tiny drops of sweat on it.

"This is rather beastly. I happen to know who was in the library. All right. I'll do it. Nothing will stop you now you're on the go."

The second experiment had the same result as the first, inasmuch as Macdonald, studying his calculation, did not see Manton cross the lounge, neither did he hear him.

It seemed evident that Denzil Strafford could have stood by the lounge fire while some one crossed either way, without his being aware of it. Consequently Graham Coombe, Ashton Vale, Miss Delareign, and Strafford himself might any of them have entered the telephone-room just before or just after the "black-out" without being observed.

Manton, having done what he was asked, returned to Macdonald in the lounge.

"I know it's pretty futile to ask questions," he said, "but I suppose one can take for granted that there was dirty work at the cross-roads. Some one chose this evening's party as a good opportunity to get rid of Gardien. I'm not lamenting that. He was the type of merchant whom I personally disliked at sight, but I hate the idea of your considering that Mr. Coombe had a hand in it. He's about the last person in the world to emulate the Borgias and slay one of his guests at a banquet."

Macdonald studied the young man's troubled face, and then said, "Dirty work there was, of that I'm certain. Any ideas on the subject?"

"None, but I've remembered something that may have a bearing on the subject. Early on, just after he'd come, Gardien tried to pump me about who was who. He said he'd never met any of Coombe's authors, and would like to have some notion as to who did what in the writing line. I explained that he'd hear all about that later. After Mr. Coombe had said his bit about the six questions to be allowed all round, Gardien said to me again that he hadn't the vaguest notion who anybody was—but he had. He knew somebody here. When he first went downstairs I was just going up to the small library to see if I'd remembered to put out the right Quarterlies. I heard Gardien say, 'Get a move on, and don't make such a palaver about it. I'm bored stiff with all this.' From the way he spoke, it was obvious that he was talking to some one he knew, not some one he'd just met. He mentioned some name, but I didn't catch it. Might have been Nell, or Ell or Ellie. Something with an L in it, that's all I could be certain of."

"You'd be willing to swear to it that you heard those words—or the gist of them?"

"Yes. The exact words, and a name that had an L in it. I can't tell you who they were addressed to, because I went upstairs again, having obviously overheard something not meant for me."

"Thanks for telling me. If you have any further recollections, let me know. It's possible to piece sounds together some time after you've heard them on occasion. The sense of the sound dawns on you later."

Manton nodded. "I know what you mean. For the moment that's my only contribution."

"It may be a very important one. Getting back to the moment of the fuse. You were in the study upstairs. I was in the small library, and I came out on to the half-landing within thirty seconds, I believe, of the lights failing. I saw Bourne standing by the drawing-room door, and I heard Mr. Coombe's voice below. The door of the study was pushed to, wasn't it? I didn't see you come out."

"No. I was in there a couple of minutes after the fuse. Miss Woodstock had asked me a few minutes earlier if I could find Professor Raeburn's address for her, as she'd lost it. I'd got a letter from him in a drawer, and I was fumbling among a lot of papers when the lights failed. The first thing I did was to jerk the drawer right out of the desk as I tried to jump up in a hurry, and I stopped for a minute or so, trying to get the damned thing back. I'd got a box of matches on the desk somewhere, but I couldn't find them. In the dark all I could do was to knock things over. Some people have eyes like cats, I believe. I haven't. I just get clumsy and helpless in the dark."

"Quite a usual failing. Besides, every one is as blind as a bat in the dark after being in a strong light. It's the sudden contrast that's so bewildering. When you said just now that you disliked Gardien, did you mean that you felt an aversion for him when you first met him this evening, or had you met him before and felt like that?"

"I met him once before at Elliott's—his agent's—and disliked him quite unreasonably."

"Elliott? I shall have to get hold of him in the morning. What is he like, by the way? Old? Young?"

"Elliott? Fiftyish, I should say. An ugly fellow with an interesting face and uncouth movements. Very able."

"Is he flat-footed?"

"Yes. Noticeably so. Walks with his feet at a quarter to three. You've met him?"

"I've heard of him, I think. Sorry to have kept you up so long. Thanks for helping with the reconstructions."

Manton grinned. "All right. I'll leave you to it. Was that really the kitten playing at ghosts?"

His eyes turned to the corner by the service stairs, and Macdonald nodded.

"Yes. It was the kitten playing with a reel of sorts."

"It got me rattled. A funny thing, when you know something queer's been afoot, you're always alert for the next thing. If I can't help any more, good-night."

After he had gone, Macdonald walked towards the door giving on to the service stairs. It would have been very easy to tie a cotton on to that plug and dangle it over the stairs to attract the kitten's attention. "People are being helpful," he meditated.

"Ellie—Ellie. Elliott, or perhaps Dellie, or even Val. I wish he'd remembered his little piece before. It sounded like an inspiration on the spur of the moment. Ellie, Nellie, or Dellie—I wonder?"

He took out his list of the guests and studied them with a thoughtful face. "Some of these names would have made quite good clues. I wonder if Coombe thought of that."

VI

GRAHAM COOMBE CAME DOWN TO BREAKFAST ON THE morning of April 2nd, looking distinctly the worse for wear. He was in the frame of mind when he would gladly have sat through his breakfast without speaking a word, but he knew that his chances of sitting and silently nursing a very accentuated hump were of the slightest, when Susan sat facing him over the coffee-pot with her alert and irritatingly intelligent look. After a polite exchange of good-mornings, she allowed him to drink his first cup of coffee in peace, and then, with her elbows on the table and her chin in her hands, she said:

"Well, my dear, I think we'd better talk it over."

"Talking won't mend matters," said Graham morosely, and then, illogically, began to talk with gusto. "I'm aware that it's in the very worst of taste to say so, but I've been saying 'Confound the fellow' all night. I hope to God he hasn't got a wife and family, as the inspector suggested. I'm very sorry he's dead; I've good reason to be, but I'd feel in a more suitably charitable frame of mind if he'd died somewhere else."

"Quite so," said Susan firmly, in the tone of voice which made her such a valuable chairman at committee meetings. "You and I can afford to say what we like to each other, knowing it will go no further. The whole thing's maddening, but we might as well be competent over it. I thought all along that that fuse was extremely fishy, and when I pulled that length of flex out of the lost-property box I knew I was right. Some one was up to tricks. Electric power is an alarmingly potent source of supply, so to speak. There's no need to elaborate the thesis. A fuse, a length of bifurcated flex and a dead man. It speaks for itself. I could do the same kind of thing quite competently. I don't know if it'd be any comfort to you to assure you that I didn't."

"Don't be so idiotic," he expostulated.

"I prefer to look facts in the face, Graham. We shall all be suspects, particularly you and me. It's unfortunate that we were both by ourselves when the fuse went. You were in the library and could have got to the telephone-room in a very few seconds. I was in the basement, having just sent Mrs. Hayes into the kitchen to make some China tea for Mr. Bourne. Obviously I could have slipped up into the telephone-room between the time Hayes left me and the time of the fuse. One comfort is that all the servants were in the kitchen at the time, so they can be disregarded. Of course, from the chief inspector's point of view, I've done the wrong thing all along the line."

Coombe's eyebrows shot up. "Why? I thought you kept your head admirably."

"Thank you. I'm not given to screaming or throwing hysterics, but I wish I'd been more competent over getting some candles discovered more quickly. I ought to have found them at once, whereas anybody might believe I'd hidden them deliberately. Hayes kept on saying, 'I *know* I saw them in the top right-hand corner last week. Some one's moved them.' And as I keep the keys of the store cupboard, it doesn't look too good. Then I thought I was being very competent over sending off Miss Delareign's frock to the cleaners and telling them to do it at once. I've no doubt the inspector would have liked to know what was spilled over it. Finally I pulled that length of flex out of the box under his very eyes, and the look he gave me was a poem. I thought I'd better go to bed after that. Taking it all round, it looks as though I'd done my best to act suspiciously."

With great deliberation she poured out another cup of coffee for herself, and took some more toast.

"I do wish you'd tell me exactly what you know of Mr. Gardien. I told the inspector that I'd never seen him before, and I thought I was telling the truth, but I woke up this morning with a teasing sense that I'd seen him before, and I can't place it."

"Really, this is the first time I've ever known you give way to nerves, Susan," said her brother. "For heaven's sake don't go imagining things. It's not like you. As for what I know about Gardien, it's next to nothing. We've had three of his books in the last eighteen months. He was first published by Steven Bond. Then Pellier's got him. He was doing very well with them, but he had a row with them over advertising, or publicity, or something. Mardon-Elliott—Gardien's agent—came in to see me some time before last Christmas twelve-month and suggested a contract with Gardien. I was glad to get it. I first met the chap six months ago, when I asked him to come in and discuss some point which Janet Campbell had raised over his MS. Damn it!" he exclaimed, and suddenly banged the table. "I'd forgotten. That discussion was about electricity, electrocuting a fellow, in one of those gas-pipe chairs. What was it? *Killed in a Cabaret.* Something to do with the high voltage from Neon lights. You remember it?"

"I certainly do not," she retorted. "You know I never read your thrillers. They're much too wild for my taste."

"That's all very fine. I saw you with your nose inside one of Miss Rees's only last week. Funny about that Neon light business. I wonder if Gardien intended to bump off some one here, and got muddled up with his bits of string."

"And, having electrocuted himself very competently, his corpse conveyed the flex to the lost-property box, and rolled itself back to position in the telephone-room. Do stick to the point, Graham."

"I am," he expostulated. "The person he meant to kill must have done that, or else the flex you found was a red herring Gardien introduced to prove he couldn't have done it. Well, never mind. As I was saying, I had that interview with him six months ago, and then didn't see him till I met him by chance in the Haymarket a month ago and I took him to my club for lunch. He was talking about India and rope tricks and optical illusions. I found him amusing. It was then that I sounded him on coming to a Treasure Hunt, and it was he who originally suggested having a mixed party—detective writers and others. I thought it a very sound idea."

"I've always said you were very competent—at acquiring ideas," said Miss Coombe. "When you get to heaven and are refused admission—or vice versa—your first comment will be, 'Now, can we use that?' We're getting along nicely, Graham, but I'm wondering what expression the inspector's expressionless face will assume when he hears all these interesting reminiscences. I suppose Gardien suggested that so and so would be a good person to invite, and that he was anxious to meet so and so. I take it that it wasn't Gardien who suggested that a C.I.D. man might round off the party pleasantly?"

"No. Certainly not. That was entirely my own idea," protested the publisher. "I thought of it after Parsons told me that the man I met at Simpson's was Macdonald. Gardien didn't suggest any names at all. He admitted frankly that he knew no other writers on our list, and said that authors generally bored him. They talked of nothing but royalties and circulations. Not that he ever struck me as being indifferent to his own royalties."

"That," said Miss Coombe, "is very different from other people's royalties. You are quite sure that Mr. Gardien didn't suggest any name at all when you discussed the party with him?"

"Quite sure," replied her brother.

"Very good. Now the next point is this: You broadcast a little information to various people about the guests whom you were inviting. You'd better go into that pretty thoroughly. It seems germane to the case, emphatically. Nobody came here with a length of flex and a plan for fusing the lights just in order to commit murder in general. Murder is always particularised, selective and limited."

Graham Coombe uttered a sound of expostulation.

"Must you keep on repeating that unpleasant word? There's no proof at present that Gardien was murdered. These C.I.D. men have to be suspicious. It's their trade. *Chacun à son métier et les vaches seront bien gardées.* I'm still hoping for a verdict of natural causes myself. Macdonald may have got a bee in his bonnet for once, and the whole thing turn out to be a mare's nest."

"Optimism is an attractive trait, Graham, but if you ever saw a man whose bonnet looked less likely to be bee-infested than the inspector's, then lead me to him. You asked Macdonald here off your own bat, and in doing so you destroyed in advance any hope of a verdict concerning natural causes. However, what about answering my question?"

Coombe stroked his chin. "I have always regretted that you wouldn't write a thriller yourself, Susan. You have a very clear brain, and a pleasant natural idiom. I did do a bit in the advisory line so far as our guests were concerned, I admit. It's no use setting tests which are too difficult to have entertainment value." He pulled a diary out of his pocket. "Here we are. I got young Vernon to go and call on Macdonald and tell him—"

Miss Combe interrupted firmly. "Never mind about Vernon. The inspector didn't kill Gardien. Tell me about the others."

"I got Manton to look up Digby Bourne and tell him that Vale might be coming, also a C.I.D. man, and V. R. Woodstock, the historian."

Fiddling with his spectacles, Coombe's face lit up with his puckish smile again as though he had forgotten his present perturbation in reminiscent pleasure at his own astuteness.

"I reckoned Bourne would place Macdonald as Vale, and

Mrs. Etherton as V. R. Woodstock. I must ask him if I was right. I saw Miss Woodstock myself and told her that Gardien and Miss Delareign were coming—two of the most ingenious writers on my list, and that I hoped she would outdo them both. I dropped a word to young Bartram at the club, knowing he is a friend of Strafford's, and told him to mention that V. R. Woodstock and Ronile Rees had accepted, and I hoped that Bourne would come."

"As Bartram was up at Balliol while Strafford was at Trinity and Miss Woodstock at St. Elizabeth's, and as they all took part in the mixed debate at the Union after the 'King and Country' affair, I imagine Bartram must have grinned a bit *sub rosa*," said Miss Coombe. "Go on. What did you tell the Delareign woman?"

"I mentioned Gardien, Bourne and the C.I.D.," replied Coombe, "and to Miss Rees I mentioned Mrs. Etherton and Denzil Strafford. Finally I told Elliott—Gardien's agent—that Vale and Miss Delareign and Miss Woodstock would be present. So everybody had something to go on. There's one peculiarity in common among all those eight writers who were here last night, Susan. They all dislike publicity. None of them will have their photographs published. Miss Rees is accepted by the critics as a man you know. They always review her as Mr. R. Rees. She has a dry mordant style—"

"Be damned to her style!" snapped Miss Coombe. "The thing sticks out like an organ stop, and I sent her dress to the cleaners. Well, I'm glad I did. Speaking as a feminist, I'm quite willing to believe she had justification. I've just remembered where I once saw Gardien. It was in the divorce court. I went to hear the Stebbing case and got there too early and heard the fag end of the previous one. Gardien was in the witness-box. A nasty bit of work."

Graham Coombe stared. "Could you be a little more explicit and a little less elliptical? I was talking about Miss Rees."

"Yes. I know you were. Go on talking about her. I like it," said Miss Coombe, lighting a cigarette. Her brother followed her lead and sat puffing away in silence, obviously cogitating profoundly.

"You sent her dress to the cleaners—Miss Delareign's, not Miss Rees's. I told Gardien that Miss Delareign would be here. I see all that. There was a broken glass in the telephone-room, I remember. Miss Delareign was talking to Gardien in the drawing-room for quite a while, too. Do I understand you to mean that the same lady was concerned in the divorce case you mentioned?"

"No. You do not. Nothing of the kind," snapped Miss Coombe, but her brother went on:

"Well, as evidence I call it a bit thin, though I know Miss Delareign camped out in the alcove for a surprisingly long time, considering she's a gregarious body. Of course I didn't say so to the inspector, but the probability seemed to me all against it. I wonder if the C.I.D. does any practical psychology. No man with any understanding of human nature would believe that Miss Delareign spent twenty minutes by herself among calf-bound sets of minor classics, when there was a selection of very passable men folk to be impressed by her very striking gown, her nimble wit, and her comely person."

"That will do, Graham," said Susan coldly. "Psychology, as a scientific study, is one thing. Your fatuous rakings of the

Freudian rag-bag simply nauseate me. You are neither psychic nor logical."

"Then I am all the better qualified to assess the mental processes of Miss Nadia Delareign on that account," retorted Graham, and his face showed that he felt he had scored a point at last. "I had a very disturbing dream last night, Susan. I thought that I had married Miss Delareign in a moment of aberration, and she was sitting opposite to me at breakfast, stark mad in gold lamé."

"My God!" groaned Susan. "You'd better go to a psychiatrist yourself, or else—Really, Graham, I have not by nature a ribald mind…"

"No, my dear, but you have a robust Rabelaisian wit on occasion, which is both illuminating and logical, if not psychic. Don't go yet. It was you who started this discussion, and it's contrary to your nature to execute a strategic retreat. I grant you all the evidence which, to use your apt metaphor, sticks out like an organ stop. I am aware that Miss Delareign has recently travelled in India, as has Gardien, and that she has coincided with him at Colombo. *But*, my dear Susan, and it's a very large *but*, you omit an integral part of the evidence. What about the grey-haired man? You can't dismiss him by saying that Miss Delareign invented him, because there is corroborative evidence of his presence. I am really grateful to the chap whoever he is. His intrusion takes the edge off an otherwise nasty situation. Perhaps he helped to beguile that incomprehensible twenty minutes among the minor classics."

Miss Coombe lighted another cigarette.

"Yes," she said thoughtfully. "It's all very obscure. You saw the inspector before he left last night?"

"I did. He was very non-committal. He regretted that it was necessary to leave a man stationed in the telephone-room for the time being, but said that the phone could be used. He said that in his opinion Gardien's death from heart failure was caused by some tampering with the electric current, but it seemed improbable that any decisive evidence could be obtained from his researches here. With so many people at large in the house it was impossible to formulate anything but possibilities."

"Precisely," said Miss Coombe. "Possibilities, including you and me. I wonder if it occurred to the inspector's coldly acute mind that for us to have asked him here when we intended to commit a murder would have been an exceedingly subtle move. On paper it can be made to look most convincing. You asked him to go to the telephone with you when you rang up the Borough Electricians, and since he failed to discover the corpse for himself at a first go, you led him to it a little later. He must have thought it very poor staff work when I produced that flex."

"Very subtle, my dear, but, if you'll pardon the reiteration, what about the grey-haired interloper? Ah, here is Manton." The door opened and Geoffrey Manton came in.

"Good-morning! I'm sorry that I'm so late," he said to Miss Coombe. "I didn't get to bed until lateish."

"I'll ring for some more coffee, and leave you to it," she replied. "The servants are sure to be agitated, and the sooner they see that I intend to behave perfectly normally, the better. Will you be in to lunch, Graham, or are you going to the office as usual?"

"I shall go to the office. I asked the chief inspector if he wished me to remain at home, and he said that it made no difference provided he could get me on the phone."

Miss Coombe nodded to Manton and walked from the room, after gathering up the letters which lay unopened beside her plate, and the publisher turned to his secretary.

"We got more excitement than we bargained for, Manton."

"Definitely," murmured the young man, as he investigated the hot plate on the sideboard. "Looking back at it, the whole evening seems to have a Mad Hatter quality. I can't help believing that the murder idea is a mare's nest. It seems completely crazy when you regard it with the cold common sense of first thing in the morning. At midnight one is much more disposed to melodrama. I got absurdly worked-up last night. The very fact of having C.I.D. men snooping round gave one a guilty feeling, and I found myself jumping at every sound."

"We all did, old chap," replied Coombe. "I left Macdonald to wander about uninterrupted. I thought it the most sensible thing to do, but damn it all, I got the dithers over turning out my own electric fire, and even my sister's got wind-up. That shows you."

"It does indeed, sir," agreed Manton, looking with distaste at the kidneys on his plate. "The inspector came and routed me out from the study and got me to play reconstruction games. Pretty eerie. I remembered one point which seemed to interest him."

He related the incident of Gardien's remark which he had overheard on the stairs, and Coombe's pointed ears twitched a little.

"Ellie?" he repeated. "Elliott, you mean?"

"Good Lord," Manton fairly jumped. "What a fool I was not to tumble to it. Elliott—and Macdonald was asking me about him, too."

"The grey-haired man—flat-footed," exclaimed Coombe. "But this is simply crazy. Why on earth? Elliott? It's plain crazy—but I *did* tell him about the party. He knew Gardien was coming here. Well, that's crazier than Susan's idea about Miss Delareign."

"The whole thing's crazy, sir, but I believe Macdonald's dead certain that Gardien was murdered, and he's not the sort of chap to make mistakes. How would it fit anyway? Elliott's been to this house and into the telephone-room, too. You remember when you were away in January—he came here to ask me for your phone number, and he rang you up then and there in the telephone-room."

The two men stared at one another, and Coombe burst out:

"But even if all that's true, how did Elliott get Gardien to go to the telephone-room like that?"

"It wouldn't be difficult, sir. Elliott may have made an appointment with Gardien for the latter to phone some one up at a given moment in the evening, some bait like a fat American contract coming through. Gardien was a demon for dollars. Elliott would have known that Gardien would have used that phone."

"Yes, but damn it, according to your argument, Elliott was in this house, on the stairs somewhere, and Gardien spoke to him. Look here, Manton, have we missed something important? What if Gardien and Elliott were both a pair of blackguards and made a plan to lift something out of this house and get away with it? There was that open bureau, remember. Was there something in it which we didn't realise—something that Elliott may have seen when he was in the room last January? Did you leave him alone in there to telephone?"

"Yes, of course, sir—and I opened the bureau for him, and put out some writing paper because he wanted to write a letter."

"Good God! We're getting down to it, I swear we are! Now what the devil is there in that bureau? There's my old stamp collection for one thing."

Manton grinned; he couldn't help it. "No go, sir. There's nothing in that that any schoolboy could get excited over."

"Don't you be too sure—you're not an expert," retorted Graham, "and rare stamps are worth a fabulous sum. Now, I wonder—"

"Easy enough to make sure, sir. Let's go and look."

"We can't, damn it. There's a C.I.D. man there. Yes, we can, though. Macdonald said we could use the phone, so I don't see why I can't use my own bureau. What did we keep in there, Manton? I'll ask Susan. She'll know. There was that dud astrology lot—six volumes, 1665, Fabricus press. Christie's man said they were no go, but you never know. I got 'em in Amsterdam—I always believed they were valuable, and meant to have a shot at tracing their pedigree. So many of these experts are too arbitrary."

"To the best of my recollection the Fabricus books aren't in the bureau, sir. Some of them were in very poor condition, and you moved them to the chest in the library."

"Rubbish! They were in the cupboard of the bureau a week or two ago. I know, because I was hunting in there for that old Mudie's catalogue to look up popular novels in the nineties. If they've disappeared, I shall be pretty certain I'm arguing along the right lines."

"I'll go and look in the chest in the library, sir. I feel sure they're there." Manton got up and went out of the room, and Graham Coombe prowled about the dining-room. He paused in front of an illuminated scroll which had been presented to his father by certain City magnates.

"Gules, two swords in saltire proper. Not a bad clue. Nobody remembers heraldic terms," he murmured. "Confound it, I've got that damned Treasure Hunt on the brain. Clues in the running brooks, treasures in stones, murder for ancient books, motives in tomes… Well, Manton, found 'em?"

The young man came back to the table and shook his head.

"No, sir. I remember now that you had that chest cleared to hold the big Merriton folios."

"I knew it!" said Coombe cheerfully. "Susan's always telling me that I never know where my books are, but I do. I can put my finger on anything after a moment's thought. I'm going to have a look at that bureau, Manton. When it comes to deduction I'm not so slow in the uptake as you might imagine. There's this point to consider. Those Fabricus books were in a bad state as you said, the leather was crumbling, and if they have been taken out of the bureau, it's probable that traces were left—tiny scraps of the leather, bits of the ribbon markers and that sort of thing."

"Wouldn't it be better to inform the detective on duty, sir? The one thing these C.I.D. fellows seem to hate is for any one to use their own initiative. I got a snubbing from the chief inspector on that account last night."

"Is this my house or isn't it?" inquired Coombe plaintively. "I don't care a fig for the inspector's snubbings, and that's flat."

Full of zeal, the publisher thereupon hastened to the telephone-room and opened the door, all the more boldly because he felt an uncomfortable qualm when he recollected the last time he had entered the room. A young man was sitting in a chair by the window, and he got up promptly as Coombe entered, and stood to attention as it were.

"Good-morning. I am Graham Coombe. The chief inspector told me that he would be leaving one of his men in here, but that the room could be used for telephoning and so forth. The fact is, I've remembered that I left some old books in that bureau—very valuable books. There was an idea that burglary might have been at the root of our troubles last night, and I am checking up my more valuable books. I want to look through that bureau. All in order, I take it? I believe your fingerprint experts have finished with it?"

"Yes, sir. Of course you can look through the bureau, but nothing is to be taken from it."

"Quite so, quite so. I only wish to ascertain if the books are there, or if there are any traces of them. Quite small books, about four by three, six of them in all. Now I wonder!"

Graham Coombe looked through the bureau very carefully. He pried, he sniffed, he fumbled, and all the while a very alert young detective watched him with an interest which was the more intense because he had not dared to hope for any incident which would enliven his vigil in a room which reminded him of a specialist's waiting-room, save that it contained neither *Punch* nor *The Tatler* to cheer the spirits of those who awaited a verdict.

VII

MACDONALD ONLY GOT THREE HOURS' SLEEP ON THE night of Coombe's party, but he woke at his usual hour with the exactitude of an alarm clock, and became aware that a sense of uneasiness was in his mind.

Running the feeling to earth, he discovered that the worried undercurrent of thought which had persisted even while he slept concerned the vague nature of his present case. A dead man, a length of flex, an adjustable power plug, a few shreds of copper wire, and a great deal of surmise. Was there enough evidence to convince anybody that Gardien had been murdered? Was he really convinced of it himself?

Going over all the evidence again while he was shaving, he sorted out his thoughts and came to the following conclusions:

He (Macdonald) felt certain that Gardien was killed by an electric current, and that the fuse had occurred through the sudden break in contact when the dead man's hands dropped from the handles of the bureau. In order to convince the authorities that any such scheme had been put into operation, it would be necessary to connect up the bronze handles with the current again, by means of the flex and power plug which he had found, and to let the electricians measure the result, with particular reference to the heating of the steel beading which edged the circular handles. If this experiment worked according to Macdonald's ideas on the subject (and he did not believe there was much room for doubt), then it was probable that the authorities would accept his own theories on the subject.

Meantime, whether Gardien's death were due to accident, natural causes, or murder, it was necessary to establish who he was, where he lived, and the state of his heart and general health recently.

The bottle of tablets found in his pocket might prove to contain a heart tonic, a bromide, or a dyspepsia corrective. Poison seemed improbable in view of Dr. Wright's observations. Gardien had certainly seemed in normal health shortly after nine o'clock. If he had felt ill, there was a bell-push in the telephone-room whereby he could have summoned assistance, and Wright as an experienced police surgeon had had too much acquaintance with the workings of rapid poisons, such as the hydro-cyanic group, to have been mistaken should one of these have been the cause of death.

When Macdonald had asked Graham Coombe if the name Andrew Gardien were a pseudonym or the writer's legal name, Coombe had replied that he did not know. Gardien was the only name by which the writer was known to him, as Mardon-Elliott, the agent was the only channel of communication between writer and publisher. For all he, Coombe, knew,

Gardien might be called Charlie Peace or Andrew Carnegie, in his other dealings with the world.

"Not my business," said Coombe. "I dealt with Gardien as an author using that name, and his pursuits in any other direction were no affair of mine."

An odd association, thought Macdonald, and chuckled when he remembered Miss Susan's cool aside about locking her bedroom door. Perhaps she had had some disillusioning experience of writers, whose pseudonyms covered unexpected eccentricities of conduct.

Arrived at Scotland Yard, Macdonald was greeted at the entrance to his own department by Inspector Jenkins. The latter, though below Macdonald in rank, was his senior by a dozen years, but between the two men was a bond of very real affection. They had worked together in a variety of strange cases, and understood one another perfectly. Jenkins, stout of person and cheerfully rubicund of face, met the chief inspector with a grin.

"What about that Treasure you were going to split with me? Landing in a job of work on your night out. Not my idea of a good party. Reckon it was a put up job, getting you there to help with a nice water-proof alibi for somebody?"

"Deuce knows," replied Macdonald. "I've got an alibi for an eminent historian, but judging by the quality of her wits I reckon she'd have pulled off a trick with admirable sang-froid. I've been wondering if she was really employed to keep me quiet while the doings were done. A low down thought, but her remarks were unpleasantly apropos. We had an almighty fine fuse, and just before the whole house went black she asked me for the origin of the phrase 'darkness which may be felt.'"

"Exodus," said Jenkins promptly. "I know that one. Well, if eminent historians take to crime they oughtn't to try being funny. Is your case a case?"

"At present it resembles a coffin," replied Macdonald, "complete with one detective writer, dead, and the reputation of one detective, living. Ask me another, Jenkins, or wait till you've read my report. It's a corker of a case, but I'm not expecting anything but worry out of it. Nebulous and nerve trying. It reminds me of that case at Deptford, when we knew just what had happened and just who did it by a process of pure reasoning, and yet we couldn't bring a charge because there was no tangible evidence."

"Pure reason's no good when it comes to putting it before counsel," agreed Jenkins, "because opposing counsel can always dispose of it by purer reason. I've got a book on logic at home, cost me sixpence, and by gum, it's an eye-opener."

Macdonald chuckled, and set to work on his report. The next move in his case would be to see Elliott, the literary agent, and since that gentleman would not be likely to turn up at his office at Thavies House much before ten o'clock, Macdonald had best part of an hour to fill in. As Chief Inspector, Macdonald was free to conduct his investigation as he thought fit, but his methods were occasionally the subject of mirth among the other chief inspectors of the C.I.D., because Macdonald was said to resemble Kipling's famous mongoose in his habit of running to find out. He preferred not only to interview all contacts personally, as far as was possible, but to interview them in their own environment rather than having them brought to Scotland Yard to be interrogated. There were two schools of thought on this matter.

Chief Inspector Venables, for instance, maintained stoutly that a witness came across with it more quickly and accurately under the stimulus of a summons to Scotland Yard than if questioned in his own home or office. Macdonald maintained that you arrived at a better idea of your witness's character, and might even get valuable corroborative evidence, by seeing him in his own surroundings.

On this occasion he dispatched a sergeant to Thavies House to find out and report immediately on the time of Elliott's arrival, so that Macdonald's own time should not be wasted.

His report was only in the outline stage when Sergeant Brading rang up, and Macdonald slid his papers together and was out of his room a very few seconds after he had hung up the receiver. With Inspector Jenkins at his side he drove up the sunny Embankment, and turned into the Strand by way of Norfolk Street, arriving at Thavies House within a few minutes of Brading's message. The building where Elliott carried on his business was a narrow slip of a block recently constructed, let out in offices and rooms to a large number of different tenants. The entrance to the block was in Arundel Passage, just off the Strand, and a constable on duty at the door had already attracted the attention of the inevitable loungers of the London streets.

"Top floor, sir," said the constable as he saluted the two C.I.D. men. "The sergeant is up there."

Macdonald and Jenkins went up in the lift—an automatic one, independent of a lift man, and they shot up to the seventh and top storey. There were three sets of offices opening on to the landing, and Macdonald rang at the door which showed

Elliott's name; the door was opened by a C.I.D. sergeant. He stood back to let the two officers enter a lobby, in which stood some chairs and a table with books on it, denoting a waiting-room. Two people were in the lobby, sitting at the table and they stared at Macdonald and Jenkins. One was a white-faced young man, thin and startled looking, the other a girl whose face *might* have been white under its make-up, but whose expression denoted a lively curiosity. There were three doors opening on the lobby. One, with glass panels, was labelled "Inquiries," another, of solid wood "Private."

"In there, sir," said Brading. "This is Mr. Elliott's secretary and his stenographer."

Macdonald nodded pleasantly to the pair who sat at the table (both looking quite unaccustomed to being relegated to a waiting-room), and said:

"I want to talk to you both later. I won't keep you waiting longer than I can help," before he went to the door indicated by Brading and entered it followed closely by Jenkins.

It was a pleasantly furnished little room, with light, clean walls, and bookcases round three sides. A grandfather clock stood by the fireplace. Sunshine gleamed through the opaque glass of the window and rendered the electric light which was burning in the pendant lamp a sickly powerless yellow. The beam of sun shone on the grey head and dark clad shoulders of the man whose body had slumped forward over the desk, shone too on an overturned inkpot and the coagulated trickle of blood which had flowed from the head.

Macdonald touched one of the rigid hands which was thrust forward on the desk, but after that he stood still and looked round the room.

"Well, that's a facer and no mistake," said Jenkins, and Macdonald nodded.

"Yes. About the last thing I should have expected. Shot through the right temple, but no sign of a gun. Well, that's plain enough—nothing nebulous here."

Mardon-Elliott, Gardien's literary agent, if this were he, was fully dressed for going out. He wore a black top-coat of fine cloth, and a white silk scarf showed above the collar of it. An opera hat lay on the ground beside him with a clean chamois glove just beside it. The other glove was on his right hand. The blotting pad on the kneehole desk was pushed away to the edge of the table farthest from the body, and a blue pencil lay just by the gloved hand. Across the clean blotting paper a word had been scrawled in the blue pencil, the big letters trailing across the surface and ending in a series of spasmodic illegible jerks. The word written was GARDIEN.

"A touch of originality about this," said Macdonald. "One is led to believe that they killed one another, which as the geometry book says, is absurd. Phew! It's hot in here."

It was very hot. An electric stove stood in the fireplace behind the chair in which the body sat, and all its bars were alight. The radiator beneath the window formed another focus of heat and Macdonald guessed the temperature of the room to be over 80° F.

"We'll just make certain that the pistol hasn't rolled into a corner anywhere," he went on, "and then I'll go and talk to the pair out there. You can stay here until the surgeon comes and see that he doesn't move anything more than he can help."

Jenkins nodded. "There's a tumbler under that chair, might

as well mark it and pick it up. What do you bet it's got Gardien's fingerprints on? That'd about put the cap on it."

"It's so damned difficult not to theorise," said Macdonald, bending down to peer into every corner of the carpeted floor. "It suggests that the same person killed both Gardien and Elliott, and planted evidence to prove that they killed one another. I wonder how a jury would like that—pure reason again."

"No gun here," said Jenkins, grunting a little as he straightened himself after perusing his section of the floor, "and I'll bet my head to a china orange the chap didn't live long enough after he got that bullet in his head to play any tricks with hiding guns. I wouldn't have thought he could have written anything, either, but that blotting pad's not been moved since he fell forward. There's a mark of blood all round one corner—not smudged."

Macdonald made a swoop into a corner of the room, where there was a space between a small revolving bookcase and the wall. Using his handkerchief to hold it, he picked up a small round clock, the glass of which was cracked in and forced against the hands. The hands stood at eight o'clock.

"Oh, ho!" said Jenkins. "What time did your party start last night? Perhaps it was friend Gardien after all."

"Convenient of him to leave all the tokens and sign manuals," said Macdonald. "Having shot Elliott, Gardien went on to Caroline House and later died of a heart attack, when Elliott walked into the telephone-room, alive and well. Quite enough to give any one a heart attack. Banquo, being buried, should not have come out on's grave. All right, Jenkins. Stay and ponder over it according to the rules of logic. Losh keep's! You'll need 'em."

Going back to the door and opening it without handling the knob, Macdonald looked at the pair in the waiting-room. The girl was calmly reading a magazine, but the young man sat twisting his fingers miserably together.

"Damn it, I don't see why you won't let me smoke," he was complaining, and Macdonald put in:

"Mr. Lethem? I understand that you were the first to find the body, I should be glad if you'd answer a few questions. We could use your own office, perhaps."

The young man jumped up as though relieved to hear the sound of the chief inspector's quiet pleasant voice.

"Yes, sir. Through 'Inquiries' there."

Macdonald, after a word of instruction to Brading, crossed the little waiting-room and opened the glass-panelled door. This gave on to a narrow slip of an office, in which a typist's table stood under the window. A door in the farther wall stood open, showing a larger office beyond, into which Macdonald walked with Lethem just behind him.

"Sit down—and smoke if you want to," said Macdonald, seating himself at the table. "I expect you had a pretty nasty shock."

"I should say I did," replied the white-faced young man, his face twitching as he spoke. "I thought things were a bit odd here lately, but I didn't expect that. I suppose he shot himself?"

"Suppositions aren't much good at this stage," said Macdonald. "I'd like your name and address first, please, then you can tell me about your arrival here and finding the body."

"Gerald Lethem, 190 Mayfield Grove, Harrow," was the prompt rejoinder. "I've been with Mr. Elliott for six months.

I generally get here by half-past nine in the morning and Miss Burton comes at the same time. I have the key and open the door. I got here a bit earlier than usual this morning as I'd got a lot to do. When I opened the outer door, before I turned the electric light on, I saw a line of light under the door of Mr. Elliott's office, and thought he must have left the light burning. I went straight in and saw him."

He broke off, his face puckering up oddly as though he would have liked to cry. "I'm not much good at horrors," he went on. "It made me feel sick. I went up to the desk, near enough to see the blood, and then I bolted out again and rushed on to the landing. Wilson was there, the porter, and I told him that Mr. Elliott had shot himself. He, Wilson, went in and had a look and then some one came to the outer door— the sergeant there. Then he took things in hand, and I was jolly glad he did. I'm willing to face up to most emergencies, but the sight of blood makes me feel sick."

Macdonald nodded sympathetically. He had been studying the young man during the foregoing speech and was in two minds about him. Lethem was a tall slim fellow, very neat and stylish with black hair which gave the impression of being set like a girl's, so immaculate was its regular wave. His face was certainly pallid and his hands unsteady, but his narrative was singularly direct. He had taken the trouble to explain, without waiting to be asked, exactly why he had gone into Elliott's room, as though he had foreseen the question and been ready for it. Most witnesses, in Macdonald's experience, when under the stress of agitation in a situation like this one, rushed straight into a description of their grim discovery without thinking to explain their own actions.

Lethem showed a mixture of excitement and carefulness which seemed contradictory.

"When you went into Mr. Elliott's room, did you touch anything?" queried Macdonald, and Lethem replied promptly.

"Nothing at all. I just thought 'he's done it then.' I was going to lift him up but I realised he was dead, and then—well, I got panicky. I just bolted out to get help."

"You say that you assumed he shot himself. Could you see a pistol or revolver anywhere?"

"No. I didn't stay to look."

"What made you think of suicide?"

"I knew Elliott was pretty depressed and I believe his affairs are in a fine old mess. He's been down with 'flu just lately and hadn't taken enough time off to recover properly. He said only a few days ago, 'I'm fed up. I reckon it'd be easiest to blow my brains out'—I didn't take much notice at the time. He was always a bit odd and given to extremes. Frightfully bucked with life one day and thoroughly depressed the next."

"Difficult to work with?" queried Macdonald.

"Yes and no. Pretty maddening if you're methodical and businesslike, but he had flair—temperament you know. He never made a mistake in estimating the market value of a manuscript, but he made mistakes every other way. Nearly drove his auditors mad. I got on with him all right personally, but he'd had a new secretary every month before I came, more or less."

"Do you know what he was depressed about?"

Lethem shrugged his slim shoulders. "You'd better look at his ledgers. He'd got a good business all right, both here and in the U.S.A., but it's my opinion he's in Queer Street. If you want to know, I was hanging on in the hopes of buying him out if he went bankrupt."

"I see. Now, we'd better get on to the facts about the last person who saw him alive."

"Probably me," replied Lethem gloomily. "No. Wait a minute. It'd have been Mr. Gardien, if he turned up. It was like this," he went on, explaining with a touch of condescension in his voice. "I stayed a bit later than usual last night. The char had come in to clean up, she does it after office hours in the evening. Mr. Elliott was here, too. He'd brought a suitcase with him so as to change here as he sometimes did, when he was dining out. He told me I could use his room until I was through, as Mrs. Gadds, the char, could leave cleaning it for once and give it an extra doing to-day. I was here until half-past seven. Mr. Elliott changed in his own cloak-room and told me to bung off. He rather expected Mr. Gardien was coming in about eight o'clock. That's Andrew Gardien. You may have heard of him?"

"Yes. I have," replied Macdonald, and Lethem went on, "I left just after half-past seven. Old Gadds had gone by that time, and there was nobody in the place but Mr. Elliott. The porter's on duty till eight, because he organises the cleaning of some of the offices. The main entrance was still open when I left, but the lights on the stairs were off."

A thoughtful witness this one, mused Macdonald. He produced, unprompted, most of the details which had to be asked for as a rule.

"Had Mr. Elliott told you previously that he had an appointment with Mr. Gardien, or entered it in his engagement book, so far as you know?"

"He hadn't said anything to me about it at all, and there was no entry in the diary I keep for office use." The young man indicated a loose-leaf calendar block lying on his own desk. "It struck me as a bit odd, after office hours like that and so on, but Elliott was given to doing surprising things."

"Such as—?"

"Well, stopping here till all hours and then not turning up till tea-time next day. I can tell you he needed some one with a spot of method to help him run this show. I reckon his business has improved fifty per cent since I came."

Macdonald sat silent and studied the young man again. Mr. Lethem's nervousness seemed to have quieted down now, and he lit another cigarette with quite a nonchalant air.

"If you ask me, I should say the poor chap was a bit batty," he added. "That go of 'flu was the last straw. It does get some fellows down."

Again Macdonald nodded agreement, pleasantly.

"You can give me Mr. Elliott's home address, and Mr. Gardien's, I expect?"

"Mr. Elliott had just moved to a place in Surrey—Boxleith Hall. It's one of those residential country clubs, I believe. I've never been there, myself. He was rather close over his own affairs. Took it amiss if I tried to ring him up when he was away from the office. A maddening fellow in some ways. If he'd have given me authority to act on my own initiative— however there it is." He shrugged his shoulders and blew out a cloud of heavy fragrant smoke.

"And Mr. Gardien's address?"

"I rather think he's at the Savoy this time," replied Lethem, putting the accent on the first part of Savoy and somehow contriving to infer that it was a haunt of his own. "Gardien's always travelling about—the devil of a nuisance to act for."

"Can't you do better than rather think?" enquired Macdonald. "Don't you forward Mr. Gardien's letters for instance?"

"Letters come for him here, but I haven't forwarded any lately. Elliott saw to it. Sometimes we have been out of touch with Gardien for months, even his bank didn't know his address. In my opinion Gardien likes doing the mystery man touch. Seeks publicity by avoiding it, if you see what I mean."

"Has Mr. Gardien been here frequently of late?"

"He's been in three or four times in the past month to see Elliott personally. I know very little about him really. Never exchanged more than a dozen words with him."

"So far as you can judge, were he and Mr. Elliott friends, apart from their business association?"

"Yes, I should say they were. Lunched and dined together, and so forth. Elliott would always put off any other appointment to suit Gardien."

"So far as you know, they hadn't quarrelled?"

"Quarrelled? Good Lord! You're thinking Gardien shot him?" Lethem stared at Macdonald with his mouth open, and then went on, "If they quarrelled I never heard anything about it. Elliott was all over him. Had good reason to be. Gardien's books sold all over the world. What you'd call a profitable proposition."

Macdonald glanced at his watch. "I am sure that you will be able to give me a lot of assistance, Mr. Lethem, but there are certain routine matters which I must attend to now. I shall need these offices for the time being. Is there anywhere else on the premises where you can work? I expect you can carry on with some of the usual business, in spite of this deplorable happening."

"There's dispatch," said Lethem. "I can work there. Can I open the mail?"

"Quite shortly," said Macdonald.

Lethem gave his characteristic shrug. "All the same to me. I've got an MS. to go through, so I may as well get on with it. Business is Business."

"It is. I have to know just what you did when you left here last evening, of course."

"Certainly. I went into Byng's for a snack—just off the Strand. Got there at about twenty to eight. Met a man named Crome and went to the Academy Cinema with him—and so to bed."

"Crome's full name and address?"

"Walter Crome. Photographer on the staff of the *Morning Mail*. Lives in Bloomsbury somewhere."

"Thanks. That's all for the moment. You will have to stop in the waiting-room for a bit, but I won't keep you there long."

For the next quarter of an hour Macdonald heard the report of Detective Green, who had followed the two inspectors with the C.I.D. photographers and fingerprint men. Green and Brading had been making inquiries of the other two employees in Elliott's office, Miss Burton, the stenographer, and Hands, the boy in charge of the dispatch room. Both of these had left the building the previous evening by six-fifteen, and since they had no evidence to give of immediate importance they were told to go home, as Macdonald wanted the offices left empty for the investigation. The porter of the building turned out to be an ex-policeman of D division, who gave evidence with police court precision. He had seen young Hands and Miss Burton leave Thavies House at their usual time, shortly after six. Holland (the porter) was on duty in the entrance hall at the time, where he stayed until half-past six, by which time most of the occupants of the offices had left. Between six-thirty and seven-thirty, Holland was about the building, superintending the cleaners. At seven-thirty these also had left, and Holland had seen Mr. Lethem go out of the main entrance just after seven-thirty. The lights on the stairs were off, but those in the entrance hall were still burning. Holland had shut the entrance doors shortly after Lethem had gone, but had remained in the building until eight o'clock, his official hour for going off duty. Between seven-thirty and eight o'clock he had been on the ground floor, putting to rights a piece of rubber floor cloth which had been torn by some furniture movers: Holland was certain that no one entered the building between seven-forty, when he closed the doors, and eight o'clock.

Asked if he had ever admitted a visitor for Mr. Elliott after the front doors were shut, he said that some weeks ago the former had tipped him to remain on duty until eight-thirty to admit a visitor. There was a bell at the front door which Holland would answer if he were in the building. His description of Elliott's visitor on that occasion fitted Gardien's appearance very well indeed. Holland agreed that it would have been possible for any one familiar with the building to have slipped in between the time that Lethem went out and the time that the doors were closed for the night.

It was at this point in the relating of the evidence that Jenkins put his large cheerful face in at the door and said:

"Got a moment, Chief?"

Macdonald promptly got up and followed his colleague into Elliott's office. Here were the surgeon and the fingerprint men, and Macdonald could see from their faces that something unusual had occurred.

"This is what you might call a signed murder," said Jenkins. "I've read some of Gardien's books, and he was a fair conjurer with his bits of string and what-nots. I often wondered if they'd work, but this one did anyway. Have you ever seen a grandfather clock in an office before, Chief?"

"No. I haven't," replied Macdonald, and Jenkins went on:

"Neither have I. Have a look at the workings of this one, you'll want a torch to see it properly."

Macdonald went and opened the long door of the "grandfather." Familiar from boyhood with the mechanism of such clocks he noted at once that both weights were down and the bob of the pendulum unusually high. Turning the beam of his torch up into the works behind the clock face, he saw that a small pistol was fixed among the mechanism and that a cord was wound round the circumference of one of the big wheels. Jenkins fairly chuckled with glee to himself.

"I haven't figured out how the shooting was done, but I can see this. If that pistol was lying on the ground when the works of that clock started and a piece of cord attached to the pistol had its other end adjusted over that wheel, then as the wheel revolved and wound up the string, the pistol would be drawn along the floor and up into the case through the space at the bottom—(the bottom panel having been removed as you can see)—and finally have come to rest where it is. That good enough?"

"That part of it's all right," said Macdonald. "Just a few

tricks to make grandfather revolve twelve hours by the clock in twelve minutes and the pistol would go on moving—at the end of a string. Murder by Andrew Gardien, including his own, signed proof copies."

"Talk about tricks, I've never seen one to compare with that," said Jenkins, but Macdonald was looking puzzled.

"Tricks—" he murmured. "I suppose that *was* Gardien who died last night. Coombe was the only person who knew him by sight, and the Delareign lady, and she's said to be short sighted."

"By gum!" said Jenkins, as the idea permeated. "By Gum! That opens out avenues so to speak."

Macdonald looked again at the workings of the "grandfather," and then gave a sound very like a chuckle.

"A battle of wits, as Coombe said. It's time we found out who's who in this game."

VIII

MACDONALD, WHEN HE SNATCHED A FEW MINUTES FOR a belated mid-day meal in the course of his investigation of the double problem of Gardien and Elliott's death, felt that he had collected so much curious evidence that he would have been glad of a few hours in which to do some concentrated thinking. The difficulty of a murder case was that the trail had to be followed while it was fresh, and the detective engaged on it had little leisure to ponder while he was hot foot after essential facts.

The surgeon's report on Elliott's death stated that the agent had been killed by a shot fired at close quarters, with the barrel of the pistol almost touching the temple. The shot might or might not have been self-inflicted, and the bullet found in the dead man's head was fired from a pistol of the same small calibre as that of the weapon found in the grandfather clock.

Since this was an American pistol of the "mass production" school, the experts who submitted bullet and weapon to the "comparison microscope" test were chary of giving a decision as to whether the bullet must have been fired from that weapon and none other. It was different, they told Macdonald (who knew it already), in the case of a Webley or pistol of similar excellence, in which the breech markings were identifiable. In this case only a probability could be declared, not a certainty.

The pistol found in the clock was without fingerprints of any kinds, but the tumbler which Jenkins had picked up on the floor gave prints of Gardien's fingers. Another tumbler was found in Elliott's cloak-room which had been wiped free of prints. All the polished surfaces in the office where the body was found had been carefully wiped also. The obvious deduction from this was that Gardien, having planned a murder according to his own formula had carefully removed all traces of his visit, but had failed to see the tumbler which had rolled out of sight under the table.

"It's just like the chap's own stories," repeated Jenkins, "seems idiotic at first, so that one feels superior, but the end is never idiotic. It's always damned clever, and you realise he was smarter than yourself."

"It looks as though he hadn't finished this one, then," replied Macdonald, "unless we're too dense to see the ending. Elliott was shot sitting in that chair, so far as you and the surgeons can see. He hadn't been moved. Well, where's the booby trap that held the pistol? There isn't a thing which suggests one. If some one came and cleared away the booby trap, why didn't they take the gun, too, or else leave it beside the body to suggest suicide?"

"In other words, some one with a mind less astute than Gardien's committed a crime and left his signature on it," said

Jenkins, "and then walked out, went along to Coombe's and killed Gardien too."

Inquiry from Mr. Lethem elicited the fact that the grandfather clock had belonged to Mr. Gardien. It had only been in Elliott's office for a week, and was being kept there until such time as Mr. Gardien could find room for it. Corroboration of this statement was unobtainable, (in so far as Gardien's ownership was concerned) Elliott having merely mentioned it to his secretary—as he had mentioned Gardien's expected visit the previous evening.

One other interesting discovery was made. In Elliott's cloak-room an enamel basin was found in which were the charred remains of burnt papers. A considerable amount of letters or other documents must have been burnt, and the resulting ashes afterwards pulverised. So thoroughly had they been ground down that nothing remained but pulverised ashes. Lethem was able to throw no light on this affair. Not being acquainted with Elliott's private papers he could not tell what was missing from his desk. In the cloak-room was also found Elliott's lounge suit and the other clothes from which he had changed into the evening suit which he wore at the time of his death. "The time" of his death was another knotty point. Twelve hours was given as the probable interval that had elapsed between Elliott's death and the time when the surgeon had examined his body—thus pointing to ten p.m. The heat of the room made it difficult to be more precise over the point. If the electric fire had been burning all night, thus maintaining the temperature of the body and deferring the onset of rigor, death might have occurred fourteen or fifteen hours previous to examination.

"Can you tell me if the temperature of the room was constant, more or less, all night?" inquired the surgeon, to which Macdonald could only reply that he assumed the fire had been burning all night, but obviously couldn't be certain. On the other hand, if the fire had been lighted later, death might not have occurred much before midnight.

Once the body had been removed and the photographers and fingerprint men had done their work, Macdonald sent for one of the solicitors attached to the C.I.D., and set him to examine the mass of papers and files in Elliott's office, a job, which in combination with the ledgers, promised many hours, if not days of work. Lethem was kept on the premises to assist when he was needed, and Macdonald and Jenkins were then free to concentrate on investigating the lives of the two men whose deaths seemed so oddly connected, and to discover some factor which could account for both.

Lethem's suggestion that Gardien had been staying at the Savoy Hotel was promptly disproved. The Savoy knew nothing of that author. While some of his men were occupied in telephoning to all the London hotels, Macdonald went to see the manager of the Strand and Counties Banks where Elliott had his account and had a stroke of luck immediately in finding that Gardien had banked at the same branch, having been introduced there by Elliott. The manager was unable to give any address of Gardien's save that of the agent himself, but one of the clerks who knew Gardien by sight was more helpful. On several occasions he had seen Gardien entering or leaving a block of chambers in Martlet Street, Piccadilly, near to the famous "White Jade" restaurant. Macdonald immensely relieved at having one problem on the way to solution, promptly asked the clerk if he could identify Gardien unquestionably. The young man (named James Harris) was certain on this point, and he was dispatched to the mortuary. The bank manager having expressed his very proper consternation at the news of Elliott's and Gardien's deaths, undertook to seek authority to prepare a statement of their accounts for the Yard auditors to inspect.

The manager was a suave but colourless man, so far as his character was concerned, and seemed to Macdonald far more able in the realm of ledgers, stocks and shares, and pure mathematics than in the observation of human beings. Perhaps it was professional custom and exactitude which made his account of his two dead clients so meagre, but Macdonald left him to obtain his authority from the board and hasten westwards to Regency Chambers, Martlet Street, in the hope of coming on some information concerning the life and habits of an author who eschewed publicity.

Regency Chambers was a small block, the ground floor of which was tenanted by an Estate Agent. A side door led to a staircase and small lift (automatic) and a plate over a bell-push indicated "porter." Ringing this, Macdonald asked the man who appeared in answer to his summons for Mr. Andrew Gardien.

"Not at home just at present, sir. Can I take a message?"

Macdonald showed his warrant card. "Is there a manager here?"

"Yes, sir. Mr. 'Obbs. Top floor. I'll take you up. Nothing wrong, I 'ope."

"Mr. Gardien met with an accident last night. Have you any idea what time he left here?"

"Just after seven o'clock, sir, on 'is way out to dine. Told me 'e 'oped to come back rolling—in money, that is, sir. Treasure 'unting, 'e said 'e was. Street accident, sir?"

"Heart attack," replied Macdonald.

"Ah, 'e was troubled that way," said the porter as the lift came to rest.

"Mr. 'Obbs"—Julian Barton-Hobbs was his full name—turned out to be a bit of a character. "Manager" was a misnomer for him. He was in reality the lessee of the house, occupying the top floor himself, and letting out the sets of "gentlemen's chambers" below at a considerable profit. In the course of conversation, Mr. Barton-Hobbs told Macdonald that he had always lived in the west end, but a contracting income had made it impossible for him to pay the rents required by the "sharks of landlords" in Mayfair. With a combination of shrewdness and optimism he had decided to turn landlord himself, taken a lease of Regency Chambers as a final speculation, and contrived to let his premises in small units to such advantage that he was now in the happy position of living rent-free.

A man of forty-five, with the clipped accent of the huntin' and fishin' sportsman, Barton-Hobbs had an unexpected business and administrative sense of a domestic kind. Some of his chambers were let furnished, with service provided, and it was in one of these *pieds à terre* that Gardien had been living for the past two months.

"I knew the fella's name as a thriller writer, of course, and he paid his rent in advance. Good enough for me," said Barton-Hobbs, studying Macdonald through a monocle. "What's he done? Glad he didn't do it here, whatever it was."

Hearing that Mr. Gardien had died, Barton-Hobbs murmured, "Saved me a spot of trouble by dying somewhere else, what? Want me to identify him?"

Of information concerning the writer, Mr. Barton-Hobbs could provide nothing. "Fella paid his rent and didn't give me any trouble. Not what I'd call a pukka sahib. Couldn't stand his ties, and he bought his boots ready-made. Woolworth's, from the look of 'em. Relatives? Lord alone knows. I'm not his aunt, you know. Where do I bung his stuff to? I could let that set again to-morrow."

"Presumably his belongings and private papers will supply us with information about his next of kin," said Macdonald. "This is the key-ring from his pocket. I expect one of the Yale latch keys is that of his apartment downstairs."

Barton-Hobbs glanced at the keys.

"That's about it," he said. "The one with the triangular end is the street-door key, the other's for his own oak. Like me to help you?"

He stood up, wrapping himself in the folds of his superb and flaming silk dressing-gown.

"Wish I'd taken to writin'," he observed. "The chap must have been rollin'. Always feedin' at Oddy's and the Ritz and that. If a fella with a face and a voice like that could boil up plots and sell 'em for all that, I reckon it's easy money."

"Mr. Gardien struck you as being well to do?"

"Well, I ask you! I didn't much cotton on to the look of him. I get eight to ten guineas as a rule for those rooms of his, with service, heatin', valet, and that. I asked him twelve—per week, y'know—and he paid up like a lamb, and I bet he's not slept in his bed here more than one night in three. Ask

Dean, that's the man who does Gardien's rooms. He's about somewhere."

"Good. Can you arrange for Dean to be free in an hour's time, so that I can talk to him then? I want to have a look round Mr. Gardien's rooms first."

"Right. I'll see to it. By the bye, just remembered. Gardien had a man in to vet him a month or so ago. Dr. Brace, that's the chap. If he died of heart disease, might save an inquest, what? Don't want any journalists rollin' round; not good for trade."

"Quite," said Macdonald. "I shall be very glad to see Dr. Brace. Thanks for your assistance."

"Not at all. Always believe in keepin' on the right side of the police, what! Anything I can do and all that—" murmured Mr. Barton-Hobbs.

Andrew Gardien's rooms consisted of a small sitting-room, a smaller bedroom, a luxurious-looking bathroom, and a tiny kitchenette or pantry. The place was admirably furnished in ultra-modern style with furniture built to take up as little room as possible. The discreet buffs, browns, and creams of the colour scheme were restful and harmonious, and there was a minimum of ornament and oddments. Mr. Barton-Hobbs had good taste, meditated Macdonald. The rooms were comfortable and pleasing to the eye, admirably kept, well heated, and efficiently ventilated. Bookcases were built into the walls, and a let-down bureau was similarly fitted. It was in the bedroom that Macdonald found the only piece of furniture which looked as though it had not been part of the original scheme of furniture. This was a cabinet, in fumed oak, doing duty as a bedside table. The keys on Gardien's ring opened the wooden cabinet and disclosed within a modern safe, which when opened disclosed stacks of neatly arranged files.

When Macdonald first began to work through the contents of these files, he thought that he had found nothing more than a series of schemes for the author's work, notes of plots, summaries of characters, and so forth, but gradually another idea dawned on him, and by the end of an hour he was certain that he was right. There was one set of sheets, neatly pinned together and labelled JANE X, whose contents gave the wretched story of a drug addict. Certain names of restaurants and night clubs were mentioned, some in England, some in Paris, and Macdonald recognised the references so that he was able to place the story as that of a girl drug-addict who had committed suicide when put under restraint and deprived of her unknown source of supply. Another neatly filed set of papers dealt with a case of cheating at cards which had been hushed up after a threatened libel action. The whole elaborate set of notes suggested one thing—the work of a systematic blackmailer. Such, then, in Macdonald's opinion, was the activity which had enabled Gardien to live in a style to which his admitted popularity as a writer could not attain.

The final section of the last file contained what was, from the point of view of Macdonald's case, the most interesting find. It was a series of notes on the guests at Graham Coombe's party and on the publisher and his sister.

Miss Coombe, denoted by the letters S.S., was recognisable by the notes on her books and her social activities, in addition to which were a series of pencil names indicating a tour in Provence: "Avignon, Hotel des Anglais. Hyeres, Hotel d'Europe. St. Raphael, Hotel Cote d'Azur. See 27B."

Another note which interested Macdonald very much was "D.G." Here, contrary to his usual practice, the writer had entered a name. Diana Geraldine. S.S. *Ophelion*. Agra. Simla. Delhi. See Orient list outward passage. J.L.? Both of Manchester.

The last set of sheets referred to V. W. Woodstock, and this was a comprehensive piece of work. "Born 1911. Mallingham, Wilts. Wraden Hall School, Reading, 1922–1928. St. Elizabeth College, Oxford, 1928–1931. July and August, 1932. Skye and D.S., J.L., etc. Easter, 1933. Majorca, ditto. August, 1935, Anncey. September, Long Lough, Braemar." There were some photographs clipped together with this sheet. One was a photograph of Valerie Woodstock, which had been published in the *Mallingham Herald* after she had taken her degree and been awarded a post-graduate research scholarship. "Brilliant academic career of Colonel Woodstock's daughter. Highest university honours won by Mallingham girl," ran the printed comment beneath. Another photograph was a snapshot taken at the seaside, by the Mediterranean, Macdonald guessed, judged by the intense lighting and the background of pines on a rocky promontory. This showed Miss Woodstock standing poised for a dive on a bathing raft, her magnificent slim body, taut and fine in its exiguous bathing suit. Beside her stood a sun-tanned young man, apparently as dark as a Moor in the strong light, one arm lifted as though to caress the girl's shoulders. It was a beautiful photograph of two beautiful young people, and Macdonald felt a moment of rage against the dead man who had included this record of wholesome physical delight among his collection of evil reminiscences. All that was human in the chief inspector's mind urged him to the view that if Gardien had been murdered, he had probably richly earned his fate. As he put the papers back in the workman-like files, Macdonald had to remind himself that murder could never be justified. The legal system of this country provided for redress against the blackmailer with protection to the blackmailed, and the man—or woman—who took the law into his or her own hands had to answer for the act.

So rich was the field of surmise offered by the contents of the files that it took a positive mental effort on Macdonald's part to leave that section of his researches and to turn to the other contents of the rooms in the hope of finding papers which would answer the still unanswered question: Who was Andrew Gardien, where had he previously lived, who had been his associates, and what was his past?

Nobody so far had been able to give any indications which would supply a background. Graham Coombe's acquaintance with the writer was (if he spoke the truth) of the slightest. Elliott, who could probably have answered these questions, was dead. (Was this why he was dead?) None of the guests at Coombe's party, save Miss Delareign, had ever seen Gardien before—according to their own accounts. Here was a man living luxuriously, concealing his address even from his own bank manager, well known by name to thousands, yet apparently living in a void of his own creation.

By the time Macdonald had worked through the contents of Gardien's admirably tidy rooms he was no nearer to a direct answer to his questions. There was nothing, in either bureau, deed-box, bookcase, or cupboards to supply a background to the man who had lived there. The metal deed-box which

Macdonald found in a cupboard in the bedroom contained Gardien's recent contracts with his publishers, the agreement with Barton-Hobbs for his tenancy of the Chambers, his pass-book and papers relating to income-tax. It also contained an envelope stuffed with Spanish and South African currency notes, to the value of about £200 so far as Macdonald could make out, at a rough-and-ready computation.

The pass-book showed credit entries of cheques from Elliott, and a balance standing at £300 odd. The credits shown in the pass-book for the past year amounted to about £800—certainly not the total income of a man who paid twelve guineas a week for rooms in Mayfair and who was given to dining expensively at the Café Royal.

The bureau contained a pile of typescript and a quantity of stationery, but no correspondence other than a few bills and letters from travel agencies concerning tours in South America and the States.

There was a portable typewriter in a case on a shelf and in a portfolio beside it the last pages, apparently, of the novel Gardien had been engaged on. The word "blackmail" caught Macdonald's eye, and he read the last page.

"The successful blackmailer must needs be a good psychologist. He must read between the lines, probe beneath the surface. It is axiomatic to him that no man or woman is without a secret which it is worth their while to conceal. No life, however seemingly virtuous, no character however seemingly estimable, but has some point which is vulnerable. The more able, the more vital, the more well known be the individual,

> *the bigger chance there is that in their past history lies*
> *some secret worth concealing—and worth an infini-*
> *tude of trouble on the blackmailer's part to acquire."*

"A pity you didn't live to be blackmailed yourself," thought Macdonald, and took up the small key-ring which had been in Gardien's pocket. There were six keys in all. The two which gave access to Regency Chambers, those of the safe and deed-box and the cupboard which contained the latter, and one other, a small door key similar in shape to a Yale. This fitted nothing in Gardien's room, and Macdonald believed that it would open the way to the facts which at present eluded him. Gardien must surely have some other establishment where he kept his main possessions. Here, in Regency Chambers, were a few clothes, a few pairs of boots, and a few books (nearly all new). With the files from the safe packed into a dispatch-case, and the packet of foreign currency in his pocket, Gardien could have walked out of his rooms at any time, leaving noth-ing behind him of any real value, and leaving no clue at all to his own whereabouts. There, under Macdonald's hand, lay the extra latch-key, giving admission perhaps to another life.

Gardien had been a tenant of Regency Chambers for the past two months, since he had returned from India, in short, and Macdonald envisaged a long hunt on routine lines before he could get any information which could lead to a recon-struction of the man's life. And when he got it would he be any nearer to solving his problem of who killed Gardien—and Elliott? There was plenty of motive to hand for the murder of the one, and it looked as though the second were inter-twined with it. Elliott had been killed to stop him giving any information about Gardien, but the problem remained of who died first.

Macdonald sat for a while and pondered over the problem. Since Gardien had reached Caroline House at half-past eight, it was obviously possible for him to have been at Thavies House at eight o'clock, shot Elliott or arranged some contraption which engineered the shooting, and then gone on to the party. If there *had* been some mechanical arrangement for the shooting, Macdonald had to admit that he failed to see how it was worked, and his mind refused to allow the possibility of such a thing. The weakness of such arrangements (often ingeniously described in detective stories) was in the assumption that the victim would oblige by taking up the exact pose—to within a fraction of an inch—required for accurate shooting. A man sitting in a chair may assume any one of a thousand poses so far as the position of his head is concerned, and this variation militated against the fixed pistol theory of the crime.

If the pistol could have been fixed in the receiver of the telephone, and arranged to fire a few seconds after the receiver had been lifted, a lethal result might be counted upon; but the combined mouthpiece receiver fitment of the telephone on Elliott's desk could not have been used in such a manner. Yet what could be the sense of shooting a man and arranging for the pistol to be wound up into the workings of a grandfather clock? If the point at issue were to dispose of the weapon so as to avoid carrying it out of the building, it would have been infinitely more sensible to have left it beside the body so that suicide could be assumed.

Leaving that side of the problem, Macdonald went back

in mind to Caroline House. The grey-haired flat-footed man had been seen there shortly after nine o'clock. Assuming that this man was Elliott, he could have been presumed to leave Coombe's house just after the fuse occurred at half-past nine, and gone straight back to Thavies House, let himself into the building with the key (one of which all the tenants possessed), gone into his own office and been shot—thereafter scrawling down the name of the man whose death he had just engineered. "That makes wilder rubbish than the other way," said Macdonald to himself. "Yet here we have the murder of Elliott—signed Gardien—so to speak, and the murder of Gardien with an indication of Elliott. The probability is that the same person killed both and arranged indications that they killed one another, doing it in such a way as to suggest a thriller writer as the perpetrator—on account of the funny business involved—from which suggestion it seems reasonable to argue by contraries that a thriller writer had nothing to do with it."

At this stage in his conjectures, Macdonald was interrupted to hear the evidence of Dean, the man who was responsible for the cleaning of Gardien's rooms. From Dean came the following statements: Gardien had been an ill-tempered but generous tenant. Apart from a habit of grumbling at alleged defects in the service rendered him, he had given very little trouble and had tipped handsomely. He had had coffee and rolls served to him in bed each morning he had been at home, had always lunched and dined out, never ordering in a meal as did some of the other tenants, and never entertaining, so far as Dean and the porter knew.

He had frequently been away for week-ends, often from

Friday to Tuesday, but had always given explicit notice of his absence, telling Dean that after such-and-such an hour his services would not be required until a given time. He was not in the habit of taking a suitcase away with him, as Dean could tell because of his duties as a valet. The only peculiarities that Dean had noticed about Gardien were as follows: He had very few letters by post, and those which did come were fairly bulky packets with a typewritten address. (Forwarded by Elliott, Macdonald surmised.) Gardien's other peculiarity was that he left no papers in his waste-paper basket. There was no open fireplace in his rooms, but he had habitually burned a small amount of papers in a pail in the kitchenette, a custom which had annoyed Dean, as it indicated "a nasty suspicious nature" on the part of the tenant.

At the conclusion of his inquiry at Regency Chambers, Macdonald tabulated the following suppositions for future reference:

Gardien was probably a blackmailer whose mode of life at Regency Chambers made it possible for him to flit from his *pied à terre* at any moment, leaving no evidence by which he could be traced. There was a strong probability that he had an alternative establishment under a different name, of which no evidence existed save the latch key on his key-ring. There was evidence in his files which indicated more than one line of research concerning those present at Caroline House the previous evening.

IX

SHORTLY AFTER HER BROTHER HAD LEFT CAROLINE House for his office, Miss Coombe was called to the telephone. The C.I.D. man on duty in the room apologised politely for the necessity of his presence, to which Miss Coombe replied in her cheerful, practical manner.

"Very nice of you to say so, but I don't mind in the least. Very boring for you, I'm afraid. Conversation over the phone always sounds so foolish. Hallo. Miss Coombe speaking."

It was Miss Delareign who had rung up, "full of chirp and chat," as Susan put it. "I am *so* sorry to bother you, but I'm afraid I left my gloves behind me last night, rather a favourite pair. Might I call for them some time to-day?"

"By all means, though I could send them if you like," replied Miss Coombe. "I think there is an evening bag of yours, too, black brocade with a diamanté clasp."

"No. I didn't leave a bag. I have my own, gold mesh to match my frock. The cleaners did the frock so beautifully.

It doesn't show a mark. I am so anxious to know if you have any news about poor Mr. Gardien's accident."

"No. Nothing whatever," said Miss Coombe firmly. "In any case, I couldn't talk about it over the phone."

"No. Of course not. If I looked in—say after lunch—could I see you for a few minutes? I have a little idea I should like to discuss with you."

Miss Coombe meditated before she replied, so that the lady at the other end put in "Hallo, are you still there?" in a surprised tone, and Miss Coombe replied abruptly, "Yes, I beg your pardon for keeping you waiting. I shall be in at two o'clock if that will suit you."

"Thank you *so* much. Good-bye."

Miss Coombe replaced the receiver and turned to the polite young man who stood looking out of the window.

"Would you like *The Times*, or do you prefer the *Daily Mail*? I'm afraid that bookcase hasn't anything readable. I'll send you in some papers."

"Please don't trouble—" His sentence was cut short by the telephone bell ringing again and Miss Coombe murmured:

"Do you prefer to answer it?"

"No, madam. I have no instructions except to be on duty here until I am relieved."

Once again she lifted the receiver.

"Could I speak to Miss Coombe, please?"

"Speaking."

"Good-morning. This is Valerie Woodstock. May I come in and talk to you for a little while? I very much want your advice about something. I should be so grateful if you could spare me a few minutes."

"Certainly. Come as soon as you like," replied Miss Coombe. "I shall be in all the morning. Say in half an hour? Excellent. Good-bye."

With a word and a smile to the detective, Miss Coombe went out into the hall, but when she had closed the door behind her, her expression altered to a frown. Really, with the best will in the world it wasn't easy to talk to people with the powers of the C.I.D., vested in a nicely mannered young man, at your elbow. And what did these writers want to talk to her about? Last night, of course. Miss Coombe made a sudden decision which had been playing about in and out of her mind ever since she woke up. What about a feminist conference on the events of last night? A committee meeting, so to speak, with herself in the chair? If Miss Delareign wanted to talk, let her do so in the presence of the other women who had been at the party last night.

Making a quick decision, Miss Coombe put on her hat and coat and hurried to the telephone box at the corner of Caroline Street.

"That young man in there gets my goat," she said to herself. "I'm not going to ring up these people under his nose."

She put through three calls at top speed. One each to Mrs. Etherton, Miss Rees, and Miss Campbell, asking them to call on her at two o'clock—an invitation which was accepted by all three ladies. She then returned home and awaited Miss Woodstock in her own study.

Valerie, in a tailored suit and a neat hat, looked much older than she had done in her gold and green evening-frock on the previous evening, and the laughing flippancy of her expression was altered to a look which was most serious and troubled.

"It's awfully good of you to see me," she said as they shook hands. "I know a lot about you because of all the work you've done on different lines, and I feel that I can talk to you freely. You don't know anything about me, but I can assure you I'm quite a serious-minded person."

Miss Coombe laughed. "My dear, I do a spot of reading sometimes, you know, and I'm not quite an ass when it comes to summing people up. What's it all about? Last night?"

"Yes. I'm worried. Can you tell me this: Did Mr. Gardien die a natural death from heart failure, or was he killed— murdered, in short?"

Susan Coombe studied the girl opposite to her with very shrewd eyes. She liked Valerie Woodstock very much on the strength of their short acquaintance, liked her spirit and level-headedness, her able mind, and her detached manner of looking at things. Susan Coombe belonged to the generation of woman who had fought—literally fought—for women's rights. She had come up against all the unfairness and unreason and obstinacy of men who saw their privileges threatened, and though she had left far behind the bitterness and preju- dices of those hectic years of her girlhood, they had left their mark on her character. Susan would rather listen to a woman's point of view than a man's, rather back a woman than a man. She had liked Macdonald and thought him competent, but she had been very much aware of his official attitude: "It will be much better if you don't interfere." Common sense bade her acquiesce, but the old suffragist spirit revolted. Looking at Valerie thoughtfully, she replied:

"I don't know why you ask that, but I am sure that it isn't mere curiosity or a desire to get sensational news. You saw the chief inspector last night. He didn't actually tell me that it would be better if I were to hold my tongue, but it was implicit in his attitude. However, I intend to use my own discretion in the matter—as you have decided to use yours. Now don't you think you had better tell me the reason underlying your question? I can only be frank with you if you are frank with me."

"That's perfectly reasonable," agreed the girl. "Incidentally, I liked the chief inspector. He struck me as fair, courteous, and very able. I'm certain he's a first-rate man, with something more than keen eyes and an observant brain. He's one of those Scots who seem to have a telepathic sense; he guesses—or feels—what you are thinking as he listens to what you tell him. I could have gone to him with my question, but I was afraid. It's just this: *If* that man *were* killed deliberately last night, I've got an uncomfortable feeling that I might guess something about it. That's why I should be very glad to learn that his death was due to natural causes, as the phrase goes."

Miss Coombe sat very still, but her face showed deep concern. "My dear girl," she said at length, "have you realised just what you are saying and what it implies? It's the law in this country that any one who shields a murderer becomes accessory after the fact. If you have any evidence—"

"I haven't. Not a shred," returned the other coolly. "I may be absolutely wrong in the conclusions I've drawn. No. Conclusion is too strong a word for my vague mental processes. But won't you answer my first question? Or have you answered it already?"

"I see no reason why I shouldn't tell you my own opinion in the matter," replied Miss Coombe. "The chief inspector was much too cautious to make any definite statement, but he obviously believed that Mr. Gardien was killed by some one interfering with the electric current; in other words, he was murdered. It's a grim thought, you know."

"It is, and the consequence entailed is even grimmer, but it's a wise thing to try to look at the matter objectively, and not to be swayed by emotional excitement over it. It's so easy to say, 'How ghastly!' so easy to be conventionally censorious, and to forget that there are two points of view over every controversy, and it's not always the popular point of view that's right."

"There can't be two points of view over murder," replied Miss Coombe, and Valerie Woodstock retorted:

"You're a pacifist, are you not—and I assume a logical one? You don't admit any circumstances in which it is justifiable to take life?"

"I do not."

"Good. Then you don't approve of capital punishment?"

"No—but—"

"There's no but about it." Valerie faced the older woman with as cool a front as though she were arguing a purely academic point.

"The chief inspector is quite logical in his attitude. If he is convinced that murder was done, he'll pursue the murderer until he gets him or her in the dock—if he can; 'thereafter to be taken to the place from whence they came and hanged by the neck—' You know that piece of legal pronouncement. Now, I also am a pacifist, and I am against capital punishment; but while I assure you that I'm not holding a brief for murder, I should hate to think that anybody I met here last night might be hanged for arranging a painless exit for that very unpleasant person, Andrew Gardien."

"You knew him, then?"

"Before last night? No, I did not, but I saw enough of him to make me realise that I've no tears to shed over his death."

Valerie had been sitting with her hands along the arms of her chair, very upright, a little tense; and suddenly she changed her attitude and her voice changed too into a tone less sharp.

"I'm awfully sorry I'm doing this so badly. The last thing I want to do is to make you feel more uncomfortable than you're feeling already. I came to you because I knew that I could trust you. I feel that so strongly that if I'd killed the man myself—and felt justified in doing it—I should not be afraid to tell you how or why I did it, knowing you wouldn't give me away. You're like that, in spite of reminding me about accessories and all the other paraphernalia. If *you* had killed him, and I knew it, I should take great pains to avoid sharing my knowledge with the C.I.D."

Miss Coombe stared at the girl's calm face. "Is that it? You imagine that my convictions of non-aggression might go to the wall in case of expediency?"

Valerie Woodstock laughed outright. "I like the way you say that! I know your militant record, you know, and the leopard doesn't change his spots. You're only pacifist from intellectual conviction, not from moral inertia, like most of them. You could hit as hard as I could if you felt justified in doing it. Do you do cross-words?"

"I do."

"So do I. I find it's symptomatic of a certain type of mind.

Some people like puzzles as others like physical exercise. Excess of biological energy over immediate needs, I suppose. Regarding this problem as a cross-word and putting all passions and 'isms' aside, can you tell me that you haven't fairly puzzled your brains to know what happened last night, and who caused it to happen?"

"My dear girl, of course I have."

"And are you going to write out your ideas in detail and submit them to that admirable chief inspector, and say, 'I think this is what really happened?'"

"There," said Miss Coombe, speaking with great deliberation, "you have me. I may have made wild guesses, but I'm going to keep them to myself. Now don't go drawing erroneous conclusions. Don't think that your arguments about logical pacifism and capital punishment have impressed me. I've heard them before, and I admit your point, but there are two things I should like to make clear. I do *not*, under any circumstances, approve of murder—mass murder or otherwise—nor do I approve of capital punishment, but this seems clear to me: Nobody, man or woman, who possesses an ethical sense, can make light of perjury. If I am to be put in the witness-box I shall tell the truth to the best of my ability."

"So should I," put in Valerie, and Miss Coombe went on firmly:

"There is a C.I.D. man on duty in this house at the present moment. It's his business to notice things. He's probably phoned through to his superior officer already and reported that you have called here. Don't you think it's probable that the chief inspector may ask me what you had to say? Please don't put me in an impossible position by telling me things which you don't want repeated."

"I see," replied Valerie. "You'd rather I didn't discuss the matter with you at all."

Miss Coombe reached out her hand for the cigarette-box and offered it to her visitor, and Valerie took a cigarette with a smile and lighted it, while Miss Coombe went on:

"My dear, I know of no one with whom I should find it more interesting to discuss this matter than yourself. You've got a clear head. There are two sides in most of us—certainly in myself. On the one hand is the woman who prides herself on her civic sense, her desire for justice, and her respect for the truth as a fundamental of justice. In association with her is the more primitive woman who is chock full of curiosity and as liable to err as ever a woman was. I'll talk the whole thing over with you, provided you won't burden my conscience with difficulties. You said just now that I was militant *au fond*. That's a good suggestion. Let it be understood that you suspect me of playing tricks with the electric power, and I will tell you frankly that I suspect you. Is that quite clear?"

"Quite—as a basis of argument. You can assume that I vamped the chief inspector and kept him interested in my bright conversation until my booby trap worked. I believe that idea occurred to him, and I don't wonder. Moreover, if he is looking around for a competent and ruthless avenger of women's wrongs, he is bound to consider you. If either of us is questioned about this conversation, we can plead that we are not bound to incriminate ourselves. The law does not require us to do so."

"Then let's get down to it," said Miss Coombe. "You were

busy yesterday evening in finding out unobtrusively where every one was at the time of the fuse—and earlier on, as well. You probably know as much about that as Macdonald does. There are two points worth considering which occurred after you had gone."

She then described the finding of the flex, and the articles she had put away in the "lost property box." "Those things—the bag, the cigarette-case of yours, and the gloves of Miss Delareign's are no longer in the box. I looked for them just before you came. I only hope the chief inspector took them away himself. While I can bear with equanimity the glance of suspicion *you* turn on me, I'm not wholly anxious for Macdonald to consider me seriously in that light, because it seems to me so very difficult to disprove one's complicity."

Valerie nodded. "Yes. I see that. From what you say, it looks as though somebody arranged an electrocution outfit in the telephone-room and removed it hastily afterwards. I suppose the oddments like the flex would be so difficult to trace—their ownership, I mean—that it didn't matter about their being found."

"Put it like this," said Miss Coombe. "The murderer expected Gardien's death to pass as heart failure. The flex had to be removed from the telephone-room, obviously. After that the idea would have been to rescue it from the box later and drop it down a drain or something. Somehow Macdonald spotted the trick. Once it was spotted, as you say, the flex became unimportant."

"Gardien *must* have been killed in the telephone-room," mused Valerie. "No one could have hauled his corpse around in this house, so whatever was done had to be arranged in the telephone-room. It may have been something that only took a couple of minutes to organise, but some one had to go in there and do it between the time they entered the house and the time of the fuse."

"Unless some one living in the house arranged it beforehand," said Miss Coombe—"myself, Graham, or Manton."

"I think that any one living in the house would have made some better arrangement for disposing of the flex than putting it in that box," argued Valerie. "That strikes me as a hasty improvisation. With plenty of time to think it out beforehand and the whole resources of the house at one's disposal, one could have done better than that."

"Perhaps one could," said Miss Coombe with a smile. "However, it's obvious that an outsider *could* have done it— the electricity business, I mean—if he'd had a look at the room first. I don't pretend to understand how it was done..."

"I haven't seen the room, so I can't enlighten you," said Valerie. "But, given a flex and a power plug, something could be arranged with very little difficulty in a minimum of time; I expect I could organise something with your fire curb and the poker, which make a complete circuit. Of course, a transformer would help—you could get a real high voltage and make a certainty of it. I wonder if the grey-haired gentleman carried a box under his arm?"

"Not that I've heard of. You seem to know a lot about this sort of thing."

"One did physics at school," murmured Valerie reflectively. "You've been very patient with me, Miss Coombe, and I'm honestly grateful to you. I wish that I could tell you exactly what's in my mind, but—"

"*But* you think it wiser to keep your own counsel, and I think I rather agree with you," said Susan. "Incidentally, I have been trying to remember where I have seen you before. You were up at St. Elizabeth's, weren't you?"

"Yes, but I don't remember having seen you there. The only time I ever saw you was when I was in the sixth form at school. You came down on Speech Day and made a really good speech—the only good one I ever heard on any of those occasions."

"Oh, that was it! Of course! You were at Wraden School, near Reading, weren't you? I remember now."

"Clever of you! Now, in addition to your other kindnesses, will you do one more thing for me—let me use the phone in your telephone-room?"

Miss Coombe stared. "Use it, by all means; but there is a C.I.D. man on duty there."

"That doesn't matter at all. It's quite a trivial message, but I want to send it now."

"Very well. I have no objection if you haven't," replied Susan, and immediately led Valerie across the hall. At the door of the telephone-room she said:

"I will say good-bye for the moment. Let me hear from you again soon."

"I will. Good-bye, and thanks so much. I'm expecting to go abroad quite shortly—to Germany—but I'll let you know."

Detective Parton, C.I.D., who was still on duty by the phone, watched the fair-haired girl with a very lively interest. Macdonald, who liked his men to be well informed over the cases on which they were employed, had given Parton a list and description of the guests at the previous evening's party, and Valerie Woodstock, with her fair bun of hair and little golden fringe, was easily identifiable.

When she had dialled her number and was waiting for an answer, she sat with her back to the window observing the little room, and it seemed to Parton that it was the bureau and the electric point which seemed to hold her attention.

"1596? Can I speak to Miss Leyland, please?... Is that you, Anne? Valerie speaking. Can you give me a shampoo and set at 11.15? I know, love, but then I must have it done this morning. I've got a lunch at one-thirty. Oh, can you? Thanks ever so. Oh, by the way, what's the address of that palmist woman you told me about? Hold on just a moment. I want to write it down."

There was a note-pad and pencil on the table, but Valerie Woodstock got up calmly and went to the bureau, opened it, and drew out a sheet of note-paper. She then returned to her place and took down an address—number ten, somewhere. Parton got no opportunity of learning more. After that she hung up the receiver, smiled charmingly at the young man, and hurried out.

Parton jumped at the chance of a little activity. From the exchange he got the number and address of the subscriber who had been connected—a hairdresser's in Wilmot Street, just off Wigmore Street. Then he reported to the Yard. Miss Valerie Woodstock had told Miss Coombe that she was shortly going to Germany. She had then rung up and made an appointment with Anne Leyland, a hairdresser, and had inspected the bureau in the telephone-room, opening it and getting out a sheet of paper. She had left Caroline House driving in a Morris eight, XXX5656. The inspector at the Yard grunted.

"We might as well see if she *does* keep the appointment with her hairdresser," he observed.

Thus it came about that when Valerie Woodstock entered Anne Leyland's very up-to-date beauty parlour, her entry was duly observed, the telephone and the C.I.D. together working with a celerity which Miss Woodstock would have approved of as "very snappy." She had parked her car nearby in Manchester Square, and she seemed rather jolly and pleased with herself.

Anne Leyland had been at Wraden Manor School with Valerie, but instead of a university training, she had insisted on being apprenticed to a beauty specialist. Now, in her own premises, she was doing very well on the patronage of her former school friends.

When Valerie went into Anne Leyland's private and particular cubicle she said:

"Sorry to exploit you, darling. That phone call was eyewash. I don't want a shampoo; I want to put off a particularly limpet-like male. Be a saint, and let me out by the Mews at the back, and if anybody inquires during the next hour and a half, tell them I'm being 'set.' I'll come back before then—and pay up like a lady. It's really rather important."

"Really, Val, I'd never have believed it of you," replied Anne Leyland. "You were always such a hopeless highbrow that even little Audrey couldn't get one on you. Have you been raided, or dunned, or what?"

"All three, including what," replied Valerie, surveying herself in a mirror very carefully. "Is my face all right? Give me a spot of that cream rouge of yours and some flesh tint—and I want to phone. Private like. Bad for you to know who I'm vamping."

"Oh, that's all right, then. You've gone all human. Who'd have believed it?" replied Anne Leyland cheerfully. "But you do have your own way of running your affairs. Is the cast-off in the street?"

"I expect so. Play up, Anne, and be a sport. I'm *here*, see, for the next hour and a half. You just run in and out with shampoos and towels and combs. Don't give the show away."

Valerie put through her telephone call, "private like"; but she had had the temerity to rouse the interest of the C.I.D., and she did not realise how thorough those patient men could be. Her call was private, inasmuch as no one overheard it, but the numbers put through from Anne Leyland's were reported to Scotland Yard, and when it became known that a connection had been made with Mardon-Elliott's office, the interest of the C.I.D. was not diminished.

When Valerie rang through to Elliott's office, her call was answered by Inspector Jenkins, for Macdonald had left by that time.

"I want to speak to Mr. Mardon-Elliott, please," she said firmly.

"Who is it speaking?"

"Jane Seymour."

"Mr. Elliott is not here just now."

"When will he be free, please? I want to see him as soon as possible. It's very important."

Jenkins, at the other end of the line, scratched his chin. He wanted to learn all that he could about Mr. Mardon-Elliott.

"A personal matter, madam, or business?"

"Personal," was the firm reply.

"Very good. If you could come here immediately?"

"Certainly. I'll get to you about twelve o'clock."

By the time that Miss Woodstock arrived at Elliott's office (via the mews at the back of Anne Leyland's salon, and thence into Wigmore Street) Jenkins had heard all about the visit to the hairdresser's. He went in to Lethem (nervously busy in "dispatch") and told him that a Miss Jane Seymour was calling on Elliott, and that he, Lethem, could interview her in his own office and find out what she wanted without giving any information concerning recent events. Lethem agreed without further comment, but there was a wariness in his eyes which made Jenkins thoughtful.

"Do you know who she is?" he inquired.

"Never heard of her," said Lethem, "at least, not since I was at school."

When Valerie arrived at the office and entered "Inquiries," she found Lethem there and said that she had an appointment with Mardon-Elliott.

"Yes. I'm afraid he's late," said Lethem. (The accuracy of this statement caused Jenkins, who was listening in from Elliott's own office, to grin.) "He may not be here this morning. Is there anything I can do?" He had seen the tell-tale parcel under her arm—manuscript, undoubtedly. "I am Mr. Elliott's secretary," he added.

"Well—we might explore avenues," said Valerie sweetly. "I was advised to come here by Simon Grand."

Lethem bowed politely. Simon Grand was a name to conjure with.

"Please come in, Miss Seymour," he said, leading the way into his own office.

The beginning of the interview was of no interest to Jenkins. It concerned a novel (historical) written by Miss Seymour, but presently things began to look up.

"Seymour is a pseudonym, I take it," said Lethem. "Do you write under another name?" He had unpacked the MS. and glanced through the first page. "This doesn't strike me as a beginner's work," he added.

Again Valerie smiled. "Very acute of you. But does it matter? It's quite usual to write under two names, isn't it? Some one told me that Andrew Gardien does."

"Does he? It's the first time I've heard of it," said Lethem. "I doubt if your informant is accurate. With a name which commands the sort of contracts that Gardien does, it seems silly to think he'd bother about a pseudonym. Who told you that, might I inquire?"

"I was told in confidence," she replied; and the sweetness of her voice might have made Lethem optimistic on any other day. "Your job must be awfully interesting," she went on. "Everybody wonders who Mr. Gardien really is, and I suppose you really know him."

"I see him here fairly frequently," said Lethem, and she bent forward across the table.

"Do tell me, who is he really? Do you know where he came from? Some one told me that he'd been a don before he wrote thrillers, and that he lives on Boar's Hill, and all the Oxford people know him under another name, without guessing about the Gardien business."

Lethem smiled. "It's not an agent's business to tell secrets out of school," he parried. "If any one asks me who Miss Jane Seymour really is, of course, I shan't know."

She looked at him sadly. "I hate lemons."

He laughed and looked again at the MS. sheets.

"Why do you want to know? Have you been reading rumours in the press?"

"Oh, no—but I'm just inquisitive. It annoys me when people tell you things with an air of authority and you can't decide if they're making it up or not. Mr. Gardien lived in Australia until four or five years ago, didn't he?"

"Did he? You seem to know more about him than I do. About your own MS. Shall I hand it on to a reader, or would you prefer—?"

"I think I'll leave it with you, and call again to see Mr. Elliott, if I may," she put in, before he had finished his sentence. "You think that there's no chance of my seeing him to-day?"

"I'm afraid not."

"All right. I'll ring up again to-morrow."

"Thanks. That would be best. I hope Mr. Grand is well."

"Quite well, thanks." She smiled at him again. "And thank you very much for all the trouble you have taken."

Jenkins had done some quick thinking towards the close of this interview. He decided that this was Macdonald's affair. The chief inspector would manage Miss "Seymour" in his own way. Jenkins let Lethem show her out. The only inquiry he made was:

"Who is this Simon Grand she mentioned?"

"Search me," retorted Lethem. "I don't know. Never seen him. There's his last thriller on the table if you'd like to see it."

"Thriller? Gardien again?"

"I tell you I don't know," said Lethem, his face puckered up irritably. "And, what's more, I don't know any one who does."

"Lots of things you don't know," said Jenkins genially as he stretched for the telephone.

X

MRS. LOUISE ETHERTON, THE GIFTED AUTHOR OF *PATIENCE on a Monument* (first impression sold out on day of publication), had recently taken one of the new service flats in Belinda Place, Hampstead. The block was advertised as "designed by women, run by women, for women only." In accommodation and service, Belinda Place was the last thing in comfort and modernity for those professional women whose purses were sufficiently elastic to meet the charges of the establishment. Sound-proof floors and walls, double windows with a system of scientific ventilation, heating adjustable to all tastes, and the most luxurious of modern furnishing and plumbing ensured peace and comfort for all, while the restaurant and service department claimed an excellence and expertise which no man's club could outdo. "Belinda" specialised in all directions, including the choice of its tenants or members, for election was necessary before the committee granted a lease in that exclusive establishment. Miss Rachel Dainton, whose energy and initiative had brought "Belinda" into being, had often said:

"I'm sick to death of all the everlasting aspersions on the 'bun and cocoa' woman. It's been said again and again that we have no idea how to live comfortably. We've no palates, no sense of food, no notions of real comfort and so *ad infinitum*. Well, we're tired of all that. We're going to make a start with an establishment that will show what real comfort means."

Mrs. Etherton, who, since she had been left with no means of support save her own abilities, had met plenty of the "bun and cocoa" school. She had "pigged it" (to use her own expression) in lodgings, wilted in women's hostels, wearied of boarding schools, boarding houses, and women's clubs of the "bed and breakfast from thirty shillings weekly inclusive of bath" variety. In short, Mrs. Etherton realised to the full the unique value of "Belinda's"—"when your royalties ran to it." She was old enough to disregard scoffs at "pusseries" and "henneries," experienced enough to know that a man in the house does not always spell complete bliss for the wife who darns his socks, and in the autumn of a strenuous life she regarded "peace, comfort, and cuisine guaranteed by women for women" as the desirable factors in life.

On the morning after Graham Coombe's treasure hunt, having breakfasted in bed and finished *The Times* cross-word with her cigarette, Mrs. Etherton was about to settle down to the great scene of *Penelope in Paradise* when Miss Coombe's telephone call came through. Having replaced the receiver, Mrs. Etherton looked down at the manuscript of *Penelope* and sighed. It was really very difficult to concentrate on tickling the palates of her public while this Gardien business was at the back of her mind. "What a nuisance men are," she complained to herself and put her writing materials away. "I expect I'd better leave it alone, but I should like to make sure. I don't suppose she'll bless me, but I'll risk it. What a small world it is!"

The decision which Mrs. Etherton had just made concerned one of her fellow-guests at the Coombes' party. Priding herself on her independence of mind, Mrs. Etherton had so far kept aloof from her fellow-residents at Belinda Place. Without being prejudiced against her own sex (her choice of a dwelling was assurance of that), she had yet had too much experience of women's society to wish to form friendships which might develop into the tiresome familiarities of communal life, and she had avoided even passing the time of day with the residents whom she saw in the restaurant and in the lifts and entrance lobby of her new home. Nevertheless, when she had recognised Miss Rees last night as a resident at "Belinda," Mrs. Etherton had been interested. There was something familiar about the other writer's square face and intelligent grey eyes which had made Mrs. Etherton say to herself:

"Now, where have I met you before?"

Without being inquisitive or pushing, Mrs. Etherton had determined to call on Miss Rees and have a talk with her. Taking up the service telephone, she got through to the office and inquired for the number of Miss Rees's flat. "7B, top floor," was the prompt and businesslike answer of a secretary who prided herself on not wasting words.

Putting on her hat and coat, Mrs. Etherton went up in the lift and rang at the door of 7B, which was opened to her by one of the maids on the service staff of Belinda.

"Would you ask Miss Rees if she could see me for a

moment, Lily?" said Mrs. Etherton, who was on excellent terms with the service employees.

"Miss Rees has just gone out to the post, ma'am. She won't be more than a few minutes. Would you care to come in and wait for her?"

"Yes, I think I will," replied Mrs. Etherton. "It seems silly to go downstairs again if you think Miss Rees will be back in a minute or two. How is your indigestion, Lily?"

"Much better, thank you, ma'am. Those pills you gave me did me a lot of good."

"I'm so glad," said Mrs. Etherton, as she was shown into the sitting-room. She reflected that it was an excellent thing to be on good terms with the servants. The housemaid, Lily, would have been considerably surprised, however, if she could have seen the behaviour of the much-respected Mrs. Etherton when she was left alone in another woman's sitting-room. After a glance round which indicated nothing more than general curiosity, Mrs. Etherton crossed over to the bureau, let down the flap, and looked quickly through the papers she found in it. She then went to the typewriter—a portable which stood on a table by the window—and inspected the sheets of typescript which lay beside it. Next she drew out one or two books from the bookcase and considered the names on the fly-leaves. After that she opened the door of the room and called to the maid. There was no answer. Lily had finished her work and gone on to the next tenant on her list.

Leaving the sitting-room door open, Mrs. Etherton next opened the door of the bedroom, which had communicating doors with both sitting-room and entrance lounge, in the manner of all the "Belinda" flats, and looked round quickly.

She opened one or two drawers, without touching anything, until she came on one which contained a black evening bag. Her hand was just closing on this when she heard the lift doors open on the landing outside, and she then hastily shut the drawer and retreated to the sitting-room, closing the bedroom door after her.

When Miss Rees came into the sitting-room she gave a start of surprise when she saw Mrs. Etherton sitting by the window.

"I do hope you'll excuse this intrusion," said Mrs. Etherton pleasantly. "I came up to see you just a moment ago, and the maid, Lily, who knows me very well, suggested that I should wait, as she knew you were just coming in again." Seeing the astonishment on the other woman's face, she added, "I am Mrs. Etherton. We met last night at Graham Coombe's."

"Oh, of course! How stupid of me not to recognise you; but a hat makes such a difference," said Miss Rees. "Do sit down."

"Thanks so much. I came to return a handkerchief of yours which I foolishly picked up and brought away with me yesterday evening. It's rather a beautiful one, and I thought you would like to have it back. Although I have seen you in this building once or twice, I hadn't realised that we were fellow-writers until last evening. Belinda is such a comfort."

"Yes. Thank you so much. It's very kind of you," said Miss Rees, as she took the lace handkerchief proffered. "These flats are lovely, but I don't live here. I couldn't afford it. Miss Duncan has lent me her flat for a week or two."

"Belinda is admirably run," said Mrs. Etherton in her deep sensible voice. "Easily the best thing in the way of solving the domestic problem that I have met. I was sorry that I missed you last night. I was going to ask you if I could give you a lift back."

"Very kind of you. I am afraid that I left as soon as I possibly could," said Miss Rees. "It was all so upsetting. A dreadful thing for the Coombes. I was so very sorry for them."

"Yes. Indeed. Most upsetting," said Mrs. Etherton. "Upsetting for everybody."

She had been studying the face of her companion thoughtfully, and she added abruptly, "You don't remember me—before last night?" And the other stared back.

"I'm so sorry. Have we met before? I'm so bad over faces."

"It was a long time ago, just after the war. You were only a young thing then, and I had black hair, not white. We were only together for a term. It was in 1920. That place near Reading. I did a temporary job when some one had broken down."

"Good gracious!" Miss Rees gazed wide-eyed at her visitor. "Mrs. Etherton—of course. But how wonderful of you to have remembered me after all that time!"

"You were very kind to me," said the older woman, and then broke out into her deep, pleasant laugh.

"My dear, this is really very comic! The young people of to-day call detective stories 'escape literature'! All stories are a means of escape—from the trivial round and common task. The little typists and tired suburban mothers who write to me about my unspeakable books are kind enough to say that they take them out of themselves. They've taken me out of a lot of tiresomeness and keep me in 'Belinda.' I'm grateful to them."

Miss Rees looked rather shocked. "But why unspeakable? I know you have a tremendous circulation. I've read your reviews."

"But not my books, I hope," chuckled the older woman. "I've no illusions about them. When I first began writing I was very high-minded and very poor. After a few disappointments I resolved to put my aspirations behind me. I read all the most popular rubbish I could get hold of. I analysed it and got the essentials. Then I began to write a book to the recipe I'd synthesised. Emotions and wish-fulfilments earn me my living, and it's not nearly so toilsome as teaching the young, and much more profitable. There you have my motive. I'm old enough to like peace and quietness. No more aspirations and agitations for me."

Miss Rees smiled. "You're very frank, but I agree with you in your conclusion about liking peace and quietness. I'm beginning to remember you now. You'd been through a bad time, hadn't you?—losing your husband and having to start work anew."

"Yes, I'd been through a bad time all right. I did lose my husband—not in the normal sense, though; he just walked out and left me. It was all very embittering at the time, but I lived through it. One can live through anything if one's tough enough." Mrs. Etherton's deep voice was quite calm and reflective, and she smiled at the expression on the other woman's face. "You're wondering why on earth I'm here, calling on specious pretences to make abrupt confidences so early in the morning. The sight of your face—although you've changed a lot—reminds me of those old troubled times. I'm not usually so intrusive. I'll own up to my real reasons for coming to see you. I wanted to make certain that I had been right in placing you, and to find out if you had recognised me. The circumstances of last night seemed to make it desirable to get that clear."

"I'm very pleased to see you again," said Miss Rees, "but I don't quite follow your last argument. Forgive me if I'm stupid, but I was always a slow thinker."

"Were you? It's not reflected in your books, then," replied Mrs. Etherton. "I mean this: The fact that that Scotland Yard man was on the warpath so promptly and politely last night indicated that he thought there was something fishy about Andrew Gardien's death. You, as a detective writer, probably know much more about police procedure than I do, but if the C.I.D. think they've spotted a murder, they'll get busy investigating the lives of all those who were in the house last night. It's a tiresome thought. Personally, I consider I've the right to my own reticences, but I like to know where I am. If you *had* recognised me, I thought it probable that you might tell the chief inspector so. Quite frankly, I'd rather you didn't. Nothing like putting things plainly. I'm prepared to trust you completely, you see."

Miss Rees turned very pink, and her forehead wrinkled up, showing a deep crease between her eyes. She sat with her chin in her hands, and it was some time before she answered.

"This is all very bewildering," she said slowly. "I think it's better to leave your statement exactly as it stands, and not to ask for explanations. You want me to avoid telling the police that we've met before. I'm quite willing to agree to that."

"Good!" said Mrs. Etherton heartily. "That's all I wanted. One thing about talking to a woman whom you've known when life was difficult is that you can trust her not to let you down. Rather oblique, but in spite of your assertions about slow thinking, I'm certain you're very quick in the uptake. I'm so glad I came and had a talk with you. Miss Coombe rang me up a short while ago and asked me to go and call on her this afternoon. She has got some idea of having a conference between the women who were at her party last night. Of course, she's a great feminist—a believer in the superiority of women's brains to men's."

"Is she?" said Miss Rees. "I think arguments on that score are so futile, but I liked Miss Coombe herself very much. She rang me up also, and I agreed to go, though really I would much rather have refused. I'm no good at discussing things; I always see the other person's point of view and either capitulate or lose the thread of my own argument. I like working out a line of thought, when I have the leisure to develop my own point of view. Besides, I think it's rather feeble, as well as distressing, to go over the same ground again. Surely we all discussed it enough last night?"

"Possibly Susan Coombe has come upon further evidence and wants to check it up with those who were present," said Mrs. Etherton. "I'm quite prepared to be intelligently interested in hearing what's said, though I haven't anything to add on my own account. I was upstairs when the lights went out, so I can't be helpful. It was you and Miss Delareign who produced the only evidence of any importance. If Gardien were murdered, it stands to reason that it was the unauthorised stranger who did it. Men don't sneak uninvited into any one's house unless they're out to do something they've no business to do."

Miss Rees sighed. "I hate the whole subject, Mrs.

Etherton. I wish most sincerely that I'd never seen the grey-haired man. It's only going to cause me a lot of trouble if this mystery does develop into a murder case. If Miss Delareign held her tongue about it, I should have felt disposed to do likewise."

"That would have been a great mistake," said Mrs. Etherton firmly. "I didn't care for the Delareign woman myself; she is much too effusive, and her books are too atmospheric for words—all tears and dither—but I'm very glad she produced that piece of evidence, and that you could reinforce it. I know I'm being an awful nuisance to you, bothering you over all this, but I do wish you'd describe that man to me again. I have very good reasons for asking you."

Seeing the distressed look on her companion's face, Mrs. Etherton added, "Really, if any one overheard this conversation they would be justified in believing that I was the culprit. I wasn't. To the best of my belief I never saw Mr. Gardien before last night."

"Such a thought never entered my head, Mrs. Etherton," interposed Miss Rees decidedly. "My own opinion is that Mr. Gardien died of heart failure after some sort of shock. If the man I saw was a burglar, it seems not unlikely that he engineered the fuse in order to be able to carry out his plans in the confusion caused by the darkness and something happened during that time which gave Mr. Gardien a fright—something colliding with him perhaps, or even knocking him down."

"Quite reasonable," agreed Mrs. Etherton. "You remember that that was what Miss Delareign said happened to her. She collided with some one in the dark."

There was a second's tense silence, and then Mrs. Etherton went on.

"It's better to be quite practical over this. The Scotland Yard man—Isaak Walton was really a brilliant nom de guerre for him—didn't make all those inquiries without good reason. He suspected something, and finally he suspected everybody. Miss Delareign was very near the centre of activities, so to speak. She was very agitated and admitted to colliding with somebody in the dark. Young Strafford was downstairs too, and also appeared to have been in the wars. Miss Coombe was in the basement—alone. I was upstairs, alone. You were resting on that little Empire couch on the second floor landing—at least you were when I went upstairs a couple of minutes before the fuse."

"I didn't see you," murmured Miss Rees.

"No. I know you didn't. Your eyes were shut," said Mrs. Etherton. "I've no one to corroborate my whereabouts! There's only my word for it that I was upstairs. Mr. Coombe was in the library, also alone, as was Mr. Vale in the dining-room. Really, the Scotland Yard man must have thought us a most fruitful field of suspicion. After all, we don't know how Mr. Gardien was killed."

"No. I was only saying so to myself just now," agreed Miss Rees. "He may have been shot with one of those silencers on the pistol."

"Silencers don't exist except in fiction," said Mrs Etherton unexpectedly, and Miss Rees stared. "I'm so tired of that silly business," went on Mrs. Etherton. "After I'd read that thriller of Stokers, which depended on a silencer, I went to every gunsmiths I could find and asked for a silencer. They only laughed at me."

"Good gracious!" exclaimed Miss Rees. "I'd always just taken it for granted that a silencer could be used."

"Conceivably it might, if you could get hold of such a thing," replied Mrs. Etherton, "but the point is that the only weapon which can be effectually silenced is an air-gun. I quote the gun-makers, and they ought to know their business. However, that's rather beside the point here. We don't know how Gardien was killed, but I think that we can take it that he was not shot. The point which really interests me is your evidence about the strange man who entered the telephone-room. I said just now that several of us, including Mr. and Miss Coombe, Mr. Strafford and Mr. Vale, Miss Delareign and myself, will all come under suspicion because we were alone at the time of the fuse—the time the C.I.D. man obviously considered the crucial point. It's not a comforting thought, but the fact of your having seen a strange man in the house makes just all the difference. The probability of foul play so evidently focuses itself on the interloper."

"I see what you mean," said Miss Rees, "and I quite agree with you. I have been so thankful that I was not the only person who saw that man. Miss Delareign noticed him first, so it can't be suggested that I was imagining things."

"Exactly. Now have you considered this point carefully? Is there any possibility that the man you saw was a member of the party in disguise? Neither of the men present was grey-headed, but a wig is very easily obtainable. I must admit that such a point occurred to me."

"It occurred to me, too," admitted Miss Rees, "and I've thought it over very carefully. I'm quite certain that the man I saw was *not* a member of the party. Mr. Vale and Mr. Bourne are both men of unmistakable physique, the one so tall and thin, the other so powerfully built. Mr. Manton is very tall, and Mr. Coombe has a beard. The man I saw was of middle height, and though I did not see his face I could see his ears and the side of his cheek. He had no beard. I am certain he was not one of the party, and so was Miss Delareign."

"Could you recognise him if you saw him again?"

"It's very difficult to recognise a man's back. I saw that he was flat-footed and walked clumsily, and that he had very close-cropped grey hair and a rather high colour."

"Good gracious!" exclaimed Mrs. Etherton. "Have you ever met Mardon-Elliott, the literary agent?"

"No. Never. I hardly ever meet anybody."

"Elliott was Gardien's agent. Mr. Coombe told me so. John Brand pointed him out to me one day—Elliott, I mean—and suggested I should go to him. I don't believe in agents myself. It would be a most remarkable thing if it turned out that Elliott was at the Coombes's house last night."

"Really, the whole thing becomes more and more confusing and distressing," said Miss Rees, but Mrs. Etherton went on:

"On occasions like this, one can't afford to get confused, and it's a waste of energy to get distressed. I think you ought to find out about Elliott, Miss Rees. It sounds astonishingly like him, and there's a sort of probability about it, you know, with Elliott knowing both Coombe and Gardien. Why not go and call on Elliott—make the excuse of asking him if he deals with Russian rights or something like that—and satisfy yourself on the matter?"

Miss Rees looked very thoughtful. "I don't mind going

to call on Mr. Elliott to see if your suspicions are anywhere near the mark," she said slowly. "I think I should recognise the shape of that man's head again. If I have given a description which seems to reflect on some person connected with Gardien, the sooner I prove or disprove the suspicion the better. After that, however, I shall consider that I have no further obligations in the matter." She sighed and then gave a diffident little laugh. "It's almost pathetic—I've always enjoyed what I call my nice quiet little murders so much—the ones I write about, you know—and yet the thought of appearing as a witness in a real criminal case fills me with horror."

"Yes, I think I can understand that," replied Mrs. Etherton. "It's a publicity of a sort that one doesn't care about. As I told you, I have not the least wish to have my affairs dissected in the witness-box. When my publishers have asked me for 'publicity' matter—my life story, and all that nonsense—I have consistently refused to oblige them. If ever it gets to the point of their insisting on a photograph I shall send them some one else's."

"Do you really think we shall all have to give evidence?" inquired Miss Rees, and Mrs. Etherton replied:

"I should think it is highly probable. You know, it seems a thousand pities to me that you did not happen to open your eyes when I passed you on the stairs a moment or so before the fuse happened."

Miss Rees went very pink. "I don't quite follow you. I am sorry—"

"It's so simple," said Mrs. Etherton briskly. "I was upstairs, but I have no means of proving it. You were noticed—fortunately—as you came downstairs. I was not. If you had seen me as I passed you on the couch—"

"But I didn't," said Miss Rees, getting pinker still.

"No. It seems a pity," said Mrs. Etherton. "Do think it over. You may remember something—a movement, or a slight draught as I passed you. I find that I can often piece small impressions together after an event. I was saying so to Ashton Vale last night. He was the only member of the party whom I had met before. I did think of ringing him up to talk things over, and then I decided against it. If he *did* have anything to do with it, he won't want to talk about it. If he *didn't*, he doesn't know any more than you or I."

"Mr. Vale? but why—?"

Mrs. Etherton broke in on the other's shocked surprise.

"Why not Vale as well as any one else? He's clever, *very* clever, and economists aren't sensitive. If you come to think of it, Coombe collected a most interesting set of men from the point of view of the inspector who's investigating the business. Ashton Vale is cool, cynical, and competent—clever with a capital C. Digby Bourne has seen so many strange things among his travels amid primitive people that a murder more or less would leave him quite calm. His principal reaction to Gardien's death was disappointment that the Treasure Hunt was cut short. Young Strafford is of the hot-tempered, romantic variety, and his books display such virtuosity in strange ways of killing people that he'd have had no trouble in improvising sudden death for any one, on any occasion, anywhere. In fact it's a very pretty problem. Now I hope that I shall see you at Miss Coombe's."

"Yes," said Miss Rees, "I said I'd go, and I'll stick to it. You don't want me to mention our talk?"

"I'd be very glad if you didn't. It's neither here nor there—but do go and see Mardon-Elliott. You'll have plenty of time before lunch."

When Mrs. Etherton had re-entered her own flat, she stood by the window for some time in deep contemplation. "I don't know if I was a fool to go or not," she said to herself. "It's all very difficult—but I think she'll go and see Elliott."

Miss Rees also stood by her window and gazed out unseeingly at the rolling Heath.

"What exactly did she mean?" she murmured to herself. "Have I got to go and see this man Elliott—and why did she tell me about her husband? Really, it's all too confusing for words."

She looked at the table where lay her neat pile of manuscript, *The Clue of the Silencer*, and sighed again.

"Human contacts aren't your strong point, my dear," she said to herself.

"It's easy enough to attribute motives on paper, but when it comes to assessing real people, I'm all at sea. What *did* the woman mean me to think? and why did she want me to say I saw her when I was on the landing?"

XI

THE INQUESTS ON ANDREW GARDIEN AND MARDON-
Elliott were presided over by a coroner "who knew his job,"
as the C.I.D. would have put it; in other words a coroner who
knew that when the police wanted an adjournment following promptly on the necessary formality of identification,
they were not to be embarrassed by untimely questions and
answers in a coroner's court. The only witnesses to be called
for the Gardien inquest were Mr. Barton-Hobbs, and Dean,
the manservant from Regency Court, who identified Andrew
Gardien as a tenant of that address, followed by Graham
Coombe and Chief Inspector Macdonald, who gave evidence
as to finding the body, and Dr. Wright, who attested to the
time of death, and the probability of its cause as heart failure,
conceivably following electric shock due to some contretemps with the fitting of the electric fire. The doctor whom
Gardien had previously consulted as to the state of his heart
was abroad and could not be communicated with in time to
give evidence. The coroner promptly seized on this fact as a

reason for adjourning the inquiry until full evidence could be produced concerning the state of deceased's heart prior to his death. There were a number of journalists in court who had to make the best of this meagre story, among whom was Peter Vernon, who paid more attention to those present than to the quick question and answer of the proceedings. Ashton Vale and Denzil Strafford were both in the court, the former looking interested but quite unmoved, as he studied the different speakers with a thoughtful eye. Strafford had a wary look. He glanced round the court once or twice as though he expected some one else to appear, and the rapidity of the proceedings left him apparently nonplussed.

News travels swiftly in London, especially among the journalist confraternity, and the news of Gardien's death, followed by that of Elliott, had made a number of journalists jump at the thought of a scoop. Vernon had the advantage of his fellows inasmuch as he had some inside information. Macdonald, knowing Vernon's ability to get information of a sort which the police find hard to come by, had let the journalist know of the two inquests and at the same time indicated than any news-gossip, rumour, or suggestion, concerning Elliott and his associates, would be gratefully received. Vernon, with a certain amount of information concerning Graham Coombe's party, looked around the court during the brief Gardien inquest, and felt his journalistic ears pricking with interest. He wanted to know more about the party, and yet knew that to approach Macdonald when the latter was hard on the trail would be completely useless. He looked at Strafford with a speculative eye and concluded that if it were a choice between him and Ashton Vale, the younger man would be the more hopeful proposition from the point of view of news value. At the conclusion of the proceedings, the journalist left the court side by side with Strafford and addressed him cheerfully.

"Funny business. More in it than meets the eye. Heard the rest of the story?"

Strafford looked at him with suspicion, and yet a lively curiosity, and Vernon went on, "You don't remember me. My name's Vernon. I met you at the Scribbler's Club last autumn. I expect you're interested in this, as you're on Coombe's list too."

"Naturally. What do you mean by the rest of the story?"

"Ever heard of Mardon-Elliott, the agent? He dealt with Gardien's stuff."

"What about him?"

"Well, he's due for an inquest on himself in about an hour's time—not here, at the Strand Court. Funny business when you come to think of it."

"When did Elliott die then?"

Vernon looked round cautiously. He had limed his man, but did not want his fellow journalists to join in the conversation.

"Inquests always make me thirsty," he said. "What about you?"

"It doesn't need an inquest in my case," said Strafford, "although a thirst in the afternoon's a poor business. I don't like coffee and I loathe tea. Are you going on to the other show?"

Vernon nodded. "You bet. If they don't hang together, I'm a Dutchman."

"Then come to my digs for a quick one. It'll be on your way—just off John Street."

"Thanks. Nothing'd please me better."

The two men strode off together as by common consent, knowing that they could cross the west-side streets more quickly on foot than the slow procession of buses or taxis in the crowded roads.

"Fact is, I feel I've missed the bus badly," went on Vernon. "I had a card for Coombe's party and couldn't go because I had to cover a damn dull labour party meeting at Liverpool. Came back by the mail train and found I'd been put on the wrong horse."

Strafford gave him a quick glance. "And you're hoping to lay off your bet after the race has started?"

"Why not?" queried Vernon. "Nothing for nothing's a good motto. You were at Coombe's party, and the old ears are just about flapping for the why and wherefore of a heart attack, aren't they? If Elliott had a heart attack too, you might like to hear about it, and I've given you a tip before starting prices."

Strafford laughed. "Right oh. Nothing like knowing how we stand. Did you know Gardien?"

"No. No one seemed to know him. That's what's so intriguing. No one knows much about Elliott, either. I've had a busy morning. Ran his typist to earth in Cricklewood and took her out to lunch. Got a few names to get busy with. Elliott ran Jake Duncan's stuff, and Simon Grand—the chap who got away with *Channel Crossing*. It sold like blazes and they're filming it now. Ten per cent on those doings is a nice little spot for any agent to get on with."

Their conversation broke off as they crossed Trafalgar Square and forced their way through the perpetual crowd outside Charing Cross. Vernon caught sight of a familiar lean face a few yards away and risked a grin—he was behind Strafford—Macdonald looked preoccupied, but Vernon had hopes of talking to him later if he had to go and sit beside his bed in the small hours. A few minutes later Strafford stopped, and let himself and Vernon into a house close to John Street, saying:

"Hope you're in good training. Eighty-seven stairs. No lift."

They made short work of the stairs and entered a small bed-sitting room, obviously "let furnished," in which Strafford's books were piled on every available surface.

"I've got about twenty minutes," said Vernon as Strafford got busy with glasses. "Thanks. Salut! Lord, I wanted that! Well, my typist lass was out to spill the beans to the quickest bidder. She told me that Elliott had an appointment with Gardien at 8 o'clock last night. Every one left the block where Elliott's office is by 7.30. Elliott was found shot in his room there this morning. That's my little lot."

"Good Lord!"

Strafford's interest was the more apparent because, having mixed his own drink, he forgot to swallow it.

"You think Gardien shot Elliott?"

"No. If Gardien had been going to shoot anybody, he wouldn't have been such a mutt as to make an appointment to draw attention to himself. Looks more like a frame-up to remove them both. What happened last night at Coombe's?"

"Want it for your paper?"

"No. Not just like that. I'll undertake not to publish anything you tell me without permission. Honest to God."

Strafford hesitated, and then caught sight of the drink which he had forgotten. As he raised it to his lips a telephone bell rang outside the door, and Strafford jumped at the sound and put down his glass again.

"Sorry. Won't be a moment."

He was across the room in a few long strides, and Vernon murmured to himself, "You were expecting that call. Some one ringing up to ask how the doings went? I wonder. This sort of game makes one as suspicious as sin."

He got up and began to prowl round the room, looking at the books which were piled up anyhow. In the waste-paper basket there was a heap of half torn up sheets—galley proofs, as Vernon knew at a glance. A title page caught his eye and he fished it out of the basket.

High as Haman, by Simon Grand.

"The blighter! So he's Simon Grand, is he? Must be. Wouldn't have proof sheets kicking about else. That means he knew Elliott, and he's been letting me babble on like the brook and never given a thing away. I'll just jolly well rattle him up a bit before I've done."

Shoving the title sheet from the waste-paper basket into his pocket, Vernon looked around for any further evidence concerning the surprising young man who lived in this untidy room. A letter stamped and ready for posting lay on the mantelshelf addressed to "Thomas Strafford, Esq., The Hall., Bishop's Wraden, Reading."

It was not until later when Macdonald pointed it out, that Peter Vernon saw anything apposite about that address. He was still standing by the mantelpiece, when Strafford re-entered the room, saying:

"Sorry. I rang off as soon as I could. Take a pew and have another drink. You were asking me about Coombe's party."

He gave a quick description of the party, mentioning the names of those present and the essential points about their positions at the time of the fuse; Coombe, in the library, himself and Miss Delareign in the lounge but not within sight of one another, Vale in the dining-room, Miss Coombe in the basement and the others upstairs. He also mentioned the stranger seen entering the telephone-room, quoting Miss Rees's brief description of him. The brevity and conciseness of the narrative struck Vernon as remarkably able; Strafford had a reporter's knack of putting essentials into a few words and avoiding irrelevancies.

"'Curiouser and curiouser,'" said Vernon in reply. "The description of the gate-crashing bloke just about fits Elliott, doesn't it?"

"Does it? I've never seen him," replied Strafford and Vernon promptly put him down as a liar, but didn't challenge the statement.

"Well, according to Elliott's typist—who ought to know—he was flat-footed and had a close-cropped grey head. What d'you make of that? Gardien pipped off by heart failure following electric shock, Elliott shot in his own office the same evening. Some story!"

Strafford frowned at the floor. "The whole thing's crazy," he said, and it seemed to Vernon that he was communing with his own thoughts.

"The thing to do is to discover the link between the two—Gardien and Elliott," went on the journalist. "Some one who knew Gardien was going to Coombe's party got Elliott to gate-crash there. Kept him in the house for long enough for him to be seen by two other members of the party and then told him to quit—presto. Organising mind then eliminated Gardien and later paid a call on Elliott to tell him the news, and plugged him in the head. Ergo, Elliott killed Gardien at Coombe's—I bet he didn't—and Gardien shot Elliott in his lair. I.d.t.! Query. Who was there at Coombe's who knew Elliott? I'd eliminate the women from this act. A woman would never have risked going to Thavies House late at night in evening dress, ringing the bell and all that, when the copper on the beat would have noticed her for a cert."

"Aren't you going a bit fast? Why do you assume that one of Coombe's guests killed them both?" asked Strafford.

"A. Gardien died in Coombe's house, and the coroner wouldn't have nipped the doings in the bud if there hadn't been something fishy, so obviously Gardien was killed by some one at Coombe's party. I don't believe Elliott did it, because he let himself be seen. Coombe knew him by sight, so did other people, perhaps. Too risky, altogether.

"B. Elliott was killed after making some appointment with Gardien, whereby I argue Gardien didn't kill him. When two men who've been associated are both killed, with indications that they killed one another, you can bet some one's being funny."

"Crime your speciality?" queried Strafford.

Vernon's ears, alert to catch every shade of meaning in the other's voice, sensed a change of tone; something ironical, and at the same time inimical, sounding in the question.

"Oh, so so. I flap the ears and roll the eyes over these enter-tainments. I wonder if the two ladies who saw a flat-footed merchant with grey hair were seeing visions, if you take me."

"I take you. I can't answer that one, but I can tell you neither of them went to Thavies House and shot Elliott after Coombe's party," said Strafford.

"Oh ho! How d'you know that?"

"I gave one of them a lift home—she lives in Barnes, and I had my car and offered to drive her home—Miss Delareign, if it interests you. She told me she dined at the Cumberland that evening, a place where she's well known, so she couldn't have shot Elliott before the party and described his ghost. Miss Delareign saw the gate-crasher first, and drew the other lady's attention to him. Miss Rees was driven back to Hampstead, right out on the Heath, by another member of Coombe's party. If she wanted to shoot Elliott, she wouldn't have gone back to Hampstead first."

"That night we went to Bannockburn by way of Brighton Pier," murmured Vernon. "Did Miss Rees dine at the Cumberland, complete with favourite waiter, too?"

"No. She dined at Belinda, in the restaurant, Belinda's..."

"The Pusseries. I know. Do themselves well, I'm told," said Vernon. "You were rather on the spot, young fella me lad."

"So so. Like you. Thought there was something odd somewhere," said Strafford. "Saw what I could, asked what I could, and imagined what I could."

His eyes were on the waste-paper basket as he spoke, and Vernon saw the involuntary move forward of a neatly shod foot, and the slight recoil as Strafford changed his mind and sat tight in his place.

"What about that inquest?" went on the latter. "Might as well hear what we can while we've got the chance."

"Why not?" replied Vernon, trying to assess the meaning

in the other's voice, and caught up his hat. "Better foot it. Buses in the Strand drive the cabby to drink. What about the coupla' yards of intellectual at Gardien's inquest? Another of Coombe's party, wasn't he?"

"Why do you assume that?"

"One of your push—tailoring, hair cut, and all that. Not one of us. Not a lounger. Not a novelist looking for copy. Obviously interested. Didn't roll in casually, so to speak."

Having run down the eighty-seven stairs, the two men turned up towards the Strand again, and Strafford replied:

"You're right as it happens. That was Ashton Vale. He's a clever devil. Notices things. He's a sort of mental conjurer, keeps half a dozen lines of thought in his head simultaneously and never muddles them up."

"Then the only man among the guests who didn't show up at the inquest was Bourne."

"What about it?"

"If I'd bumped Gardien off, I think I should have gone to the inquest, just to see which way the cat jumped."

"Let sleeping dogs lie is a better motto. I should have kept away."

The tone of the last sentence was casual, but Vernon was aware that Strafford had given him a quick sideways glance before he went on.

"I bet if Vale did it, no one will ever prove it. His wits are as good as that chief inspector's, if not better."

"Remains to be seen. If 'twas murder, the murderer's lost the first round already."

"How so?"

"Because the whole show's being investigated. Gardien's

death was meant to pass as heart failure pure and simple, and Macdonald didn't pass it. His reputation is that he doesn't pass much. Damn all, this must be an easy one for him. Some one at Coombe's party did the doings. That some one knew Elliott."

"You're simply jumping to conclusions over that. The evidence that Elliott was the chap going into the telephone-room's too thin for words."

"Just seen that?" said Vernon coolly. "You seemed to take it for gospel when I first suggested it."

"What the devil d'you mean?"

"Nix, or just what I said. Nothing subtle about me. Simple sort of chap. Don't lose your wool. Here we are. What do you bet they'll dispose of little Elliott in ten minutes, in order to get his doctor's opinion about the impenetrability of his skull to projectiles proceeding from pistols? I get a front seat in this act. Freedom of the press and all that. If you'll wait for me afterwards, I've got some beer at home. Cheer-ho!"

"Dirty look the blockhead gave me," said Vernon to himself as he sat down at the Press table and looked around. "Can't make the blighter out. He's as quick-witted as they make 'em and yet behaving like a flat. Hullo, here's old coupla' yards again. Taking an intelligent interest is Ashton Vale. Wonder if his legs ever get into knots. Slimming, by one who knows. Gawd, why are juries so plain? They ought to provide bags to put their heads in."

The proceedings concerning Elliott, if not quite so brief as those at the Gardien inquest, were marked by the same reticence on the part of the police. Identification by Mr. Gerald Lethem, secretary to deceased, who also attested to finding the body at 9.35 that morning, was followed by evidence from Sergeant Brading of the C.I.D. concerning the position of the body. The police surgeon stated that death was due to a shot, which might have been self-inflicted or might not, and that the time of death was difficult to ascertain owing to the temperature of the room. Twelve hours, with a margin of error of four hours, was his non-committal opinion. Inspector Jenkins followed, saying that the police had not yet been able to get into touch with deceased's relatives, and an inquiry was proceeding into his affairs, which seemed involved. The most interesting item of evidence was also produced by Jenkins in reply to the coroner's question.

"When examining the room was any firearm found there?"

"A pistol had been found in the room," replied Jenkins, "but the experts had not completed their investigations into it. It was one of the same calibre as that which shot deceased. The police were anxious to have time for the investigation to be carried further so that their evidence could be more decisive."

The adjournment followed immediately, and Vernon snapped the band round his notebook and grinned at Frazer of the *Morning Mail* who was sitting beside him at the Press table.

"Short and sweet, what!" said Campbell, "keep off the grass, and all that. I'd give a lot to get hold of some one who knew this Elliott bird. Kept himself to himself, they say."

"Gardien knew him," said Vernon.

"Did he an' all? How did you get on to that?"

"Rang up Coombe's office saying I was speaking for Paramount Studios, and asked for Gardien's agent."

"Bright child. You deserve jam on your bread and butter for that."

"Got any inside dope, Vernon? Your pal at the Yard might tell you a thing or two."

"So he might, when it's all over bar the shouting. Thomas by name and oyster by nature, that's our Scottie. See that long-legged nut-cracker wallah over there? Try him. Graham Coombe told me he was going to his little party last night."

"Vale? Glory! Thanks quite a lot. Do the same for you another day."

Frazer dashed off in pursuit of Vale, and Vernon looked round for Strafford, but failed to see him. Hurrying out on to the pavement he saw Strafford's long figure bending to enter a taxi, and an impish demon in Vernon's head caused him to become unreasonably inquisitive. He said afterwards that if Strafford had stayed to speak to him and then shaken him off, he wouldn't have bothered about him any further, but the other man's hasty retirement made Vernon wonder. He got into another taxi and bade the driver follow the old blue Unic into which Strafford had bundled so hastily.

"A mug and a mutt, that's myself," said Vernon, "but I've a yearning to know if he's going to see his lady friend in Barnes. Taking her out to tea at the Cumberland and all that. Do I sit at the next table behind a paper and hear how they worked the doings-oh? He's a rum bird. Simon Grand, what ho! and doesn't know what Elliott looks like. Not good enough."

The taxis worked their weary way down to Charing Cross. The Unic got a little ahead and was separated from Vernon's cab by a builder's lorry. By luck the journalist saw Strafford dive into the crowd by the Corner House, and it took some quick work on Vernon's part to alight, pay his man and dash off in pursuit.

"Just returning to his own digs, curse him. No, by gosh, he's not. Over the road and off we go, tally ho. Bakerloo tube. Change at Oxford Circus for Barnes. What a lark."

Keeping well behind Strafford, Vernon managed to see which machine he took a ticket from, followed suit and reached the platform for north-bound trains, a strategic distance behind his quarry. With an evening paper to shield him, Vernon watched the other. Strafford didn't look round and gave no sign that he was conscious of being followed. The train that came in was just right for Vernon's game—full, but not overcrowded. He got into the coach adjoining Strafford's and watched. The tall young fellow with the wide-brimmed hat was easy to observe. Oxford Circus arrived and he made no move.

"Baker Street for the Outer Circle, Hammersmith and all that, or Paddington? I wonder," murmured Vernon to his paper. It was at Paddington that Strafford made a move. He got to the door of his coach before the train drew up with the air of a man in a hurry, and Vernon had to leap out and follow at the double. As he went up the escalator he thought that the eighty-seven stairs at Strafford's lodgings certainly kept him in good training. Vernon had never run up an escalator at such a pace before, and things were complicated because he knew he had excess to pay on his tube ticket.

"Keep the change and love to the wife," he said, as he thrust his ticket and a shilling into the collector's hand. "All aboard for the Cornish Riviera. Hell! That chap can run."

Less than two minutes later Vernon was in the Great Western booking-office on the far side of the station, and heard Strafford snap out, "Reading, return."

"First-class, curse him, wasting my money and he's only going home to see mother. Well, I'm going too. I'll just look him up after dinner and ask for a few words about Elliott by one who knew him. Reading, 1st return, buck up! How long have I got?"

"Minute and a half. Number 3."

"Glory! How I won the Reading Relay. What a hope!"

Off again, tearing down number one platform and across the crowded space by the barrier, Vernon caught the train with no margin to spare, having seen Strafford jump into it twenty seconds before himself. Vernon, forced into buying a first-class ticket because he had not risked wasting time to join the queue at the third-class booking office, had got into a third-class compartment for the simple reason that he was sure Strafford would not waste his own first in such a manner.

"Non-stop to Reading. Plenty of time to realise I'm the world's fool, going whoring after mine own inventions. Still, the chap wouldn't have run like that for nix. Running away from little Peter, or fleeing from justice? What a hope!"

XII

WHILE PETER VERNON WAS JOURNEYING IN A NON-STOP train to Reading, Macdonald and Jenkins were consulting together at Scotland Yard over the evidence which had been collected by them during the day, and hearing the report of Detective Inspector Waring, who had been detailed to investigate Mardon-Elliott's rooms in the residential club known as Boxleith Hall. Both Jenkins and Macdonald were struck by the similarities between Gardien's manner of living and Elliott's. Each had lived in a "furnished suite" for the past few months, each had a minimum of personal possessions, and in neither case was there any evidence to show anything about their past life. Elliott, described as an amiable, unassuming sort of person, had been a good bridge player and billiard player, but had displayed a steady reticence concerning his own affairs. Like Gardien, he had kept no personal letters in his rooms. In fact the paucity of papers found there suggested that a clean sweep had recently been made of anything that could convey information. Detective Waring, who had examined everything in Elliott's rooms with a care which Macdonald himself could not have bettered, had only one exhibit to lay before his superior officers in the matter of tracing Elliott's origin, and that was a small, well-worn copy of Lamb's Essays, which contained a bookseller's label inside the back cover, giving the name, "Wellaby, Church Street, Reading."

"I don't suppose that it's any good, sir," said Waring regretfully, "but that book was the only thing you could describe as *old* in the place. It's been read a lot, too. I found it behind a set of Conrad's, and it was quite hidden. All the other books in Elliott's rooms were fairly new, bought at Bumpus's, most of them."

Macdonald and Jenkins exchanged a glance, and the former said, "This may be exceedingly useful. Reading seems to be indicated as a strategic point in this case. I wonder if Wellaby of Church Street is still in business."

"No, sir, he's not," said Waring regretfully. "I phoned through to find out. Wellaby's been dead for three years."

Just as Waring had finished his report, a form was brought to Macdonald giving the name of a visitor who had called to see him—Ashton Vale—and after a moment's consideration Macdonald said:

"Ask him to come up."

Turning to Jenkins he added, "I wonder if Vale's got anything up his sleeve. He was at the Gardien inquest and went off with Coombe. Vale struck me as the shrewdest male of the party last night. I had the feeling that I could cross him off the list of suspects, for the paradoxical reason that if he undertook a murder, he'd be much too efficient to bungle it. Whoever it was that contrived Gardien's death lost his or her head at the crucial moment—gave way to nerves and left those damning fragments of wire behind the handles of the bureau."

"No man's nerves are shock proof on an occasion like that," said Jenkins. "Allow that this chap Vale was human enough to get rattled, and consider the point that it was he who butted into the telephone-room when you and Coombe found Gardien. That may indicate something."

When Ashton Vale came into the room, Jenkins' beneficent gaze gave no indication of his quickened interest. The inspector had noticed Vale's tall figure at the Elliott inquest, and his shrewd mind murmured "So ho! This looks promising," even as he smiled amiably at Vale.

"Hullo," said the latter, smiling back at Jenkins, "we've seen one another before to-day."

He turned back to Macdonald, adding, "I went to the inquest on Mardon-Elliott. Coombe told me about his death, and I had a reason for being interested, which I thought you might like to hear about."

"Thanks. I should," said Macdonald, drawing forward a chair. "As you may imagine, Elliott's death took the wind out of our sails a bit. We depended on him for information about Gardien, who seems a very dark horse indeed."

"So was Elliott, if I'm not much mistaken," said Vale. "This is my story. Ten days ago I was dining at Frascati's with Brand, the essayist, and Mardon-Elliott was dining at a table near by. Something about the shape of his head struck me as familiar, although I couldn't place him, and I asked Brand who he was. Brand knows every one in the world of ink and publishers, and he told me. Ever since I've been puzzling as to where I'd seen Elliott before, and I think I've got him placed. I'm a native of Langbourne in the Thames Valley, six miles from Reading. It's a small market town with about three thousand inhabitants. About ten years ago there was a bit of excitement there which rattled the town tremendously. The chief solicitor in the place—a fellow named Robell, who did business for all the small farmers and landowners round about—shot himself in his office. His affairs were found to be in the deuce of a mess with a lot of trust money and securities missing. You can go into the details of it yourself, but the upshot was this. Robell himself was reckoned to be straight enough, and the police concluded that his chief clerk, a fellow named Mavory, was the delinquent. Robell shot himself rather than face the music which his own easygoing ways had brought about. A warrant was issued for Mavory's arrest, but he was never caught—or if he were caught I've never heard of it. To the best of my belief, Mardon-Elliott was Mavory."

"That's very interesting," said Macdonald, his mind working busily to fit in this new piece in his jig-saw puzzle. Elliott blackmailed by Gardien, for a very substantial backsliding. Elliott dead, with Gardien's name scrawled on the blotting-paper in front of him.

Jenkins was nodding like an amiable mandarin, and Macdonald flashed a glance at him before he asked Vale:

"You knew Mavory when he was in Robell's office?"

"I knew him by sight. Robell made my father's will, and did what legal business the old man needed. I'd been in and out of the office a good few times, and seen Mavory there. However, I'm not saying that I'm certain; I'm telling you what I think, and it seems to be worth looking into it."

"It certainly is. When did it come into your mind that the man whom you'd heard of as Mardon-Elliott was Mavory?"

"Last night. I was talking to young Strafford—Thomas Traherne—you know, while we were waiting to be put through it by you. Strafford told me he comes from Market Wraden, only a few miles from Langbourne. We were exchanging local reminiscences in the fatuous way one does—'remember old so and so?... and is poor old what-not still alive?'—I haven't been down there since my father died, six years ago, and Strafford was able to tell me all the latest gossip. It was while I was yarning away with him that the recollection of Mavory's face flashed across my mind. I made a mental note that I'd look into the matter, though naturally the business of Gardien's death overshadowed anything else last night."

Macdonald nodded. "Quite. Did you mention Mavory to Strafford?"

"No. I spoke of old Robell, but Strafford was at school at the time and naturally didn't remember the story."

"You know that Mardon-Elliott was Gardien's agent?"

Vale nodded. "Yes. Coombe told me so. I asked him as we came away from Gardien's inquest if he knew anything about Elliott, and had the surprise of my life at the story he told me."

"What did he tell you?"

Vale's eyebrows twitched and he pursed his mobile lips up before he replied.

"Exactly what he told you, I expect. That Elliott was Gardien's agent—and that he—Coombe—had got it into his head that Elliott was the grey-haired man seen by Miss Delareign and Miss Rees last night. When Coombe told me that Elliott was dead too, it seemed to me that the two stories might be related—so naturally I went along to hear what I could about Elliott." He ended abruptly and pulled a cigarette-case out of his pocket. "May I smoke here? Thanks. It's the deuce of an odd problem you've got. I wish you'd tell me this. Is it certain that Gardien predeceased Elliott?"

Macdonald paused before he replied. "No. It's not certain at all. There is a bare possibility that Gardien died first, but it was more probably the other way about."

"The probability being that the same murderer accounted for both?—Gardien and Elliott being a pair of rogues working together, probably originating from the same neighbourhood."

"An assumption—or genuine information?" inquired Macdonald, and Vale smiled.

"Call it inspired guesswork, to use Jane Austen's phrase of yesterday. Andrew Gardien. It's an interesting name. What is even more interesting is that several of the contacts in this case hail from the same neighbourhood."

Vale studied the chief inspector with his shrewd bright eyes. "Assuming that we're right about Gardien, then he, Mardon-Elliott, Strafford, and myself can be said to be linked by coincidence. So far as I am concerned Elliott was the only one of the three whom I'd set eyes on before. I'd certainly not met Gardien previously, nor Strafford."

"There was another person present at Coombe's party who might be said to be linked with the coincidence of locality," said Macdonald. "Miss Woodstock went to school in the same neighbourhood, which forms the connecting link."

Vale nodded. "Yes, so I gathered."

He puffed away at his cigarette, and then jerked out, "From the point of view of common sense psychology, I should be disposed to leave Valerie Woodstock outside the range of inquiry, even though she was entertaining you when that fuse went." Chuckling to himself a little, Vale went on, "I admit that the idea of the accomplice keeping you happily occupied in intelligent conversation while the principal got on with the main theme is an attractive avenue of approach, but to my mind it leads nowhere. The complement of that line of thought is Strafford, and I don't think it's a sound proposition, even though the sight of Strafford at the inquest on Elliott did make me ponder a bit."

"Ponder aloud then," said Macdonald, who was keen to know what argument had been occupying Vale's calculating mind.

"It's a matter of comprehending the youth of to-day," said Vale. "You and I are both over forty—pre-war, not post-war like Strafford and Valerie Woodstock. These youngsters haven't the same conventions that we had at their age. They're not susceptible to blackmail because they don't care a damn who knows what. Then if Strafford had been planning Gardien's murder, he wouldn't have indulged in a row with him just beforehand to point to a motive, if you get me."

"I get you," said Macdonald. "Your argument suggests that the mature are more susceptible to blackmail than the young."

"Of course. Having lived longer, they've given more hostages to fortune. They're more avid of security, more fearful of loss."

"An interesting point, psychologically, but to get down to the facts of the case, we have these factors. Gardien may have been a blackmailer—and Elliott had a particularly vulnerable point so far as the blackmailer was concerned. Ergo, Elliott got into Coombe's house and killed Gardien, and then retired to be killed himself."

"Doesn't that suggest to you that Gardien and Elliott were a couple of rogues working hand in hand, and that the same person killed both, to scotch the company at one go?"

"Yes, but the evidence doesn't reinforce the theory altogether. Some time you will be able to study it in full—it's not permissible for me to lay it before you at present."

Vale chuckled. "I don't altogether like the sound of that. Prisoner in the dock generally has the privilege of hearing all the evidence eventually. I suppose I do look a bit of a fishy party to your professional acumen."

"Every one at Mr. Coombe's party remains under suspicion until the problem is cleared up," said Macdonald cheerfully, "though that is not the point I was stressing. I think you are capable of seeing the cogent points of the evidence. Last night you had as much chance of observing events as I did."

"Up to a point. I'd say for one thing that the theory of Elliott's presence at Coombe's party is based on very insufficient evidence, a very vague description by two ladies, reinforced by leaps to conclusion on the part of Coombe and Manton."

"Quite. Disregard that hypothesis for the moment, and concentrate on those who were known to be present. The murderer had to be in the telephone-room between the time of the fuse and the time when the party reassembled in the drawing-room. That still gives us a large field of suspicion. As you observed for yourself, certain people can be said to be linked by locality. At the outset of Coombe's party we were warned by him to observe—as far as we could—the characters of those about whom we were to have six guesses at the conclusion of the evening. One or two people indulged in admonitory witticisms which could be interpreted as 'I won't give you away if you'll observe the same convention with regard to me.'"

Vale nodded. "Yes, but it was all too nebulous to be regarded as evidence."

"Yes. I agree. The next point that arises is this. I asked each member of the party if they had previously met any of their fellow guests. Leaving out Coombe and Manton, who knew all of you, including Elliott, the replies I got were as follows: Miss Woodstock knew Strafford and vice versa. Neither of them knew any one else. You had met Mrs. Etherton. Miss Delareign had seen Andrew Gardien at Colombo. That was the sum total of admitted contacts. If it emerges that any of the party were previously acquainted and took trouble to conceal the fact, I shall regard it as an indication of further knowledge on his or her part."

Vale nodded. "You get some rather interesting combinations in this case. Coombe and Manton, Mrs. Etherton and self; Miss Woodstock and Strafford, Miss Delareign and Miss Rees, Miss Campbell and Gardien. And if it was not Elliott whom those two ladies saw, then who was it? Manton with a wig on, assisting Coombe in a cunning plot?"

"Does it strike you as reasonably probable?" said Macdonald.

"No—but neither does anything else in this affair strike me as reasonably probable."

"When you were discussing local gossip with Strafford, did he mention any stories connected with Market Wraden, where he lives?"

"Stories—such items as might make a blackmailer hopeful? No. He did not."

"Was Miss Woodstock talking to you at the time?"

Vale screwed up his expressive face and said, "Talking? Listening might express it better."

"Holding a watching brief, in other words?"

"I don't quite know what you're getting at, Chief Inspector, but I hold to my original opinion that Strafford and Miss Woodstock are not concerned in this. If you are suspicious of them, it's up to you to put them through it."

"It's up to me to put everybody through it, and to try to read the evidence aright. The actual tangible facts tell us very little in this case, and by propounding the wrong guess I might give a subtle witness the chance to prevaricate truthfully. When Miss Woodstock was listening to you and Strafford gossiping last night, did you get the impression that she was prepared to short-circuit the conversation if need arose?"

Vale was silent for a minute, deep in consideration. At last he answered:

"I'll give you my honest impression. Strafford and I started yarning while you were talking to Valerie Woodstock as your first witness. When she came into the room, she joined Strafford and me."

"Who else was close at hand—listening to you two? Anybody?"

"Mrs. Etherton and Miss Rees were nearest to us—both of them very quiet. Bourne was entertaining Miss Coombe and Miss Campbell with Manton in attendance. I asked Strafford if he could tell me anything about old Wraden Hall, and he said it was in the market again after having failed as a private hotel. It was a school up till a few years ago. It was at this point that Miss Woodstock changed the conversation with a question—rather an odd question, I thought. She asked me if I had read Galsworthy's *Escape*. I said that I had, and she addressed the room at large asking them what they would do if an escaped convict appealed to them for help. She ended by saying that her own sympathies would always be with the hunted."

He broke off as a messenger came in with a note for Macdonald, and Vale got up.

"I'm afraid I've been wasting your time. The psychological approach to the problem's what interests me, and psychology's a wordy business. You're out for facts. If Mardon-Elliott proves to have been Mavory, that's a fact of sorts."

Macdonald nodded. "It is—it's also a line of approach. Thanks very much for the information. I shall be interested to compare notes again—later on. Good-bye for the moment."

When Vale had gone Macdonald turned to Jenkins.

"Miss Woodstock went to see Miss Coombe this morning and used the phone in the telephone-room before she left. I was sufficiently interested in the report I had about her to put a man on to watching her. She went down to Reading by the 3.15 from Paddington. Strafford caught the 6.30 to Reading by the skin of his teeth. It will be interesting to see if Vale follows suit. What did you think of him? You were as mute as the Sphinx."

"I think he's clever," said Jenkins, rather glumly. "He stood up for that young couple all right, but gave away indications that they looked fishy. This Elliott-Mavory story's interesting. What price Ashton Vale shooting Elliott, after having made an appointment with him as Gardien, and then going on to Coombe's to finish the business?"

Macdonald shook his head. "Won't do. It doesn't make a scrap of sense that way. The evidence in Elliott's case all points one way, to my line of thinking, and Vale's story hasn't made me alter my opinion—in fact it has reinforced it. I'm going down to Reading, Jenkins. That's the line indicated."

"Find out if Coombe was born there, too," said Jenkins. "That'd make it all jollier than ever. Why was Coombe so interested in that bureau this morning?"

"Every one has shown an interest in the bureau," said Macdonald, "even Miss Woodstock. I'm sorry for her, Jenkins, but it's time she answered a few questions."

Jenkins scratched his head, "And gave a few straight answers," he said. "I've been thinking over those witnesses of yours in the Gardien case. They're all what I call highbrows. I expect you call them intellectuals. They hate giving a straight answer, and tie themselves up in a knot with what they call the psychological approach. That long-legged fellow said one thing which was plain common sense. The assumption that the intruder at Coombe's party was Elliott is pretty thin. Coombe and Manton weighed in on it, and it was a nice fertile suggestion of theirs. Miss Rees, who seems more capable of a straight answer than most of them, described the chap she'd seen as bullet-headed and flat-footed—'I thought he was the C.I.D. man'—a bobby, like me, that is." Jenkins rubbed his well-cropped bullet head with a podgy finger and looked down at his substantial boots. "That's a plain description of a plain type. Coombe improves it to Elliott. What about the psychological approach, Chief?"

Macdonald grinned and slapped the other man's powerful shoulders. "Matter of vocabulary, Jenkins. Psycho-what-nots always get your goat. You call the sum total of your observations 'common sense about human nature,' and you succeed in being a better psychologist than any of the highbrows—your word, not mine. The Misses Delareign and Rees aren't highbrows. To invert some one else's phrase, they're more interested in Humanity than the Humanities. Capital H each time."

Jenkins groaned. "You pack off to Paddington, Chief. The G.W.R.'s. a grand line for meditations. Routine work's more in my line. Before the evening's out, I'll be able to tell you if any of Coombe's little party could have paid a visit to Thavies House before or after the party. When this case is over you can give me a report of Humanities with a capital H. Me for humanity with a small one, being your humble, as old Dickens put it."

XIII

PETER VERNON, SITTING IN THE TRAIN ON ITS WAY TO Reading, had plenty of time to kick himself—metaphorically speaking—and then turned his fertile mind to future operations before the train in which he was travelling was clear of the London suburbs. Being an optimist by nature he looked on the more promising side of his impetuous jaunt. Strafford, when talking to him in the first case after the Gardien inquest, had seemed in no sort of hurry, and had not suggested that he had a train to catch or any sort of urgent journey to undertake. He had left Vernon without any contradiction of the other's cheerful "See you later," and his behaviour after the inquest had indicated a desire to get away unobserved. Remembering Strafford's glance at the waste-paper basket and the "Simon Grand" title page in his own pocket, Vernon said to himself, "Here's a chap who was at Coombe's party and who knew Elliott and yet pretended he didn't, and he's doing a bunk from London when he's supposed to keep in touch with the police in case they need him for further evidence. Something funny somewhere. What's he going to do next, and how the devil am I going to keep up with him? Twenty to one he'll have a car waiting for him at Reading—that telephone call was probably from down there—and I shall be left standing. Taxis are as much good as a sick headache in this act. Damn! What do I do next? Even if I could hire a car I should be too late to follow the blighter."

At this stage in his contemplations, Vernon saw Strafford walk down the corridor of the train, and the journalist concealed himself under his hat as best he might. A few moments later his hat was plucked off his head by a hand thrust through the corridor door and a cheerful voice said:

"Hullo, old scout. Understudying Napoleon, or flying from the wrath to come in the shape of creditors? I'd know your legs and feet anywhere. You ought to have been a contortionist."

Vernon, much relieved at the sound of the voice—which was not Strafford's—looked up with a grin and retrieved his hat from the hand of a cheerful red-headed youth who stood at the entrance to his compartment.

"Fatty, by all that's holy!" he exclaimed, and a wild hope surged up in his heart. He jumped up and went out into the corridor, heedless of the scowl of the gentleman opposite whose feet were disorganised by Vernon's rapid uprising.

"Look here, Fatty, don't you live in Reading?"

"Not on your life, cheeild. I park in Petherington, five miles out. Want a drink, little one?"

"No. I want a car," said Vernon. "A good car with plenty of petrol, as soon as I get out of the train. Fatty, you're a godsend. I bet your opulent sire sends a bus to meet his offspring at the train."

"You're a cool one," replied the other. "The pater don't send his—a Bentley's too good for the little son. I have my own M.G. and the garage people bring it up to meet the train. Want a lift, Ugly face?"

"No. I want the car—loan of same, on note of hand only," said Vernon. "I'm on to a scoop, fat one, and you're an answer to S.P.—Silent Prayer, what! Rotting apart, old chap, be a sport and lend me your car. I'll do as much for you another day."

"Here, damn it, you're a cool one! What about me? Do I walk? Five miles. I like that."

"No, you fat ass. You taxi. I'll pay up. Lend me your car, Fatty. If you do, I'll take you behind at the 'Duchess of Kent's' and introduce you to Mae Milson any night next week."

"Said he seductively. What's your scoop, Ugly? Tell Fatty and he'll chauffeur you himself."

"Won't do, old chap. This isn't a joke. It's dead serious. I'm on the warpath, Fatty. The jolly old ed's sitting on the phone at the other end and it's going to make or break me."

"Then why didn't you order a fleet of cars?" inquired Jack Gleeson—the Fatty of fifth form days at Sherrow. "What's the use of being a big noise in Fleet Street..."

"Don't make puns, you mutt. I caught this train by the split skin of a stopped tooth, and the powers that be don't know where I am except that I'm going there fast. Damn it, Fatty, are you an answer to prayer or are you a plater, and do you want to meet Mae Milson or don't you?"

"Don't mind if I do," replied Gleeson, with a grin which lit up his square face. "I've been in uncle's office all day and I'm going home to eat the old man's birthday dinner and be

lectured on wild living. Next Monday evening, old Ugly—
and supper at the Savoy for four, what?"

"I'll work it, if you'll let me have that car, cross my thumbs
and spit on 'em. You bung out of the station, fat face, and have
your engine running and buzz off at the word go. I wouldn't ask
it if it weren't needful. Honest to God, Fatty, I need that car."

"All right, Ugly. I'll oblige. I'm the world's best at helping a
pal in a tight place. You can have my bus, my own ewe lamb,
bought with the hard-earned savings of virtuous living, but
I don't see why you should be so damn close over the story,
old lockjaw. I won't split. What's the scoop?"

"Alleged mutiny at Blagden Aerodrome," said Vernon,
uttering the first wild notion which came into his head, "and
look here, Fatty, if you split on that, I'm done for, ruined,
fallen, discredited, and hanged at dawn. It's not funny. If you
breathe a word you'll be had up for sedition. I don't *know*
anything. It's only a rumour."

Gleeson opened his eyes in a round-faced stare.

"Reds?" he whispered, fiercely yet hopefully.

Vernon, knowing that Fatty was of the true-blue die-hard-
rule Britannia type nodded portentously, though he shook
with inward giggles.

"Reds," he whispered in reply. "Mum's the word, Fatty.
O.K. about the car?"

"O.K. old chap," replied Fatty promptly. "I'll have her purr-
ing for you."

"Good man! Now bung off and don't take any notice of me
when we get out at Reading. I've got an idea there's a bloke
watching me, and I may have to make myself scarce. See you
in the station yard, old sergeant-major!"

Fatty walked off obediently along the corridor, and Vernon returned to his place hoping that his plump and patriotic pal would not drive over to Blagden in the hope of quelling a non-existent mutiny among His Majesty's most loyal forces.

"Poor old fat face," said Vernon to himself. "He always swallowed the can with the bait. Still, it's a spot of excitement after a day of tea broking or whatever it is he brokes."

Arrived at Reading, Vernon with his hat pulled well over his face mingled in the crowd on the platform until he picked out Strafford's tall figure in a less crowded section opposite the first-class coaches. Edging nearer to his suspect, Vernon had a shock of consternation. Strafford had just raised his hat to some one on the platform, and that some one was a girl whom Peter Vernon was able to recognise—Valerie Woodstock. Later Vernon had time to analyse the queer feeling which came over him at the sight of the girl's fair face upturned questioningly to Strafford's dark one. Vernon was keen enough to play the detective when it was a matter of trailing a man, but to do the same thing where a woman was concerned went against the grain. His feeling of uncertainty, however, did not last long. Valerie Woodstock had been at Coombe's party, and might have been involved in the Gardien business, he reminded himself. In any case, Strafford's attitude towards her now betokened something much more than an ordinary casual meeting on a railway platform. The crowd which had descended from the train was seeping away through the barriers, but the pair whom Vernon was following walked very slowly, their heads bent, their voices dropped almost to whispers, so that while it was evident that they were deep in some important discussion, not a word they spoke was audible to any, save one another. So slowly did they move that Vernon was constrained to linger by the bookstall to avoid overtaking them, and as he watched their close converse, curiosity got the better of every other feeling in the journalist's make up. That intent, cautious discussion indicated something both suspicious and suspecting; they were intent and they were afraid—so it seemed to Vernon's shrewd mind as he watched their slow reluctant footsteps towards the barrier.

Once Strafford and his companion were outside the station, Vernon made hasty search for Fatty and his sports model. They were not hard to find. The yellow M.G. with its chromium fittings stood out among the sober taxis and vans like some exotic flower in a back yard.

"Cripes!" thought Vernon. "Some bus for a bit of quiet sleuthing. You could see it ten miles away in a London fog."

"Fatty" Gleeson had been as good as his word. He had the engine running, and got out of his place in the driver's seat without a word of prompting. Vernon, glancing round, saw Strafford standing by a discreet Morris "Eight," a little closer to the exit than the M.G. Everybody who knew this station probably knew Gleeson's M.G. by sight; he turned to its owner.

"Bung your hat in the bus, Fatty, and take mine, there's a good chap," hissed Vernon. Gleeson did as he was bid without a murmur.

"Take care of yourself, old chap," he whispered, and Vernon slid into the driver's seat and clapped Fatty's expensive green felt on to his own head, saying to himself as he let in the clutch, "Hypnotic effect of the word 'Reds' on a die-hard! In the old days you'd have said you were out to save a maiden's honour. Now you mutter 'Reds' and the effect's the same. Oh, cheer oh! the lass is left to foot it and the gent takes the car. So far, so good. Keep behind and hope for the best."

Valerie Woodstock had set off on foot, and the blue Morris "Eight," with Strafford alone on board, was sliding slowly forward among the traffic. Vernon, a first-rate driver, settled comfortably back in the low driving seat of his luxurious little car and chuckled to himself as he followed Strafford. "Talk about a fool chasing a fool," he mused. "I've done a few dotty things in this peculiar life, but this is about the dottiest. I don't know where the chap's going and I don't care, but I'm damn well going too!"

Following an inconspicuous car in the crowded streets of a busy town takes all the driver's attention. Vernon did not know Reading and he had no time to try to get his bearings. He soon became pretty certain that Strafford knew he was being tailed and that he was doing his best to lose his follower. He drove round the town, dodging in and out of small streets, turning suddenly here and there and performing erratic feats of steering among heavy traffic. At the end of ten minutes Vernon knew several things. First, that Strafford was a good driver, but that he himself was a better. Second, that Strafford knew he was being followed and that it was therefore useless to tail him. Third, that out of sheer obstinacy, he, Peter Vernon was going to hold on and see where the other driver made for.

A moment after he had made this admittedly unintelligent resolution, Vernon had a bit of bad luck. The Morris slewed round a right-hand bend unexpectedly and a small Austin van overtook Vernon just as he was about to follow. The journalist managed to avoid a smash, but he stalled his engine and his way was blocked. By the time the driver of the van had ceased his objurgations and cleared out of the way, the Morris had ceased to be, so far as possible observation was concerned.

"Take you down a peg or two, you fat ass," groaned Peter Vernon to himself. "Now you'd better take Fatty's car home and borrow some money for your ticket back. Sleuths in fiction are never broke. I always am. Damn all! Hi! where's the Petherington Road, Charlie?"

The errand boy thus addressed gave directions which involved too many 'firsts on your right and thirds on your left' for Vernon to follow, but with a general sense of direction culled from the complicated instructions he turned down a narrow suburban road and was rewarded shortly by the sign of that gallant gentleman "Major Road ahead." Slowing up in orthodox manner at the junction he nearly let out a whoop when he saw a small green car with black mudguards shoot by.

"It's himself, or I'm a Chinaman, and he didn't see me!" he chortled to himself. "No lights on this road, no speed limit, and if I can't catch him I'll eat Fatty's hat."

The long straight stretch of road ahead was ideal for a chase. The M.G. was new, and in tip-top order, and Vernon began to enjoy himself. He was soon near enough to read the registration number ahead and to realise that his luck was in. It was Strafford's Morris all right, on a road with enough traffic to make the following car not too conspicuous, and Strafford was travelling at what Vernon would have described as "a very conservative rate." They proceeded thus for just over six miles, and then the Morris turned off the main road (direction quite unknown to Vernon) and took a narrow road whose surface betokened "B" road but none so dusty to Vernon's experienced mind. He followed carefully, took another turn into a road which should not have been classified as a road at all in his opinion, and bumped slowly on, for the car ahead seemed in no sort of hurry Vernon realised at once when the Morris stopped. He was near enough to see the driver get out, and he himself drove on past the Morris and pulled up to consider. There was a building of sorts behind a gate by the roadside; no lights showed, only the dark hulk of a gable against the sky.

Switching off his headlights and stopping the engine, Vernon sat very still and listened intently, thinking hard. He had followed Strafford on impulse in the first place, obeying the "news-finding" hunch which had often enabled him to get ahead of his fellow news hunters on other occasions. Later, obstinacy and coincidence had caused him to carry on with a chase which reason condemned as futile. Now he had to choose between the dictates of common sense which said, "Go home. You're asking for trouble," and the dictates of an adventurous mind which said "Find out what the chap's up to. There's some funny business going on, and you'll kick yourself if you don't follow it up."

The instinct for news finally got the better of cautious common sense, and Vernon got out of his borrowed car and walked softly back to the gate by the roadside. There was a full moon behind the cloud drift which covered the sky, and Vernon's keen eyes were able to make out the lines of the open gate and a shape beyond which might have been a garage door. The journalist crept past the gate, and stood on the rough grass behind the farther side of the hedge. His senses tingled as he heard a low voice say:

"Give it to me, you damned fool. What do you think I've come for? Gardien's…"

The words broke off in a groan and there was a sound of something falling and another groan. Caution fled from Vernon's mind. He had to find out what was happening behind that half-open door. Creeping forward, he reached the dark aperture. Some one's arms came round his knees from behind, and he was jerked forward off his feet and flung headlong into the darkness. As he measured his length on a pile of hay he heard the door slammed to behind him.

Sitting up, in complete darkness, cursing bitterly, Vernon realised that he had been outwitted by an opponent who had led him by the nose. His flash-lamp showed him that the barn in which he found himself was empty of any occupant save himself, and the sound of an engine outside told him that the chap who had collared him was driving off to pursue his business in peace.

"And that's that—damn all," said Vernon to himself. "But one thing I do know: Strafford's up to something that won't stand watching, and the Woodstock's in with him. If I'm a fat fool, he's another. If he hadn't been so anxious to get away without letting me see him, I should never have come loping after him. What hopes about this door?"

At first the prospects of escape from durance vile looked none too good. With the assistance of his torch and a good deal of fumbling, Vernon found that the solid double doors of the barn were fastened on the outside with a bar and staple. A vigorous attack with his boots proved quite futile, but a further reconnaissance with the torch showed that the doors had some inches of clearance at the top. Finding a stout wooden "spud" in a corner to assist his labours, Vernon managed to lever one door upwards and to lift it off its hinges, so that at last it fell outwards with himself on top of it, leaving him free with grazed fingers, a barked shin, and a flattened nose.

"Serve you right, you sanguinary ass," he growled to himself. "See anti-climax in the dictionary and look for the county asylum, lunatics, certification of... Thank Gawd he's left me Fatty's bus. More than I expected."

Starting up the amiable M.G. again, Vernon drove on. The road was too narrow to turn, and in his embittered state it seemed to make very little difference where he drove or how long it took to drive there. But Peter Vernon was not the type to remain morose or deflated for very long, and as he bumped over the execrable road his nimble mind soon began to make plans. He would not admit defeat and go back to London. Rather than that, he would spend the night in Fatty's car and do a little research into the matter of Strafford's movements the next day. "Market Wraden, that's where the chap hangs out, or his people hang out," said Vernon to himself. "I'll roll along there and get a snack at a pub if I pass one. Not closing time yet by a long way. While there's life there's hope. Why didn't I touch Fatty for a fiver?"

As Vernon expected, his byway ran eventually into a "road which looked like a road," and he turned left with the intention of regaining the route whereby he had left Reading. He had only travelled half a mile from the turn when he saw a car standing by the hedge, or, as he expressed it, "leaning against the hedge, blotto, blah, ditched," and as he slowed up to investigate, a very tall man came and stood in the light of the headlamps and signalled energetically. Vernon pulled up, ennui, heart-searchings, and self-recriminations vanishing like frost in a sunbeam, for the signaller, clearly illumined by Fatty's superior headlamps, was "the coupla yards of intellectual" who had attended the inquests on Gardien and Elliott—Ashton Vale. Descending joyously from the M.G., muttering, "Thick and fast they came at last," Vernon made his best bow.

"Dr. Livingstone, I presume?" he said politely.

Vale stared at the journalist—as well he might. Vernon had been pitched headfirst into a heap of loose hay, remnants of which stood up jauntily in his longish fair hair and adhered to a dark-blue overcoat which was plentifully powdered with dry limewash. His nose was grazed by its contact with the barn door, and a smudge of mud down one cheek added to the picturesqueness of his appearance. The battered appearance of the young man, plus the immaculateness of the shining M.G. which he had been driving, was too much for Vale's gravity.

"Mr. Stanley?" he replied, and then began to laugh as he recognised in Vernon the journalist whom he had noted twice already that day. Seeing Vale laugh, Vernon's gravity broke down, and the two stood in the light of the headlamps and shouted with mirth.

Vernon was the first to recover. "I say, what label did they pin on Macdonald at Coombe's little party?" he asked, apropos of nothing, and Vale replied:

"Izaak Walton. Not bad. Who are you, by the way?"

"Name of Vernon—*Morning Star*—collecting copy. You're Ashton Vale. Who put you in the ditch?"

Vale turned his eyes on the inebriated-looking Rover at the roadside. "I ditched myself, to avoid some young fool in a blinding hurry who thought the whole road was his own—and then some."

"Ha! That's my party, I'll swear," said Vernon. "Green-and-black Morris Eight, registration AXX9395?"

"Morris of sorts, no time to acquire specific details," replied Vale. "I think my back axle's in a poor way, and it'll take a crane to lift her out of the ditch," he went on, looking sadly at the Rover, "so if you could give me a lift in your search for copy, I should be infinitely obliged."

"Delighted," said Vernon. "Where do you want to go? Anywhere in the vicinity of Market Wraden?"

"Look here, what do you know about all this?" inquired Vale. "I was intending to go to Market Wraden, as it happens."

"That'll suit me," said Vernon politely. "Do you know how to get there?"

"I thought I did, but I must have missed my road," said Vale. "Damn it, this is a crazy business. What?…"

"Now you listen to me, sir," said Vernon, who had taken one of his sudden decisions. "You think all this looks dashed queer, and you think I'm one over the eight, don't you? Well, I'm not. I'm a journalist, as you know. I took the train to Reading all in a rush, so to speak, following a chappie who might mean news. I met a pal in the train who lent me his car—a very snappy article, as you see. I followed that chappie round in circles, and all I got for my pains was a sojourn in a barn, where I was pitched headfirst by superior strategy. I got out of the barn after chappie had melted away. I've got about five and sixpence on me, half a book of stamps and an empty packet of Gold Flake. I'll drive you where you like and swap yarns if *you* like, for the loan of a fiver. What about it? You can't sleuth on tuppence. It cramps your style."

"Let's get in," said Vale, waving a hand towards the shining M.G. "It looks a nice little bus, and I'm tired of this bit of road. There's a pub near Bishop's Wraden kept by a friend of mine. I expect he can put you up, too, if you want a bed, and I'll go bail for you for to-night. If I lend you a fiver I shall be broke myself; but we might get a cheque changed in the morning. D'you drive this contraption, or do I?"

"I do," said Vernon promptly. "We're bound to pass a garage somewhere, and you can tell 'em to go and salve the bits"—pointing to the melancholy Rover.

Seated in the M.G., progressing towards the main road with the intention of finding his bearings, Vernon said:

"About swapping yarns—I'll make first move. I went to the Gardien-Elliott proceedings and so did you. Then I followed a chappie who has also taken an intelligent interest in said proceedings. I lost him through being a mutt, and happened on you. Seems to me we must all three be after the same thing, only you know what it is you're after and why you're after it, and I don't. I hitched my wagon to a hunch..."

"And got heaved into a haystack backwards," put in Vale. "I know the journalist game of fishing in obscure waters, but before I swallow the fly I want to know if it's edible. Was the chap who heaved you into the haystack young Strafford?"

"Got it in one. Not too difficult, when you think it out," said Vernon. "What's Strafford doing which won't bear watching, and why is Mr. Coombe's party reassembling down here?"

"Is it?" inquired Vale.

Vernon chuckled. "Well, there's Strafford, and there's you, and there's Miss Woodstock."

"Is there, by jove?" Vale's voice sounded heartily surprised. "This is the main road we're coming to. D'you think your friend's left any maps in this outfit? I shall feel more disposed to be confidential when we've found my pub. It's a good pub."

Rummaging among Fatty Gleeson's belongings, Vernon found a map, and with Vale's assistance their position was located and they worked out the route to The White Dog, the inn near Bishop's Wraden which Vale had been seeking when he ditched his car.

"You know this part of the world pretty well," Vernon observed as Vale folded up the map, and the latter nodded.

"I was raised hereabouts, as the Yanks say," he replied. "Strafford knows these parts, so does Miss Woodstock, so did Elliott, so did Gardien, I imagine. The latter opinion is based on surmise. The same mental process which makes me assume that you are an optimist."

"Umps. So-so. Why that comment in conclusion?"

"How do you know I didn't account for both Gardien and Elliott? How do you know I didn't meet Strafford and leave him in the ditch? How d'you know I'm not leading you to a lonely grave?"

"Well, if it comes to that, I don't know," replied Vernon cheerfully. "One must take risks sometimes. I'm out for NEWS. If in the process I become news myself, they'll be able to put: 'He perished for his paper' on the headstone and 'One more fool gone west,' in the headlines."

XIV

WHEN VERNON FOLLOWED ASHTON VALE THROUGH THE ancient door of The White Dog, the journalist perceived at once that he was entering one of those hostelries which knowledgeable Englishmen—and women—are developing from the downfallen village pub. A huge fire blazed in the open chimney of the lounge; old oak furniture gleamed with polish; copper and brass glimmered in dark corners; and the whole atmosphere of the place had that air of comfortable sophistication which only the cultured seem able to impart to the hotel-keeper's craft. A tall grey-headed fellow in ancient tweeds strolled towards the visitors, and Vale said:

"Hallo, Charles. Got a couple of beds? Lord, you keep shrewd winds in these parts. I'm cold through."

"We'll soon have you unfrozen," growled mine host in a deep bass. "Want a meal? There's a bird in a casserole which isn't any the worse for stewing in its own juice. Are you having a conference for cultural relations, or what d'you call it in these parts? We haven't had any one but

a lost commercial in the place for days, and now you're
rolling up in couples."

"Like that, is it?" said Vale. "Get your bird on the table,
Charles. I'm half starved, and so's Vernon. My own car's in a
ditch waiting for a crane to lift it out—God knows where—and
this chap's given me a lift. Who are your couples, by the way?"

"Pair of high-browed dames in there," replied mine host,
tilting his chin towards a door farther along the lounge. "I
expect they'll be off to their beds shortly and leave us the
fire to yarn by. You can have numbers three and four, up on
the right there. Like a wash before you eat?"

He met Vernon's eye and the journalist grinned. He had
just caught sight of his own reflection in a mirror and realised
that the suggestion of a wash was not inapposite.

"Had a bit of a spill," he observed.

"Item, he's got no pyjamas and no tooth-brush," added
Vale. "You might see to it, Charles. He's picked me out of a
ditch, so to speak, and he's my pigeon."

"That's all right," replied the other. "Nothing we can't
supply here. I'll see to it."

He strolled off towards the end of the lounge and Vale
grinned at Vernon. The latter was staring at the door which
mine host had indicated as concealing his "high-brow dames,"
and Vale knew that the journalist was longing to open the
door and look into the room. Vale slapped the younger man
on the shoulder. "Look here, if you realised what you look
like at the present moment—"

"I do realise it," said Vernon. "I'm the world's beauty chorus
complete, and I don't care a damn. Lots of people may know
of this pub—it's obviously a corking good pub, and I lift the

lid to Charles and his bird—but I'm going to unsport that oak, because I'll bet my last non-existent sou that one of the dames—if not both—is leading lady in the present show. It'd be too good to find a couple of highbrows in this spot on this particular evening who're not mixed up with Coombe's party. You see!"

He walked to the door and opened it cautiously, closing it a moment later.

"What did I say?" he demanded. "You bung in and keep 'em talking. I'm all for a wash now I know the worst."

He hastened towards the stairs at the end of the lounge, and Vale walked to the sitting-room door, not without some feelings of trepidation. Closing it behind him, he walked towards the fireplace, murmuring:

"Good-evening. Jolly chilly outside, but cheery enough in here."

The calm courtesy of the "good-evenings" with which the two ladies replied spoke volumes for the breeding and self-control of the two "high-browed" dames. Valerie Woodstock was standing by the fire, having just lighted a cigarette, and Mrs. Etherton was leaning back in a comfortable chair, toasting her toes by the good woodfire.

As Vale came towards the fireplace, Mrs. Etherton said pleasantly, "This inn almost restores one's belief in the 'Merry England' tradition. I first heard of the place from James Child, and I've been meaning to sample it for a long time."

"Ah," said Vale. "Child was partner to Belton—who keeps this inn. They ran a coaching establishment together in Bloomsbury for years. Marvellous man, Charles Belton."

He caught sight of the *Morning Post* cross-word lying beside Mrs. Etherton's chair.

"Completed?" he inquired, and the white-haired lady shook her head.

"No. I'm off my form this evening, somehow. Held up by a long anagram, of all things. Perhaps you can see it for me, Mr. Vale—'Red lorry in a taxi.' One word, apparently."

Vale laughed and glanced at the paper. After a pause of only a few seconds he replied, "'Extraordinarily' will fit, I fancy."

Valerie Woodstock looked at him thoughtfully.

"Can you see any anagram at a glance like that?" she inquired.

Vale met her eyes steadily. "Generally I can. It's a sort of visual gymnastic facility, I suppose," he replied, almost apologetically. "If you have the knack, you see the transposition of letters almost automatically. Nothing clever or even reasoning about it. It just happens."

"Like the major events in most people's lives," said Mrs. Etherton reflectively. "One plans out a reasonable course of action and then something happens and the letters re-sort themselves and spell something one never intended. All very vexing when you have a tidy mind, as I have. Do you often come down here to enjoy the amenities of The White Dog, Mr. Vale?"

"No. I've only been here once since Charles Belton took it on," replied Vale, "though I know the neighbourhood pretty well. I was born in Langbourne, and I went to the grammar school there."

"And you're paying a visit to your boyhood's haunts. How pleasant!" murmured Mrs. Etherton in her deep, tranquil voice, and Vale turned to Valerie Woodstock, who still stood by the mantelpiece, fiddling with an ancient pair of snuffers.

"And Miss Woodstock is contemplating a visit to the old playing fields where she once captained the lacrosse team?" he inquired.

"I didn't. We played hockey," she retorted. "My old school closed down shortly after I left, Mr. Vale. It was unable to stand the shock of my departure, you see—or perhaps unable to weather the financial crisis of the early 1930s, which you have expounded so clearly in *Popular Economics*. Mr. Coombe told me that the book was a best seller for weeks."

"I'm afraid his use of the term 'best' was a publisher's euphemism," said Vale. "I doubt if the circulation of my pot-boiler was more than fifty per cent of Gardien's last thriller, for example."

Valerie Woodstock frowned, her fair face looking so weary and troubled that Vale felt compunctious, and was glad when the door opened and Peter Vernon strolled in.

"Good-evening," he said airily, and grinned at Vale. "Damage repaired to some extent," he burbled, "thanks to kindly assistance of friend Charles. Recent intimate contact with barn doors, ditches, and the like relegated to the far-off unhappy past."

Vale looked inquiringly at the two ladies.

"I'm not sure if you have met Vernon?" he inquired, and the journalist bowed, saying:

"Miss Woodstock was kind enough to give me an interview at the St. Elizabeth Settlement in Southwark. Mrs. Etherton chastised me under the editor's very nose…"

"For poking your own where it was not wanted, young

man," interpolated Mrs. Etherton firmly. "I think that I then told you my opinion about journalistic intrusiveness, and the rights of an author to his or her own privacy. My opinions have not changed since. With that proviso, I am very pleased to continue our acquaintance."

Vernon bowed again, very meekly, and Miss Woodstock observed: "It might be as well to ascertain Mr. Vernon's convictions—or conventions—on the privileges of pressmen in the service of publicity. They may not coincide with your own, Mrs. Etherton. I'm sleepyish. I think I'll go up to bed."

She walked across the room and Vernon, neat-footed and nimble, reached the door in time to hold it open for her, and make another of his polite bows as she passed.

Charles Belton came into the room as Miss Woodstock left it, mine host saying:

"If you two fellows want to eat, the bird's waiting. Better get down to it."

"Thanks, old boy, we will," said Vale cheerfully, and Mrs. Etherton looked up.

"Miss Woodstock didn't seem to like the cut of your jib, young man," she observed to Vernon. "Since I have an open mind on most subjects, I shall be interested to hear you give an account of yourself after you have eaten your supper—likewise Mr. Vale. Convictions, conventions, and coincidences to be the subjects for discussion."

"Delighted," said the two men in chorus, and hurried out after Charles Belton to the dining-room.

Vernon was silent, save for casual remarks commending the building and the service, until he and Vale had put away the greater part of the contents of the casserole before them.

At last the journalist remarked, "I thought my capacity for surprise had been exhausted long ago in my days of innocence. I was all wrong. The bird we're eating is the sort of surprise you don't expect to get in England. The White Dog ought to be called The Improbable Inn. Dash it all, man, did you expect all this, complete with company?"

Vale shook his head. "The company leaves me guessing," he replied. "If I'd known who were to be our fellow-guests, it's likely I shouldn't have brought you here. I didn't know. I've butted in—followed a hunch, like you—and now I wish I hadn't." He screwed up his face in a queer grimace. "I feel as though there's another surprise in the offing. What if all the lights go out, as they did at Coombe's party, and another corpse is found under the table?"

"Curiously enough, that wouldn't surprise me at all," said Vernon calmly, "though I tell you straight, the corpse isn't going to be mine if I can help it. Is there any ferocity to beat that of the logical pacifist? I doubt it."

Vale stared. "Did you get a crack on the nut when you landed into that barn?" he inquired, and Vernon shook his head.

"No. I landed into a hank of hay. Head quite intact," he replied cheerfully. "It gave the old grey matter a bit of a jolt, and it's been functioning quite well since. I've got an idea of sorts, and I'm just wondering if the same notion brought you tootling down here."

Vale's eyes were very wary. "Fishing with fat worm, old copy-scrounger?"

"Not more than usual. It's my living, anyway. Don't you think it'd have made more sense if we'd found Miss Susan

Augusta Coombe sitting warming her toes in there? Mrs. Etherton doesn't seem to fit the bill—unless—oh, great goop that I am!"

"I expect Charles has got a clinical thermometer somewhere; he's got everything any one could ever want," replied Vale. "Come up to bed, old chap. To-day's been too much for you."

"Thank you for nothing," retorted Vernon. "The more you pretend to be dense, the more certain I get that I'm seeing daylight."

"I'm not pretending to be dense. Honestly, I've not the least notion what you're driving at," said Vale, and Vernon said coolly:

"Well, I'll tell you bang out. First, I don't believe *you* killed Gardien." ("Thank you," murmured Vale.) "Not because you're incapable of it in the abstract, but because if you'd done it, your calculations wouldn't have miscarried. I know you're one of the peace-at-any-price push, so far as modern warfare's concerned, anyhow. So is Strafford. His principles preclude him fighting for his king and country under any conditions. Doubtless Miss Woodstock is of the same way of thinking, and so is Miss Susan Augusta Coombe."

Vale sat up, his face looking really animated.

"Sorry I took so long to follow you, my child," he said cheerfully. "You're really being quite interesting. Pacifism as a basis for murder, all comrades to assist with the euthanasia outfit. I grasp that bit—also that, for reasons at present unknown, we happy few—we band of brothers—are having our monthly reunion at The White Dog. I pass that. But why, oh ingenious journalist, should we have gone to the trouble of removing Gardien and Elliott from their late sphere of usefulness? *Cui bono*? The motivisation is the weak point in the drama."

"Yes," admitted Vernon. "But there's some funny stuff going on in what might be called the sewerage of the diplomatic system. The Fascist countries would do anything to discredit Great Britain—all sorts of dodges like touting for arms orders, proving supplies have been sent by this country to Abyssinia and Spain, and low tricks of that kind. There's always some nasty blackguard who's at the root of these calumnies."

Seeing Vale's expression of sceptical amusement, Vernon went on doggedly:

"You'll tell me I'm talking puerile rot. All the same, aren't there always some lowdown blackguards who'll make a living out of embroiling countries in war if they get the chance?"

"Oh, that I grant you," replied Vale. "You, as a journalist, probably hear more queer stories than ever get published in the press of this country; and in the present state of the world's politics a good deal of scum boils up on the surface and attracts attention. You argue that Gardien and Elliott were secret agents of the most poisonous kind. I won't dispute that. You may have prior information. But answer me two questions. You said just now, after you had mentioned Mrs. Etherton, 'Great goop that I am.' It did occur to me to wonder what you meant. Why were you a goop over that particular point?"

"I was trying to reason out the 'motivisation' of this reunion of literary lights in the remote village of Bishop's Wraden," said Vernon. "Miss Woodstock, Strafford, you—all members of the 'Peace in our Time' campaign. Susan Augusta's one of the most active women in the movement, but I've never heard of Mrs. Etherton in that connection. I forgot she's a friend of yours."

"Who told you that?" inquired Vale, and to the journalist's observant eyes it seemed that the older man had lost something of his complacency.

"I saw you together at Burlington House last year," said Vernon, "and you obviously weren't chance acquaintances."

Vale's face was a study. "Your observant habits may lead you into trouble one day," he observed. "Say if you answer my previous question. How do you account for the fact that we select this very inconvenient locality for our rendezvous?"

"Who is the most famous among pacifist internationalists in England?" inquired Vernon. "Who has been imprisoned for urging mutiny in the army? Who has a price put on his head in Italy and Germany? Isn't it Randolph Ramovell? And doesn't he live at Ingham-under-Isis, quite close to Bishop's Wraden—about five miles from here?"

Vale sat silent, his brows knitted in thought, his eyes cast down on the table, while he made patterns with the salt which he had spilled by an abrupt movement of his hand. When he raised his eyes he looked Vernon full in the face.

"You've done quite a nice bit of logical reconstruction," he said. "There are holes in it, as you're probably aware, and I don't think it would look very convincing after counsel had pulled it to pieces; but still it's the nucleus of an idea. And why you've chosen to air the great surmise to me, I simply cannot understand. If you're merely being funny, I think your humour is of a questionable kind. If you're serious, you appear to lack a bump of caution. You've been locked up in a barn once this evening, but that doesn't seem to have taught you the elements of self-preservation."

"I think I was depending upon *your* convictions of self-preservation," said Vernon. "If I were killed to-night, in this place where you and your friends foregather, the chances of your getting away with it would be very slim. It'd be a bit too apropos altogether. Anyway, I'm not worrying," he went on cheerfully. "You're leaping ahead much too fast. I didn't suggest that you killed Gardien or Elliott either."

"I see. In fact, you'd be the world's most surprised journalist if I told you that I did?" snapped Vale, and the tone of his voice made Vernon jump. He had not imagined that Vale's mild, humorous voice could utter a tone so trenchant.

"You'd be about the last person to admit it if you had," said Vernon, and Vale snapped back:

"You're one of those ingenious fellows who can only see one line of thought at a time. You had the great idea of following Strafford to see where the trail led. You got chucked into a barn full of hay for your pains—very suitable, assuming hay to be your natural diet, with an occasional thistle for encouragement. When you saw me with my car conveniently ditched, you thought, 'Cheer-ho! Here's more evidence to be collected!' You gave me a lift, and came to the very spot where it was most convenient for me to have you, and you crown the great work of intelligence by a reconstruction of recent events, complete with motives." Vale fairly snorted. "I only marvel you've survived as long as you have to air your optimism on serious-minded people."

Just as Vale concluded his sentence the dining-room door

opened, and Strafford appeared. Vale jumped to his feet. "Hallo, Thomas Traherne! I fancy you've seen this chap before. He's an ingenious-minded fellow, full of bright ideas. Perhaps you'd like a word with him."

Before Strafford could reply, Vale had slipped out of the door behind him. Vernon, completely taken aback, stared up at the frowning face of Denzil Strafford, and the latter said:

"Time we had a word or two. I'm tired of the sight of your silly face. What the hell and hades d'you think you're up to, trailing round after me like a pickpocket?"

"What I'm up to is my affair, Mr. Simon Grand," said Vernon coolly. "If you're interested to know, I reckon I've got my money's worth—more than I expected when I paid for a first-class ticket."

Strafford came and sat down at the table.

"Found out how I killed Gardien?" he inquired. "Or would you like a demonstration? Why don't you stay at home, muttonhead? You're out of your depth in all this. Moreover, you're a blinking nuisance."

Vernon got to his feet. There was something very unpacific about Strafford's attitude as he stood scowling across the table.

"Want some news for your paper, owl face?" asked the latter truculently, and then the door opened again and Valerie Woodstock appeared.

"Denzil, Mr. Vale wants to talk to you—at once, please," she said, her calm, decided voice as cool as though she were asking for a taxi to be called, "and *I* want to talk to Mr. Vernon."

With a tilt of her chin she indicated the door to Strafford, and with a rueful grin he obeyed her gesture.

"As you will, partner, but he's asked for a sock on the jaw, and by gad, he's going to get it some time."

With a nod to Vernon which promised a lot, Strafford walked out, and the girl advanced to the table where Vernon was standing, completely nonplussed.

"Shall we sit down and talk like reasonable beings?" she said, pulling out the chair which Vale had recently occupied. "I was very rude to you just now, Mr. Vernon. I apologise."

Vernon met her eyes and felt his face grow hot.

"*Pas de quoi*," he murmured. "I expect I asked for it. All's fair in love and war, likewise in crime and copy-hunting."

"That I'll not dispute," she said. "I know you're a journalist. I know you've got to be pretty snappy to get news, and that you can't afford to be too nice over it; but look at the matter from my point of view. I'm not feeling humorous or amused, although I admit there's something ludicrous about the present situation. Quite frankly, I feel desperate. Murders may be bread and butter to journalists, and playing at detectives may be great fun when you regard the people concerned as pawns or robots. When you realise that they're human beings—and you care about them—it all looks different."

Vernon felt abashed and uncomfortable, and his answer was made with patent sincerity.

"I'm sorry that you're distressed over it, Miss Woodstock. I do realise that it's a rotten situation for you if you're concerned with the human element in the situation. For me, it's simply a puzzle."

"The cross-word mind again?" she put in, and Vernon nodded.

"Yes, that and the instinct for news. Forgive me if I sound

callous, but when people commit murders, or concern them-selves with the concealment of murder or murderers, they automatically become news."

"And you assume that I am here on account of Mr. Gardien's murder?"

Vernon looked her squarely in the face.

"I don't assume anything about you, Miss Woodstock. I didn't follow you here, I didn't expect to find you here, and—if you'll pardon straight speaking—I haven't gone out of my way to speak to you, or to inflict myself on you in any way." Suddenly he grinned, his thin boyish face widening into amusement. "You used the word 'ludicrous' just now. Doesn't it just about hit the mark? Why should Graham Coombe's party reassemble like this at The White Dog? If you were in my place, wouldn't you be racking your brains to find an answer to that question? I've launched my ingenious recon-structions on Mr. Vale to try to test his reactions. He hinted darkly that I had better look out for myself—ergo, he was the guilty party. Strafford asked bang out, 'Do you want to know how I killed Gardien?' You rebuke me for my callousness…"

"…And ask in my turn, 'Have you guessed how *I* killed Gardien?'" Valerie Woodstock interrupted suddenly: "Have you included that in your reconstruction?"

"Is that the great idea?" asked Vernon coolly. "Are you one and all going to say, 'I killed Gardien and Elliott,' and reduce the whole proceedings to a farce? Is Mrs. Etherton going to join in the general confession, plus Miss Coombe and Miss Delareign? It's a beautiful idea, of course," he ended thoughtfully.

With elbows on the table and chin in her hand, Valerie Woodstock looked at him fixedly.

"Talking of testing reactions, what would be yours in this case?" she asked. "If I told you here and now that I killed Andrew Gardien, and gave you chapter and verse for how I did it, would you go to the nearest police station and give information to that effect? Would you treasure the recollection of handing over a fellow-human being to the hangman?"

Vernon jumped. Her voice had an intensity and depth of feeling which startled him, and he stared back at her, uncomfortably aware of the challenging power in her wide eyes.

"Answer me that!" she insisted. "It's not your job to hound down a man to the gallows—nor a woman, either. Think again before it's too late. What are you trying to do, and are you proud of doing it?"

She got up suddenly and pushed her hair back from her face with a restless gesture. "Why not go home and forget all this? It's more difficult to be charitable than it is to be clever, Mr. Vernon."

The door opened, and the large figure of Charles Belton stood in the doorway.

"If you've finished in here—?" he began, and Valerie Woodstock turned away.

"Good-night," was all that she said as she walked out of the room.

Charles Belton raised his shaggy eyebrows and looked quizzically at Vernon.

"Conference finished? What's it all about?" he inquired, in his deep rumbling bass, and Vernon held out his hands, palms upwards.

"Search me!" he replied. "If you ask me, they're a bit batty, the whole boiling of them. D'you want a front page—leaded type—exclusive last-minute write-up for this pub of yours?"

"I'm damned if I do," growled Charles.

"Sorry about that, because it looks as though you were going to get it," replied Vernon. "May I monopolise your telephone for a bit?"

"Hey, what's that? If you think you're going to spread yourself over my pub…"

"You'll bust the blooming line first?" put in Vernon. "I'm not going to mention your pub. I'm going to put in an overdue account of a London inquest—two London inquests, in fact—to my newspaper. You may listen to me while I do it and enjoy my narrative style. Likewise, if your guests would find it enjoyable, they may listen in to some delectable and edifying essay in the art of condensation, *précis* and verbal economy. At the first mention of you or your pub, you may dash the telephone from my perfidious hand, crying, 'Exinanite! Exinanite! to those privileged to attend.'"

"Well, I've met a few crazy customers since I acquired licensed premises," growled the big man, "but this evening's party beats the band. Batty? I'll believe you."

"Meaning me?" inquired Vernon.

"Definitely," rumbled Charles.

XV

MACDONALD, ONCE HE HAD GOT AN IDEA INTO HIS HEAD, was quick to act upon it for the purpose of putting it to the proof—or disproof.

Telephone communication with the police authorities in the neighbourhood of Market and Bishop's Wraden assured him a lodging at whatever belated hour he put in an appearance. Murmuring, *"His rebus adducti"* (which remnant of De Bello Gallico, Book I., returned to a mind at present concerned with scholastic reflections), Macdonald busied himself on the outline of a report which he showed to Jenkins before he left Scotland Yard. The chief inspector's abilities in the line of "précis condensation and verbal economy" far outdid Peter Vernon's when Macdonald wished to present a report in "tabloid form," and Jenkins scratched his head over the terse phrases which were offered for his consideration.

"Well, you've got a theory which accounts for Elliott's death and Gardien's, complete with names of principals," said

Jenkins; "but proof's a long way from theory. If you showed this to the old man in its present form he'd tell you not to propound nebulous theories in advance of information. The Elliott explanation's reasonable enough. The idea cropped up in my own head, I admit, but it seemed a bit silly."

"It seemed silly because Gardien was dead, too," reflected Macdonald. "If Gardien had lived, the evidence in Elliott's rooms would have forced us to look for a motive, and I reckon the evidence we found in Gardien's rooms would have gone a good way to hanging him."

"Circumstances alter cases," murmured Jenkins. "I can see the Elliott argument all right. The Gardien business is much trickier, though. Not solid at all. You can urge the locality motive in more directions than one, and the blackmail motive all round. From the point of view of deduction pure and simple, I favour the Strafford-Woodstock combination. The idea of keeping you busy chatting in the little library was good team work."

"Well, Strafford's returned to his native heath with Peter Vernon on his trail, apparently," said Macdonald, "so it's probable that I shall find them both in the vicinity of the Wradens. I only hope that Vernon hasn't made an ass of himself. He's a shrewd fellow and he's been useful to us on more occasions than one, but he goes hot-headed at things sometimes, like a bull in a china shop. I'm off to the hub of activities, Jenkins. I've got to try out my hunch as fast as I can. If it's a washout, you'll hear from me early to-morrow."

"And if it's the truth you've guessed?..."

Jenkins tapped the report in his hand and Macdonald frowned a little.

"It's the 'if' that's got to be faced by every individual who takes the law into their own hands," he replied.

Macdonald, driving in his car, did not reach the village of Market Wraden until midnight. He was met at the market cross by a constable, detailed for that duty, and directed to a house just off the main road, where a room had been reserved for him.

"Mrs. Bardon's, that is, sir," said the constable. "She's a relation of the superintendent's. You'll find he's there waiting for you."

Macdonald was admitted to the small house by a big man whose burly figure seemed to fill the little passageway.

"Glad to see you, Chief Inspector. I've often heard of you and reckon your visit's a bit of luck for me," said the superintendent cheerfully. "Come along in. There's a good fire in here."

Macdonald, tired and cold, was glad to see the cheerful fire in the tiny warm room. "It's good of you to have kept out of your bed waiting up for me," he said to the other. "I might have waited until to-morrow morning before I came down, but I thought it'd save time if I did the journey to-night and got going first thing in the morning. Since you are here, d'you feel good for a talk?"

"I do indeed," replied the other heartily. "My bed can wait. We don't often have big guns in these quiet parts."

"For which you should be devoutly thankful," said Macdonald. "I often think I'd like a job in a remote rural area, with nothing more enlivening than a spot of poaching to worry over. I'll give you a bare outline of my present case."

They pulled up two chairs to the fireplace, and lighted their pipes, and Macdonald began:

"Graham Coombe, the publisher, gave a party to ten people; here's a list of their names. During the evening Andrew Gardien, a well-known writer, was killed by a neatly-worked electrocution outfit. Any of the guests could have arranged the mechanics of the scheme, but only certain of them could have cleared away the apparatus. The names of the possibles are underlined. The others had no opportunity of doing the clearing up because they were never out of sight of their fellow-guests. Do any of the names convey anything to you?"

Superintendent Bardon studied the sheet of paper which Macdonald held out, puffing away at a gurgling pipe the while.

"Mr. Denzil Strafford is pretty well known about here," he said. "His uncle lives at Wraden Abbey. Mr. Ashton Vale, I've heard a lot about. He was born in Langbourne and brought up there, though it's some years since his father died and the house was sold. He's not been back hereabouts for a long time—not to my knowledge, that is—until this evening."

"He's down here, is he?" inquired Macdonald. "Just a minute before we get on to that, though. Do you know anything about any of the other people?"

"I've seen their names on books and in the newspapers," said Bardon; "but they're none of them local people. I don't know anything about them."

"Good. That's point one. Next, you got our inquiry about Mavory, the chap who escaped your warrant?"

"Yes. I've brought you a photograph of him. We never got his fingerprints. It was before my time. They were slow in getting the business sorted out, and Mavory had disappeared before they thought of looking for him. This photograph was taken from a group—the only one we could get of him. He belonged to a sort of literary club."

Macdonald took the photograph held out to him and studied it thoughtfully.

"Yes. I think it's the same chap all right," he said. "He had established himself in London as a literary agent—Mardon-Elliott. He was found shot through the head, having died about the same time as Gardien. I hope the group from which this photograph was taken still exists. It may be illuminating. Having got that point settled, I want to hear about Mr. Vale's visit to these parts."

"Ah! It's quite a story," said the superintendent, suddenly beaming over his broad face. "Accounts a bit for me being so happy to keep out of my bed, perhaps, until I'd seen you. That list of names you showed me was very illuminating—to use your word—very descriptive word, too. Our constables have had quite an interesting evening of it. P.C. Robins was patrolling the Wraden-Topham road when he heard a noise of sorts along a little by-road which is only used by farm carts as a rule. Robins was on his bike. As he turned into the byway he heard a car start up in front of him and thought it a bit funny. He kept his eyes open as he went, and found there'd been some queer doings at Fox's barn—doors off the hinges for no reason at all. No sign of accident otherwise. Robins thought it a bit odd, but put things to rights and rode on. About a couple of miles away, this time on the Waynton-Topham road, he saw a car which had been standing in the road move off as he sighted it. A few minutes later he found another car, capsized in the ditch and deserted. That car was

Mr. Ashton Vale's. Investigation during the course of the evening brought in the news that Mr. Ashton Vale was putting up at The White Dog, a very classy inn kept by a gentleman named Belton. This inn is in the parish of Market Wraden. Mr. Vale arrived at The White Dog in a car which belongs to a young gentleman named Gleeson (car and owner very well known hereabouts). It was driven by a gentleman named Vernon, who's also staying at The White Dog. Vernon arrived there looking as though he'd been pulled through a hedge—or a barn-door—backwards. Robins inquired if there were any other visitors staying at the inn (he knows the barman there). Here's the visitors' list: Mr. Vale, Mr. Vernon, Mr. Strafford, Miss Woodstock, Mrs. Etherton. Illuminating, eh?"

"Very," said Macdonald. "It throws light on the fact that people with first-class minds can be remarkably stupid when they get agitated. I believe that the intention inspiring several members of that party is to avoid giving information to my department, and their anxiety makes them behave as pointers to the facts they're endeavouring to conceal. How long have you been in this place, superintendent?"

"Six years come midsummer. I was up Swindon way before that."

"Six years—that ought to be long enough for you to be able to tell me what I want to know. Do you remember any one of the name of Seer living in this district?"

Bardon nodded and then looked somewhat perturbed. "Yes, I know the name all right. Don't go telling me that story's cropped up again. I thought it was just malice which started those rumours."

"Say if you tell me the story. I haven't any notion at all what it is. If I told you the reasons which caused me to come down here at the end of a hard working day to see if I could get any news of a lady named Seer you'd suspect I had a tile loose."

"Well, you seem to have hit the nail on the head in guessing that there was a story to be told," said Bardon, shaking his pipe out into the fire as the clock struck one. "In January of this year, an invalid lady, known as Miss Vera Wilton, moved into Bourne Cottage, on the outskirts of Market Wraden. A nurse-attendant came with her, as the poor lady's health was so bad that she was always confined to the house. I learnt later that the legal name of Miss Wilton was Vera Wilton Seer, the Wilton which she used as a surname being part of her baptismal name. She died in February…"

He broke off as Macdonald gave vent to an exclamation of surprise.

"Not quite what you were expecting?"

"No, not quite," replied Macdonald. "Never mind though—go on."

"This Miss Seer—known as Miss Wilton hereabouts—died of heart failure," went on Bardon. "Her heart was badly diseased, and Dr. Ingston, who attended her here, knew she might pass away at any time. She died in her sleep, and her nurse found her dead in bed. Just what Dr. Ingston knew might happen to her at any time. He signed the certificate without any hesitation. The dead woman's sister—another Miss Seer, who was known hereabouts some years ago— came and took charge of the funeral arrangements and so forth, and the body was taken up north and interred near the parents, I understand. However, shortly afterwards, the village gossips got busy—no end of rumours and stories.

Some man had been seen about Bourne Cottage, peering in at the windows, and he'd been seen on the very night that Miss Vera Wilton Seer died. You can never pin these stories down, but we got anonymous letters at last saying the poor soul had been murdered—you know the sort of thing. No solid evidence at all, just hearsay. No one had seen the man with their own eyes. All I could get was: 'So-and-so says so-and-so told him,' and you go chasing rumours round the country and never get forwarder. I tell you I'm heartily sick of the name of Seer. I don't like rumours in my district."

"So I can imagine," said Macdonald. "But tell me this: Was the dead woman's sister named Elinor Seer—her baptismal name spelt E-L-I-N-O-R?"

"That's right. So you do know something about them?"

"No, I don't. All I've got to go on is guesswork of the most irrational kind. Can you tell me anything of the previous history of the Misses Seer? They weren't strangers to the district previous to this January, I take it?"

"No. From what I've gathered, they'd both lived in Bourne Cottage some years ago. The older one, Elinor, used to teach science at Wraden Hall School, a matter of seven or eight years ago. The school—it was a young ladies' boarding school—closed down in 1932, but Miss Seer had left before that. The sister who died in January—call her Miss Wilton Seer to differentiate them—used to come to stay with Miss Elinor Seer at Bourne Cottage occasionally, but didn't actually live there, I gather, and wasn't much known in the village. There were a lot of stories—scandal, to put it plainly—mooted about the pair of them before they left, I'm told. From what I know of the gossip in these little villages, it was probably all pure malice. You know how conservative these country folk are. Elinor Seer offended the village ideas of decorum by living by herself, without a maid, being independent and a bad mixer. Wouldn't join in the life of the village, and was accounted a snob and a high-brow."

Macdonald nodded. "Quite. I expect the rumours over Miss Wilton Seer's death arose from a recollection of those old stories. Memory lives long in the country. What was actually said about them?"

"The usual yarns you get when an independent-minded spinster elects to live by herself, and offends the village busy-bodies. Scandals about a man staying there. There may have been something in it. Miss Wilton Seer lived up north prior to this spring, and, as chance had it, one of the village dames had relations in North Yorkshire, too, and heard in a round-about way that this Miss Wilton Seer had a child which died in infancy, about a year after the sisters left here in 1930. That's as may be, but I've no grounds for supposing that her death was due to anything else but what Dr. Ingston certified. Of course, if you've got additional evidence, it's a very different matter."

In spite of his interest in the other man's narrative, Macdonald yawned. He had been up most of the previous night, and sleep was creeping insidiously across his faculties.

"Sorry," he said, apologising for the yawn. "I'm addlepated with sleepiness. I'm desperately interested in your story, especially in the rumours which you say have been piling up. The facts will probably prove to be as follows: The man who was seen in the Miss Seer's cottage in 1930 was seen in the district again before her death. Some one—who prefers to remain anonymous—recognised him and said, 'Ah, I always told you there was something in it. Mark my words, that man killed the poor thing,' and without any evidence at all which *we* should call evidence, the story's been growing and growing."

Bardon looked uncomfortable. "They say there's no smoke without fire," he said. "It'll be a nasty pill for me and Dr. Ingston if the village rumours prove to be reliable. What do you suggest? An autopsy?"

Macdonald shook his head. "If you like old saws, try this one. Let the dead bury their dead. You say that Dr. Ingston signed the certificate without hesitation. You haven't arrived at any substance in the cloud of rumour, and you've got nothing to go on."

"Quite true, but I don't like to think that an evildoer's got away unpunished."

Macdonald got up and stretched himself, and then stood looking down at the fire.

"So far as I can see, no one is going to get away unpunished. I'm not going to tell you my story to-night. It's still incomplete, based on surmise, and I should only confuse you—and myself—by outlining a complex case when I'm half-witted with sleepiness. As a matter of fact, I've put the major part of the evidence before you already. I'll tell you my reading of it when I've done a little more research into the lives of the inhabitants of Bourne Cottage."

Bardon got up in his turn. "I'm no good at guesswork," he said. "Give me facts every time. You've told me that a man named Andrew Gardien was killed, and you've given me a list of names, including two that are well known hereabouts. Added to this you've identified Mardon-Elliott as a man named Mavory, wanted by the police of this county. Obviously the whole story is connected with this locality."

"And the connecting link—as the pointer to the locality—was Andrew Gardien," said Macdonald. "As Miss Woodstock said, some have the cross-word mind and some haven't."

"Confound it!" groaned Bardon. "Who *was* Andrew Gardien?"

"I don't know," said Macdonald, "probably a member of the local literary society to which Mavory belonged. I expect the Misses Seer belonged to it, too. That reminds me. I wish you'd look in at Bourne Cottage first thing in the morning. If any one is in residence, say that I shall be obliged if they will wait in during the morning, as I hope to call on them before noon."

"Right. I'll do that," said Bardon. "Anything else?"

"Nothing, thanks very much."

"Then I'll bid you good-night." Bardon sounded a little tetchy. "Your room's above this one. I hope you'll be comfortable."

"Again thanks. I'll see you to-morrow some time. Good-night."

When Bardon had left, Macdonald seemed to forget that he was sleepy. He stood and looked down at the dying fire and visualised Valerie Woodstock's charming, intelligent face as he had seen it before the lights went out at Coombe's party, and then remembered a rather tense, nervous voice saying abruptly, "Don't they keep candles in this house?" Followed the recollection of Graham Coombe peering at men's hats in the cloak-room.

"I wish I hadn't gone to his party," said Macdonald regretfully as he went up to bed.

XVI

THE SUN WAS SHINING AND THE SKY WAS DAPPLED WITH white mackerel clouds as Macdonald drove slowly along the country roads which led him to Bourne Cottage. Willows shone golden, their flowers heavy with yellow pollen, and hazel and elm were brilliant green. Even the tardy ash shoots in the hedgerows were opening their black buds to disclose the foliage within, and the ditches were runnels of clear water beneath the greenery of wild arums and jack-by-the-hedge.

A good morning, thought Macdonald, in his uneffusive Scottish way. He loved the country, and the clear, bracing quality of this brilliant April morning awoke the country-man in him, so that he would gladly have left his car and gone afoot over the wet meadows. Hedging and ditch-ing seemed a more desirable job than his own in Bishop's Wraden that morning.

The cottage he was seeking was off the main road, down a muddy byway whose rutted unmetalled surface made him decide to leave his car and to walk the last hundred yards which separated him—so he believed—from the final unravelling of Andrew Gardien's death.

With lark song above him and the sun warming his back, Macdonald wished once again that he could turn hedger and ditcher and forget Scotland Yard, the law of the land and the whole unsavoury business of Andrew Gardien.

As he strode reluctantly towards the gate in the old thorn hedge, he heard a bell ringing close at hand—a noisy, clanging, uneven beat.

"Who'll toll the bell?" flashed incongruously through the chief inspector's mind as he reached the gate.

Bourne Cottage was a pleasant old house, squat and comfortable, rose red in the sunshine. Daffodils bordered the path which led to a porch at the side of the house, and rambler roses were showing energetic green buds on the strong branches which were trained around the porch. There was no sign of any one about the place, but the old-fashioned bell which hung from the beam of the porch was still shaking, settling down to rest again after the summons which Macdonald had just heard. He put out his hand to the chain which hung beside it, and then hesitated. Some one had rung the bell and gone away. There were marks of wet shoes on the tiles of the porch, but none on the wide flagstone before the door. The visitor had rung, but received no answer. His hand still stretched out to the bell-pull, Macdonald heard a sound at the farther side of the cottage—the crash and tinkle of falling glass.

In a trice he had left the porch and was striding round to the rear of the little building. The sun shone in his eyes as he turned the angle of the walls and blurred his vision as he saw a woman's figure enter the cottage by a French window a few yards from him.

A few seconds later Macdonald stood in a sunny little sitting-room, his quiet voice saying:

"Don't touch anything, Miss Woodstock. This is my job. You oughtn't to be here."

Valerie Woodstock was standing by the writing-table, her hand resting on the shoulder of a woman whose body had fallen forward over the table with the face hidden as it lay on the bent arms. The sun striking athwart the room danced on the reddish hair of the bowed head, and showed up the lines of silver in it. An empty glass stood beside the still head, and there was a bowl of violets and primroses at one corner of the table. As though sleeping in the sweetness of a spring morning, Ronile Rees lay still and placid, about her the mingled scent of sweet violets and the queer almondy smell of potassium cyanide.

Valerie Woodstock turned on Macdonald with bitterness in her face and voice.

"Are you satisfied?" she asked. "She's dead—because you used your wits so well!"

Ignoring the accusing voice in which the girl spoke, Macdonald took her arm and pushed her into a chair by the open window, as he might have dealt with a child. It took only a touch on the hand which was clenched on the desk to assure him that the woman who lay there was indeed dead, and something in his heart was thankful that death had filled in the final word of the puzzle.

There was a fine piece of embroidered lawn lying on the work-basket beside the desk, and he picked it up and spread it over the bent head of the dead woman—a delicate pall of wrought needlework to cover the grizzled gold of that once troubled head.

Turning to the white-faced girl again, he said:

"Come outside. It's better to be in the open air. I'm sorry that you came here, for this is a thing which you won't easily forget; but, believe me, it is better so. Come."

Looking up into the lean, kindly face of Macdonald, the girl obeyed his words and the gesture of his hand, and walked stumblingly out into the fresh air of the garden.

"I don't care what you think, or what you'll say or do," she said passionately. "I'd have helped her to get away if I could."

"I know you would, but from some acts there is no escape," replied Macdonald. "If you take another person's life, for no matter what reason of private anger or vengeance, your own is surely forfeit. You may escape punishment by the law, but your own awareness you never escape."

"She killed Gardien, I know. But didn't he deserve to be killed?"

"Perhaps—and the debt is paid," replied Macdonald. "Isn't it a good thing that we needn't argue the rights and wrongs of it any more? Gardien—whoever he was—was a blackmailer. He probably wrecked the lives of both that poor soul in there and of her sister. But murder never can be judged as a good method of righting other wrongs. I believe that," he added very simply and earnestly, "otherwise my job would be an intolerable one."

"I don't see life in terms of black and white," she protested. "I shall always be troubled with the thought that I gave her away. I helped you to guess."

Macdonald was walking with her very slowly along the garden path, between the daffodils. The sad offices of death could wait, for he felt unwilling to let the girl go away in her present bitterness of mind.

"I don't think that what you said made any difference, not eventually," he said. "I did guess, from those guarded trivialities of yours at Graham Coombe's, that you knew Miss Rees—as she called herself. When you spoke to her, you became the pupil, she the teacher—yet you denied later that you knew her at all. It was the names that made the clues. We were all cross-word minded that evening at Graham Coombe's. Something in my mind made me spell 'Ronile Rees' backwards, and the name sprang out as Elinor Seer. Andrew Gardien was an anagram of Wraden—Reading. Nadia Delareign—who had no part in the story—also writes as Diana Geraldine, an anagram of her pseudonym.

"I learnt that you—who, I was convinced, knew Miss Rees—had been at school at Wraden-by-Reading, but I also learnt that Gardien was overheard speaking the name of 'Nell' or 'Ellie.'

"Elinor Seer, once of Wraden School, fitted the cross-word I was making in my own mind. Clue one. A locality—Reading, turned into the anagram, Gardien. Clue two. A school, Wraden, turned into the anagram Andrew. When Gardien chose that pseudonym to cover his first novel, he must have been very attached to Wraden—Reading. Learning that Miss Seer had taught at Wraden, the connection seemed likely!"

Valerie Woodstock pushed back her fair hair from her face in the gesture which Macdonald had observed before.

"You're clever," she said; but this time there was no

grudging in her voice. "I recognised that backward spelling of Elinor Seer when I first saw it on a book, but I've never known any one else comment on it. The anagram made by Andrew Gardien's name didn't jump out at me until after he was dead—and then I was frightened. I knew that Miss Seer had left this place under a cloud of trouble, some business about a man who had made love to herself and her sister. When Gardien was found dead, I guessed. Miss Seer taught physics; she would have found it easy enough to connect up the handles of that bureau. That man she saw going into the telephone-room—do you think he existed?"

"I think the man was Gardien himself," said Macdonald. "Miss Delareign, who originally mentioned him, is short-sighted to the verge of myopia. Miss Seer palmed off that story on to Miss Delareign as a conjurer palms a card—the stronger personality suggested to the weaker that a grey-haired man had been seen. Miss Delareign swallowed the suggestion and produced it as her own. Sound psychology, that."

"Then it wasn't Elliott?"

"I'm sure it wasn't. Nobody would have been more horrified than Miss Ronile Rees when she realised that her description of a bullet-headed man with flat feet was taken seriously to identify a real person. 'I thought he was the detective,' she said to me. Hence that inspired touch about the bullet head and flat feet. A policeman from a novelist's angle of vision!"

Suddenly Valerie Woodstock laughed, a weak little laugh, and Macdonald said:

"That's better. It's no use being bitter and miserable over a tragedy which was based on human weaknesses which were no concern of yours. Death in this case is a solvent of old miseries. Don't regret it."

"You're a sane person," replied the girl. "Perhaps as one grows older it's easier to view things philosophically. Poor Miss Seer! I've been living in a sort of crazy nightmare since yesterday. I went to Elliott's office to try to find out who Gardien was. Then Denzil and I thought that if we came down here we might find the poor thing, and get her away somewhere safe. Mrs. Etherton thought the same thing, and we all met at that inn—Mr. Vale coming chasing the Andrew Gardien anagram, as you did, and that fool of a journalist chasing Denzil because he 'acted suspicious.'"

Leaning against the gate-post, Valerie Woodstock looked at Macdonald with eyes that were wet, though rueful laughter curved her lips.

"All tragedies have a touch of the ludicrous in them when viewed objectively. I suppose that from your point of view we were rather a farcical spectacle," she added.

Macdonald smiled at her. "Perhaps I was farcical myself, especially when I worked out the probabilities of your intentions in entertaining me in the little library at Graham Coombe's."

"I realised how your mind was working," she replied. "Treasure hunting, oh dear—"

Her sigh was an unhappy one, and Macdonald replied, "Why not? Death means release from trouble—perhaps that was the treasure she found. You must go now—tell Mr. Strafford that he and Vernon needn't play boy scouts any longer."

The abrupt change of topic in the last sentence brought

a half-smile to the girl's face. She held out her hand to him and Macdonald shook it before he walked up the path again.

As he turned the corner again he seemed to hear the assistant commissioner's voice saying:

"This is all very irregular, Macdonald, very irregular indeed."

"Human behaviour is irregular," thought the chief inspector. "In this case irregularity was the rule. Material clues provided by kittens, intangible ones by anagrams—popular views on policemen—flat feet and well-cropped heads. A one-time pupil murmuring 'Archimedes' to her science mistress, and the principles of electricity and magnetism—as propounded to the fifth form—utilised to make a complete circuit with the handles of a writing bureau—only the fuse put things out and confused the issue in 'a darkness that may be felt.'"

Re-entering the sitting-room by the window which Valerie Woodstock had broken to obtain admittance, Macdonald went to the desk. There was a letter lying on it, addressed to himself, which he had seen when he first entered. Once he had realised that the woman at the table was indeed dead, Macdonald had been concerned to get Valerie Woodstock away from that grim sight. He was too humane a man to wish to investigate the problems of death with a girl standing by.

Going to the window, he opened the letter and read:

DEAR CHIEF INSPECTOR,—*Before I die I want to make clear the problem you are investigating. I killed Andrew Gardien by electrocution. He behaved very vilely to me and mine in past years and recently he* had attempted to blackmail my sister and myself. Her death was hastened by the shock of seeing him again and realising his motive in searching her out.

When I learnt that Gardien was going to be present at Mr. Coombe's party, I called at the latter's house and learnt enough to enable me to make a plan. I told Gardien that I would pay him what he asked if he met me in the telephone-room at nine twenty-five. I went in there myself earlier in the evening and connected up the handles of the bureau with the electric power. I joined Gardien there at nine twenty-five, and he opened the bureau at my request. The fuse which followed the interference with the current upset my plans, and I realised almost at once that you were suspicious. I think you have guessed what followed, and I am too weary to describe it. I killed him. That is enough. I ought to add that the grey-haired man seen by Miss Delareign and myself was imagination on her part, inspired by suggestion on mine. She really saw Gardien going into the room. I heard of Mardon-Elliott's death last night. I don't know anything about it. When one is very near to death one can't bother to puzzle things out. I am very tired, but I don't regret the thing I did. I write this to ensure that no one else shall be pursued for my crime.

RONILE REES.

Macdonald folded the letter and put it in his pocket. The superintendent would be coming to Bourne Cottage directly

246 E. C. R. Lorac

and arrangements would be made for the removal of that still body.

Looking at that shrouded head, Macdonald was glad that Ronile Rees had solved her own problem in death.

It was at lunchtime the same day that Ashton Vale saw Peter Vernon again. After a busy morning, in which Vernon had collected a lot of exceedingly puzzling stories, the journalist had returned to The White Dog for lunch, and he saw Vale looking at him with a subdued smile. Mrs. Etherton looked up at him quizzically and said:

"Have you run the great pacifist plot to earth yet, Mr. Vernon?"

With a rather shamefaced grin the journalist replied:

"That was only a try-on. I've often found that if you put up some tall story, the chap you tell it to reacts by telling you something that's very near the truth, just to prove what a mutt you are. The sillier I look, the more I learn."

"Sorry I didn't react in the proper way," said Vale. "I'll make you an offer. If I tell you the truth about the part of the story that Mrs. Etherton and I know, will you undertake not to print it? Some of it may become public later, but it's up to you as a decent-minded person not to make copy out of the story as a whole."

"All right. I'll meet you there, and you can censor my copy," said Vernon. "Fact is, I feel a spot cheap over it."

Vale gave a terse summary of the facts of Gardien's death, mentioning the reversal of Elinor Seer's name as a pseudonym and the anagram of Andrew Gardien's.

"Thickhead that I was! I might have seen that bit for

myself," groaned Vernon, and Vale went on: "Miss Woodstock guessed enough to make her apprehensive for Miss Seer, and decided to come down to Wraden to see if she could get any news of her or of Gardien.

"She phoned to Strafford to come to Reading to help her. You followed him. At the station Strafford undertook to try to lose you, as they did not want you spying on them."

Vernon flushed, and Vale added quietly, "I don't mean that offensively. If I'd been in your shoes I should probably have done what you did, only there are always two points of view. I, following up the Andrew Gardien clue, got ditched as you know. You picked me up and agreed to come on here with me for the night. All very exasperating from the point of view of the other two. Miss Woodstock was genuinely upset, and tried to make you see her point of view. Strafford was furious with you, and I, thinking that you had a bee in your bonnet, played up in my own way. That's an analysis of your dramatic evening."

"You were rather a trial," put in Mrs. Etherton thoughtfully. "I had seen Miss Seer twice yesterday, once at Belinda, once at Susan Coombe's. I realised that I had unintentionally done her a disservice in telling her to go and call on Mardon-Elliott. When I heard that he too was dead, I was horrified. I came down here to try to help Miss Seer, having guessed from something she said at Miss Coombe's that she would come here. I was honestly trying to tell her—indirectly—that I would help her if I could. The sight of your brightly-intelligent face and the knowledge that you were 'on the trail' seemed the last straw at the end of a wearing day."

"I'm sorry," said Vernon contritely, and Mrs. Etherton said abruptly:

"I believe you are—and you've a perfectly good way of showing it. If you have to write up this story, don't bring Miss Woodstock and myself into it. Leave yesterday evening out of the story."

"I will," replied Vernon. "Honestly I will."

"He's all right," said Vale a little later, when Vernon had left. "It was much better policy to tell him everything straight out and ask him not to print it. If he'd been left to guess, he'd have got there sooner or later—and his paper would have got there, too."

"Yes," replied Mrs. Etherton. "Honesty is always the best policy—within reason. I didn't tell him that I went to call on Elinor Seer at Belinda, did my best to warn her that guessing was in the air, told her she could rely on me, and offered her a perfectly good alibi, saying I'd seen her sitting on the sofa halfway upstairs at Graham Coombe's. Poor thing! She looked so bewildered. I'm glad I didn't have to swear to that alibi, though."

"Quite," murmured Vale. "Perjury's an awkward business."

"My own conscience is quite capable of dealing with its own burdens," replied Mrs. Etherton in her deepest bass. "It wasn't that, only the poor thing slipped her pliers into my evening bag, mistaking it for her own. They were rather alike—only Macdonald found mine because I left it at Coombe's and it might have been awkward." Looking up at him with her inquiring gaze, she asked abruptly, "But who killed Elliott, Ashton?"

With a shrug and a gesture of his hands he replied:

"God alone knows! I didn't. I can assure you of that."

"I'm delighted to hear it," said Mrs. Etherton. "I'm tired of trying to help people out of holes, and crime isn't my natural subject matter."

XVII

"It all seems very irregular, Macdonald, very irregular indeed," complained Colonel Wragley.

The assistant commissioner sat with Ronile Rees's letter in his hand. "You are sure that your explanation—and this letter—cover the facts?"

"I think that there is no reasonable ground for doubt, so far as Gardien's death is concerned," replied Macdonald. "You have motive, opportunity, and confession. Gardien was a bad lot from his youth upwards. I don't often feel that murder is justified, but I think in this case it was comprehensible."

Wragley frowned. "We need not discuss that," he said firmly, and a smile glimmered in his very blue eyes. "I believe they have Elders in your national establishment, Macdonald. If the opinion of an Anglican is of any value, I should be glad to recommend you for the position. Talking of comprehensibility, it will be interesting to learn what the jury make of your theory about Elliott's death. It is more subtle than substantial."

"It fits the facts, sir, and London juries have tidy minds," replied Macdonald.

Colonel Wragley, muttering the word "Irregular," dismissed the chief inspector, and the latter made his way westwards to Caroline House. He had promised to call on Graham Coombe and tell him the upshot of the inquiry.

Coombe and his sister were talking to Ashton Vale and Digby Bourne when Macdonald arrived, with Geoffrey Manton in attendance, and Macdonald sat down by the library fire to begin his narrative as soon as Miss Coombe had greeted him.

"So far as Gardien's death is concerned, the facts seem clear," said Macdonald. "Miss Rees, to use the name she was so well known by—thought out a very neat scheme which you have already heard. She arranged her flex when Gardien had agreed to meet her in the telephone-room at 9.25. When the lights fused her nerve failed her a little. She dragged the flex away from the nuts fastening the handles in the bureau and cut off the plug with her pliers. The flex she put in the lost property box. She then ran to the back of the lounge upsetting Miss Delareign in the darkness."

Susan Coombe put a word in here. "I knew Miss Delareign's evidence was unreliable. She said that it was a man who knocked her down."

"Typical," murmured the publisher. "Dramatising the situation needed a man for the aggressive act."

Susan frowned at her brother, and Macdonald went on hastily:

"That collision accounted for the dropping of the power plug by the service stairway. There was no time to look for it. Miss Rees ran up the service stairs and came out on the second floor landing. From there she descended by the main stairway coming down to meet me and to say a few words by way of alibi, proving that she had been on the upper floor when the fuse occurred. She then went to the piano, the pliers still concealed in her handkerchief, I expect. Playing the piano saved her from joining in the general conversation. Later she put the pliers in a bag which she probably thought was her own. It wasn't hers, but she was too rattled by that time to think clearly."

"Poor thing," murmured Susan. "I would have helped her if I had known."

"Really Susan," expostulated Graham, but Macdonald put in:

"This is a privileged conversation, and an unofficial one. A good many people were anxious to help Miss Rees, notably Miss Woodstock and Mrs. Etherton, who had known her years ago. Mrs. Etherton told me that she did not know Miss Rees, although they were both staying at Belinda Place. I'm afraid the fact that those who appeared to me to have known Miss Rees, denied all knowledge of her, rather put me on the right track, until the Elliott business muddled things up."

"And that is the part of the story I want to hear," said Ashton Vale. "Is it a logical corollary, as my mother used to say?"

"No. It's a quite illogical one," said Macdonald. "In my opinion the two cases are quite distinct, though I know that my superior officers don't like my explanation. Perhaps you would like to pick holes in it. These are the facts."

He gave them a terse description of the scene in Mardon-Elliott's study and then continued:

"Here is my explanation. Gardien had blackmailed Elliott,

and acquired such large sums from him that the latter was within sight of bankruptcy. Elliott also had been ill with influenza. He was utterly depressed and desperate. He shot himself, having first written Gardien's name on his blotting paper and having fixed up the contraption with the grandfather clock—a typical 'Gardien-ish' piece of mechanics. Elliott hoped that Gardien would hang for his death."

There was a moment of surprised silence, then Ashton Vale said:

"Steady on a bit here, I don't quite get you," he said. "You found Elliott dead in his chair and the gun in the grandfather clock…"

"Yes," said Macdonald. "Consider the facts as I have described them to you, remembering that Elliott was depressed and at the end of his tether owing to Gardien's blackmailing. The shot which killed him could have been self-inflicted. He wore a glove on his right hand, and there were no fingerprints on the pistol. The bottom panel of the grandfather clock was removed, and the legs of the clock were high enough to give a clearance of four inches between its case and the floor. Elliott sat in his chair, having arranged the mechanism of the clock and having wound it up so that it had started coiling up the slack of the line attached to the pistol. He then shot himself. The pistol dropped to the floor, and the clock hurried on, the big wheel revolving and winding up the line until the pistol was drawn into the works and stopped them."

"Neat," murmured Coombe reflectively. "Very neat. I bet that Gardien himself thought out that notion originally, and discussed it with Elliott."

"Possibly," replied Macdonald. "It's interesting to reflect on what might have occurred if Gardien had not been killed that evening. With the evidence of Elliott's writing on the blotting paper, and Gardien's fingerprints on the tumbler (doubtless preserved from a previous occasion) I think a jury would probably have brought in a verdict against Gardien on the probabilities. That, I am certain, was Elliott's reasoning."

Coombe nodded, and Vale put in:

"That sounds a reasonable reading of the facts, which otherwise sound crazy, but it's your own mental process that interests me. You had been given the impression that Elliott was seen in this house—"

"—And I couldn't make sense of it," replied Macdonald. "If Gardien had shot Elliott, the shooting must have occurred before Gardien came here to the party. Following that line of thought it was impossible for Elliott to have been seen entering the telephone-room here at 9 o'clock. Dismissing the idea that Gardien shot Elliott and assuming that Elliott *was* here about 9 o'clock to ensure Gardien's death, one has the ludicrous conclusion that Elliott killed Gardien and then went back to his office to shoot himself and plant evidence that Gardien had killed him. The remaining supposition was that some other person killed both Gardien and Elliott. This idea was put out of court to my mind by the fact that Gardien's murder was meant to have been accepted as natural death from heart failure. To plan Elliott's death in such a manner as to ensure an inquiry into Gardien's mode of life seemed all at odds with the careful arrangements for killing Gardien in a way which seemed to promise a verdict of death from natural causes. All these theories were contradictory. Incidentally, that statement of Miss Rees about seeing a man who resembled Elliott drew unnecessary attention to herself. Once I was convinced that

Elliott's presence here was so improbable as to be ridiculous, I naturally scrutinised the originator of the suggestion."

"Strafford seemed to think you were hot on his trail at one time," put in Manton, but Macdonald shook his head.

"No. I give Miss Woodstock and Mr. Strafford top marks for intelligence. If they had planned this Gardien murder, I am sure they would not have risked a contretemps with him earlier in the evening, or told me about it so frankly in their original statements. Strafford had wanted to thrash Gardien, and told me so. If he had killed him he wouldn't have given me a motive for his doing so."

"All very subtle," said Miss Coombe. "If I may put a spoke in, my question is this. Who *was* Andrew Gardien?"

"He started his career in a printer's office in Reading," said Macdonald. "His name was William Jones, and he became a reporter for a local paper, since defunct. We ran him down through looking up the old photographs of a Literary Society in which both Gardien and Elliott—under their original names—were shining lights. Gardien left Reading after the publication of his first novel. We have found out that he had a small house near Folkestone. We have not had time to clear up all the details of his career, but his blackmailing activities were widespread. He had taken the trouble to collect a lot of facts about the guests he was to meet at Mr. Coombe's party."

Miss Coombe looked startled. "Ourselves, for instance? How unpleasant! Really, Ronile Rees deserves recognition for her public spirit in removing such a menace!"

"You can't expect the chief inspector to agree with you, my dear," said Coombe. "The ethical standpoint…"

Vale intervened here. "For heaven's sake don't let's argue

ethics," he said. "By the way, young Vernon seemed to think he had hit on a good thing when he found that Strafford wrote under the name of Simon Grand and that Elliott was his agent," and Macdonald replied:

"Vernon once helped me very successfully in a case which he and I happened on together. Since then he has always hoped for a similar scoop. Elliott *did* act for Strafford under the Simon Grand pseudonym, but the whole association was a 'correspondence course,' so to speak. Strafford was keen to preserve the anonymity of Simon Grand, and he never went near Elliott personally. Their business was conducted through the post, and Vernon's great discovery was a damp squib."

The chief inspector here turned to Graham Coombe. "I hope your valuable volumes of astrology turned up, sir."

Susan Coombe replied for her brother.

"Those books were relegated to the attics a month ago. Graham has these lapses of memory. He was peevish because the things turned out to be quite valueless."

Grahame Coombe grinned. "Quite right, my dear. I admit it. My lapses stick out like organ stops, to use your illuminating analogy on another occasion."

"Ah," said Miss Coombe, by no means abashed. "Graham is referring to my original effort of deduction—that Miss Delareign was the responsible party."

Ashton Vale laughed. "If it's permitted to say so, Miss Coombe, I thought that *you* were just the person to evolve the subtle scheme which helped Gardien out of this world. You see I was anti-suffragist in the bad old days. I know just what women are capable of in a good cause."

Graham Coombe turned to Vale with his puckish grin.

"I thought you'd done it, Vale. Your look of scientific inquiry when you pushed your nose round the door of the telephone-room spoke volumes."

"And the chief inspector nearly hypnotised me into thinking I'd done it myself in a moment of aberration," put in Geoffrey Manton, "only I should never have had the originality to think out such an ingenious scheme as that trick with the bureau. If it hadn't been for the fuse…"

"If," put in Macdonald. "There's so often an 'if.' The unexpected, the margin of error—and a subtle scheme miscarries. It's not the modern science of detection nor the organisation of Scotland Yard that penetrates a problem. It's the emergence of some small detail which was not foreseen in the assessment of chances."

"Then you consider that if the fuse had not occurred, Gardien's death would have passed as an accident?" asked Coombe, and Macdonald replied:

"Possibly. The more imponderable evidence which was not sufficiently considered was this. The very circumstances of the Treasure Hunt sharpened the wits of the searchers. Because we had been dealing with verbal subtleties all the evening, our wits were attuned to the cross-word method, anagrams, and reversals and so forth. In any other circumstances the peculiarities of certain names might not have revealed themselves." He took a sheaf of papers out of his pocket and handed some to Coombe.

"Those are the clues of the Treasure Hunt, which helped me not at all. This is the list of the Treasure Seekers—and these names made clues."

FINISH

If you've enjoyed
These Names Make Clues,
you won't want to miss

the most recent BRITISH LIBRARY CRIME CLASSIC
published by Poisoned Pen Press,
an imprint of Sourcebooks

"The degree of suspense Crofts achieves by showing the growing obsession and planning is worthy of Hitchcock. Another first-rate reissue from the British Library Crime Classics series."

"Not only is this a first-rate puzzler, but Crofts's outrage over the financial firm's betrayal of the public trust should resonate with today's readers."

"This reissue exemplifies the mission of the British Library Crime Classics series in making an outstanding and original mystery accessible to a modern audience."

"A book to delight every puzzle-suspense enthusiast"

"Edwards's outstanding third winter-themed anthology show-cases 11 uniformly clever and entertaining stories, mostly from lesser known authors, providing further evidence of the editor's expertise...This entry in the British Library Crime Classics series will be a welcome holiday gift for fans of the golden age of detection."